PRAISE FOR EMILY R. KING'S

THE HUNDREDTH QUEEN SERIES

THE HUNDREDTH QUEEN

Winner of the 2017 Whitney and UTOPiA Awards
for Best Novel by a Debut Author

"King's debut is built on a solid premise that draws on Sumerian mythology for inspiration . . . The tale maintains a consistent thread as King embarks on a deep examination of sisterhood, first between Kali and her best friend Jaya, and later when she must fight the rajah's other wives to keep her place within the palace."

—*Publishers Weekly*

"*The Hundredth Queen* plunges readers into a fantasy world full of love, betrayal, rebellion, and magic."

—*Deseret News*

"King writes multiple strong female characters, led by Kalinda, who has the loyalty and bravery of spirit to defend her friends even if that means facing death. Strong characterization, deep world building, page-turning action scenes and intrigue, as well as social commentary, make this book stand out. This outing opens a trilogy; readers will be eager to get their hands on the next installment."

—*Kirkus Reviews*

THE FIRE QUEEN

"King treats the readers to stunning descriptions of Kalinda and her sister warriors' characters, even giving villains redeeming traits and hints of sympathy. A descriptive action-packed fantasy in a vivid world . . ."

—*Kirkus Reviews*

"The most poignant and important parts of this novel are the relationships that blossom and grow. If you're a fan of *The Hundredth Queen*, rest assured that *The Fire Queen* is definitely its equal. It's just as fascinating, heartbreaking, and exciting . . ."

—Hypable

"A great follow-up to the series. King writes with such a vivid detail that the imagery of *The Fire Queen* is stunningly real. The world she created is both extremely dangerous and invitingly beautiful. You will be drawn into this world of fantasy with ease and it holds your attention till the very end."

—*Fresh Fiction*

THE ROGUE QUEEN

"King delivers a fiery fantasy-adventure in her fast-paced third installment to the Hundredth Queen series. *The Rogue Queen* moves the series' main action from a tournament to a large-scale war, injecting a feeling of freshness and vitality to the Hundredth Queen books . . . Kalinda's crusade to save and unite her empire, regardless of the cost, will leave readers on the edge of their seats."

—*Booklist*

"*The Rogue Queen* exposes new angles on established ideas and stories that make it a really enjoyable novel. It has the perfect amount of action and strategic planning, as well as a healthy dose of female empowerment. Fans of the series certainly won't be disappointed with this new installment and, by the end of it, will be cheering 'Bring on *The Warrior Queen!*'"

—Hypable

"This book is all high-stakes action and magic. The characters come alive even more . . ."

—*Night Owl Reviews* (Top Pick)

INTO
THE
HOURGLASS

ALSO BY EMILY R. KING

The Evermore Chronicles

Before the Broken Star
Into the Hourglass
Everafter Song (forthcoming)

The Hundredth Queen Series

The Hundredth Queen
The Fire Queen
The Rogue Queen
The Warrior Queen

INTO
THE
HOURGLASS

THE EVERMORE CHRONICLES

BOOK TWO

EMILY R. KING

SKYSCAPE

SKYSCAPE

Published by Skyscape, New York

www.apub.com

Amazon, the Amazon logo, and Skyscape are trademarks of Amazon.com, Inc., or its affiliates.

ISBN-13: 9781542092258 (hardcover)
ISBN-10: 1542092256 (hardcover)
ISBN-13: 9781542043946 (paperback)
ISBN-10: 1542043948 (paperback)

Cover design by Kirk DouPonce, DogEared Design

Printed in the United States of America

First Edition

For Joseph,
My firstborn and my favorite reader

Prologue

Once upon a time, before the worlds were crafted from the heavens, two competing stars each thought they were the greatest and brightest in all the cosmos. To prove their might, the stars set off in a race across the eternities. Both were so preoccupied with flying the fastest that they collided and shattered into tiny pieces.

Only a single prong of one star remained, and she was brokenhearted.

The Creator cradled the weeping star in her hands. She pitied the star and wished to give her a new purpose. Grasping the star like a blade, the Creator cut seven worlds from the cloth of the eternities. When finished, the star no longer belonged in the heavens. She was an immortal sword. The Creator gave the sword to a protector, for, in the wrong hands, the blade could be wielded to split apart the very worlds she had molded. After a while, the sword was so content in her new calling she forgot she was ever a star.

One day, the sword was hidden away and forgotten until, years later—in a moment appointed by fate—a sad little lass with a clock heart discovered her.

As the sword rested in the girl's eager hands, she remembered that, before she was a blade, she had been a star. Although the lass was also broken, she, too, had a purpose, and together, the two of them would rival the sun.

Chapter One

Nothing and no one hides more secrets than the sea. Forgotten stories whisper over the whitecaps, lurk under the reflective surface, and dissipate in the winds. Our ship groans and creaks as her full sails elbow a path through the crests of the deep. Our course is set for the far-off thunderheads, making way for another world.

After two months of sailing open waters, neither I nor the captain nor our crew of outlaws on the *Cadeyrn of the Seas* can isolate our precise heading. My skill in reading and creating maps and my strong sense of direction are no help either. To find our destination—a portal to an Otherworld—we must lose ourselves in our own world.

I spy the marine sandglass on the navigation table. The sand has poured from the upper half of the glass through the constricting middle and down to the base. We turn it three times a day, once for each eight-hour watch. In the next minute or so, the marker will be spent.

Captain Vevina mans the helm, her wavy brown hair tied back, a tricorn hat low on her head. She wears a burgundy work dress, her bosom high and proud. The former street gambler is on the hunt for a grand treasure. I am after a prince.

The last grains of sand fall in the glass. Between the tick and tock of my clockwork heart, I turn the sandglass over, and the next eight-hour period commences.

"Will you visit Jamison now?" Vevina asks.

"He doesn't want to see me."

"He's your husband."

"He's our prisoner."

Vevina laughs. "Many people view marriage as a sort of prison. Go on. Tell him if he changes his mind and wants to join my crew, I'll release him."

"He won't. Not after what we've done."

Vevina and I were sentenced to seven years at the penal colony on a distant isle from our home in the Realm of Wyeth. The settlement was overseen by Prince Killian, known by most as Governor Markham. After the colony was destroyed and Markham fled, we boarded this ship and Vevina led a mutiny against Jamison, our interim captain. We had to detain him belowdecks or I would have lost momentum tracking the prince.

Captain Vevina grips the wheel, her attention on the horizon. "We should reach the storm within the hour. You may not get another chance to visit him."

I peer at the moody sky. The Terrible Dorcha, the monstrous whale that swallowed Markham and the ancient sword of Avelyn, travels back and forth between our world and the Land Under the Wave through mighty tempests—portals unreachable by other means. Finding the whale is our best chance of recovering my sword.

Tugging my red wool gloves high up my wrists, I descend to the main deck. Laverick and Claret are loitering by my cabin door.

"We dropped a coin," Claret says, her slight accent rolling her *r*'s softly. Her catlike eyes shine mischievously, and her yellow frock complements the golden undertones of her deep-tan skin.

Laverick's chestnut hair is pulled back, accentuating her nose, which is long and narrow like a fox's. Cannon fuses are tucked at the waist of her skirt, the tops hanging out like droopy flowers. The Fox and the Cat are always up to no good.

"We know she's in there," says Laverick. "We just want a peek at her."

4

"I have no idea to what you're referring," I reply.

Claret pulls at her friend's sleeve. "Let's go, Lavey. Everley will let us in when she's ready."

They stride off together, arm in arm, and I go inside my sunlit cabin.

"Radella?" I ask.

The azure pixie, tall as my hand, tiptoes out from behind books on a shelf, her gossamer wings tucked close to her little body.

"The Fox and the Cat were skulking around outside. If they ever get in, stay hidden."

Radella makes a motion like she's bopping someone over the head.

"No, don't hurt them. Well, not unless they're deserving."

The Fox and the Cat have guessed I've hidden Radella aboard and have taken it upon themselves to uncover her. The two have been fascinated with pixies since they learned the creatures can vanish things with magical dust sprinkled from their wings.

I spot a letter on the desk by Cleon's fishbowl. A picture of a daisy adorns the top of it, Father Time's calling card. I rush over and scoop up the letter.

"Did Father Time leave this? Was he here?"

Radella nods. I rip open the letter.

> *Dearest Everley,*
> *We're sorry we missed you, but we're pleased you're on your way to the Land Under the Wave. It's paramount that you find the sword of Avelyn. The fate of the worlds depends on you, as does any hope of your returning home. Be careful in the Land Under the Wave and take precious care of your clock heart.*
> > *Your friend,*
> > *Father Time*

I inhale the sweet scent of the daisy. Some people become seasick during long voyages. I have become homesick, and the only cure is to return home to Dorestand and my uncle. But first, I must take back the sword of Avelyn from Markham and return it to Father Time before the prince does something horrendous with the immortal blade.

Radella flies down and lands on the musical composition that she finished this morning. Her pointy ears and chin are impish and her big eyes always suspicious. Pixies are musical creatures, and Radella trills beautifully, or she did. I haven't heard her sing since Jamison was locked below. I try to slip the music out from under her, but she glares and flutters her wings in warning.

"Don't you dare," I say before she disappears the music. Last week, we had a spat and the scamp vanished my comb. "I'll tell Jamison the song is from you."

The pixie stomps her bare foot, her toes stained charcoal. Her feet are the ideal size for making musical notes, so she dipped them in ink and left prints on the lined measures to write a song. She motions at herself, then at my pocket, and finally the door.

"You know you can't come."

Her wings wilt.

"I'm sorry, Radella. You're safest here." Captain Vevina isn't fond of otherworldly creatures. Most humans believe pixies are a myth, but Vevina knows they're real. Unfortunately, she's of the opinion that any magic is trouble. Naturally, I haven't told her about my stowaway.

Radella flies back to the upper shelf, and on her way, she kicks Cleon's bowl. The goldfish swims around, oblivious to her temper. I once asked Radella why she dislikes him, and she made chomping motions with her hands.

I glimpse my reflection in the glass fishbowl and wince. My hair is tousled, and my clothes are disheveled from the wind. I discard my trousers, shirt, and waistcoat and put on a blue frock. Men's clothes conceal my ticker better, but where I'm going, a dress is more fitting.

A sudden faintness washes over me. I brace against the bunk and squeeze my eyes shut until it passes. Since Jamison replaced my water-logged parts, my clock heart has beat weaker. These bouts of light-headedness started around the same time I noticed the softening ticks. The two are clearly connected, though I cannot say which is the cause and which the symptom. Do the dizzy spells reduce the force of my heart's ticking, or is it the other way around?

I run my fingers through my tresses and scowl at my unsightly chin scar. Markham inflicted the wound, a detail that bothers me more than the pain did. Every time I look at myself, I think of him.

"Radella, I'll be back soon."

I cross the main deck under billowing sails, the waves rising to mountainous swells, and descend through the hatch. A few dissenters, former sailors from the queen's navy, are chained in the main hold. Markham's accomplice Harlow lies on the floor on her back, her feet propped against the wall. She tosses a bean sack up and catches it in her shackled hands. Her indifference about her imprisonment has left Vevina and me wondering what she knows about Markham's capture by the whale. We tried bribing her with smoking tobacco, but she wouldn't cooperate. No one else on board besides her and Jamison know about my ticker. Harlow could use this information for her gain, yet she would rather hold it over my head.

Down the dim corridor, toward the bow of the ship, Jamison's voice carries through an open door. "This is your fate line. Not many people have one, but look there. Yours is visible."

I pause outside Jamison's room near the guard on duty. Quinn and Jamison sit together by the table, her cat asleep on his lap. He's holding her right hand and studying her palm.

"The fate line is your destiny," he says. "We're all born with a purpose, and this line indicates how important that purpose is to the fate of the worlds."

"Why is mine so short?" Quinn asks. She's pinned her hair up, giving her the impression that she is older than her twelve years.

"The length of your fate line doesn't matter, only its legibility." Jamison touches her palm again. "Yours is deep, which means you're very important to the Creator."

I step across the threshold into plain view of them. Jamison lifts his chin high and glances away. Quinn pulls her hand from his.

"Everley, you came for a palm reading!"

"Perhaps another time." I survey Jamison's small quarters. The room is furnished with a hammock, a table, and two chairs. A chess game is set out on the table, and his violin case rests in the corner untouched. "We've tracked down a storm. Quinn, why don't you go up top and get ready?"

"But we're in the middle of a reading."

"We'll continue later." Jamison smiles at Quinn briefly, long enough to remind me what I've been missing.

The lass scoops her cat off his lap and drapes him over her shoulder. The big feline purrs as I scratch his head. Quinn stands taller than when we left home, but she is still the youngest member of the crew. Cradling her cat, she takes her leave.

Jamison dismantles the chess game, placing the pieces in the game box, his golden hair framing his scruffy face. His beard and sideburns grew in redder than his head hair, an imperfection that is insurmountably charming.

"You haven't touched your violin," I note.

"Did you think I would perform for you?"

"I hoped you would—"

"Forget I'm a prisoner aboard a ship of traitors, locked in the brig by my own wife? You'll have to do more than give me back my instrument and wear a dress."

My face and neck warm. "I thought your violin would help you pass the time."

"You were trying to rob me of my right to be furious with you," he retorts, shoving the chess pieces into the box faster. "This is ludicrous, Everley. Chasing a storm and seeking out a whale? The Terrible Dorcha destroys ships and drowns sailors."

"Dorcha can lead us to the Otherworlds." In addition to our world, the Land of the Living, there are seven Otherworlds, all crafted by the Creator. At least there *were* seven worlds until Markham destroyed his own.

For so long, I was intent on bringing him to justice. Now, more than anything, I want to complete the task Father Time gave me so I can go home to the only family I have left.

"We should return to Wyeth," Jamison presses, "and petition Queen Aislinn. Let her take care of her traitorous governor."

I wish we could, but our queen professes to receive direct guidance from the Creator. In truth, she executes anyone with faith in anything other than her crown or her self-made church. Jamison may be an earl and a lieutenant in the royal navy, but he's unable to promise me that the queen won't throw me back in prison to finish my sentence.

"You don't know that the queen will help us," I say.

"*You* don't know what Killian is after. You're dragging us along on your quest for revenge."

I should overlook Jamison's anger, but I see myself through his lens, and it's unflattering. "I have to finish what my father started. The sword of Avelyn was lost for centuries until he found it. He died trying to return the blade to Father Time."

"So could you. Why doesn't Father Time get the sword himself?"

"Why didn't he intercede when my family was killed, or when your mother and sister died? Why do he and the Creator let any misfortune happen?" I push the chagrin out of my voice. "You're right. We don't know what Markham wants, but he already destroyed one world. Ours could be next."

Jamison's tired gaze meets mine. "Or we could be grateful he's gone and worry about ourselves."

I cannot bring myself to say what I came to ask him quite yet, so I set the sheet music on the table. "This is for you from Radella and me."

"Are the musical notes footprints?" he asks, studying the measures closely.

"Radella misses you . . . We both do."

He sighs, expelling his temper. "Earlier, my remark about your dress—"

"I know you didn't mean it." I smooth my hand over his shoulder. Jamison's muscles go rigid, but he does not pull away, so I slide my arm behind his neck and lower myself onto his lap, putting my weight on his good knee. He smells of leather and salt water, the land and the sea. "I want you to come with us."

His eyes cool again. "You're asking me to leave our world behind."

"Only for a while." I run my fingers along the nape of his neck. "Come with me."

A large swell knocks the box of chess pieces off the table. We brace ourselves against the rocking as the pieces spill to the floor and roll across the cabin. We're closing in on the storm.

"Why do all of this?" He's referring to my dress, the music, and my sitting on his lap and caressing his neck. Touching him is something I rarely do.

"Jamison, we don't know much about the Land Under the Wave, except that it's covered in seas. You fixed my waterlogged ticker once. I may need you again."

"Ahh," he says, leaning back. "You haven't told your partners about your clock heart."

Given Vevina's dislike for the peculiar, her response would be less than favorable, and I don't trust the Fox and the Cat to keep a secret. "I'm taking precautions."

"Is your ticker the only reason you want me to come?" he asks gently.

No, I would like his company, but I already said I miss him, and he hasn't said two words about whether he misses me. He could have changed his mind and joined the crew at any time, yet he remains in his cell. "We both want the same thing. We both want to go home."

"I see," he says, his expression closing off. "You want your old life back."

"Don't you?" Neither of us wanted this marriage. I wed him to get closer to his commander, Governor Markham, and he wed me to gain a post at the penal colony. Although we have established a friendship, my clock heart is metal and wood, a machine incapable of falling in love. Jamison is a disavowed earl, but he hopes to reconcile with his father, the Marquess of Arundel. Life as his wife, as a countess, a prominent position in society, is not for a lass hiding her clock heart.

He shakes his head slightly. "Things change, Everley. Home may not be the same as when we left it."

"My uncle will be the same, and so will his shop. He would never abandon me."

Another swell scatters the chess figurines across the floor. The loose pieces could be me, rolling and reeling, at the mercy of wherever this journey leads.

As I rise, the soft beat of my ticker lightens my head, and I remember to ask: "Did you do something to my waterlogged ticker when you installed the new parts?"

"No. Why?"

"Never mind. Thank you for not telling anyone about my . . . about me."

"I gave my word." His tone hints at disapproval, but this is not his secret to tell. "Good luck, Everley."

I carve on a smile, my throat taut. "I'll need it."

Up on deck, winds shove at my cloak and skirt. As we crash through the steep waves, the ship slows. I climb to the upper deck and join Captain Vevina at the helm.

"The storm turned," she explains.

The sky ahead lightens by the second. It will take even more time to correct our course and chase the tempest. "Don't lose the storm," I say.

Vevina's mouth slides downward. "I'm more concerned about the ship following us."

"The ship?" I pluck the spyglass off the navigation table and peer past our stern at a triangle on the lip of the horizon. "Who are they?"

"Don't know. They're too far away to see their colors."

Perhaps they aren't displaying any. We took down our blue-and-green flag, the colors of the Realm of Wyeth, the second we turned rogue. "Could they be lost?"

"Doubtful. They're following our heading."

In these neutral waters, our pursuers could be merchants, pirates—or worse, a navy vessel from Wyeth. The last possibility is the least likely. We left the penal colony two months ago, and Wyeth and the isle are several months' passage apart. Too little time has passed for the queen to have discovered our desertion unless she really does receive inspiration from the Creator.

"Vevina, you don't think Queen Aislinn . . . ?"

"If that woman's a seer, I'm an elf."

Her cynicism quiets me. I was surprised when Vevina agreed to hunt down Dorcha, but her hunger for the renowned treasures in the Land Under the Wave surpassed her contempt for magic. She wants to establish herself as the pirate queen of the seas.

"I'll keep after the storm," she says. "Our pursuers will likely get nervous and change course. I'll send for you when our luck turns."

I observe the shadow ship through the spyglass again. Like the sea, luck is unpredictable. One minute it is on our side, and the next we are drowning in disaster.

Chapter Two

I open and close the hammer on my pistol. Yesterday I loaded and fired the navy standard-grade gun in thirty-six seconds. If only my aim were as good as my speed.

Again, I snap the hammer. Open. Closed. Open—

"Everley," Dr. Alick Huxley says on an exasperated groan. "I'm nearly finished. Can you wait outside for me?"

I place the pistol in my lap, sit up in the chair, and jog my knee. The ship's sick bay is a cozy cabin filled with glass bottles and wooden boxes of herbs. "I'm comfortable here."

"Then please be quiet." The surgeon's mustache twitches, his concentration returning to his patient log. Alick sided with the mutineers, staying on as our medic. He once had romantic interest in me, but we are comrades now, crewmates and coprotectors of Quinn. On the corner of his desk is one of her writing samples. Alick is teaching her how to read and write.

I brush wood shavings from my trousers. After speaking with Vevina, I changed back into my work clothes and carved a few figurines. I have been trying to replicate the figurehead of the *Cadeyrn of the Seas*, a female merrow. The half-human, half-fish creature has several complex details, from her long hair to the diamond pattern on her scaly lower half. My uncle could have carved her with little effort, whereas I tossed away my second failed attempt and came here.

"There," Alick says, setting down his quill. "You can give your foot a rest."

I shove the pistol into my belt and grab an empty bottle. "We don't have long. Vevina is chasing down a storm."

He pulls on his coat. Before he can fasten it, I drag him outside. My cloak comes to life in the wind, billowing like a curtain by an open window. The sails glow in the early evening light, the storm on the starboard side an ashen wall. Off the stern, the unnamed ship is still trailing us. Perhaps it's my paranoia, but our pursuers appear closer.

Alick and I reach the gunwale on the middeck. He takes out his pocket watch, which is attached to his belt by a gold chain. In exchange for his instruction during my firearm training, I assist him with his seasick patients, feeding them crystalized ginger and dumping out their vomit pails.

I set the bottle on the gunwale, and it stays. Here, in the center of the ship, the swaying is mildest.

"Ready?" he asks, checking his watch.

Nearer to the bow, outside the range that I will be aiming, a group of crew members huddles by a cannon. Every morning and night, Laverick and her six-man gun crew practice firing. The *Cadeyrn of the Seas* has three gun decks, each stocked and well armed. Laverick has enjoyed testing every single gun. She has a talent, even an obsession, for black powder.

Our section of the deck is clear, so I nod. "Ready."

"Prime and load, then present and fire at will," he says.

My hands and mind react as one. I measure the black powder from my horn, pour it in, and cram in the ball with the ramrod. Then I grip the pistol, yank back on the hammer, and pull the trigger. The gun recoils in my grasp, and fire sparks with an ear-popping blast. The lead ball soars out to sea, missing the bottle. Smoke spills upward for several seconds before a gust dispels it.

Alick lower his hands from his ears. "Your aim is getting closer."

My aim is rotten. "What was my time?"

"Thirty-four seconds."

At least I'm quick.

The ship slides down a steep swell, and the two of us totter for balance. Alick catches the bottle before it falls overboard.

"Perhaps we should go back inside," he remarks.

"I emptied three vomit pails this morning. One of your patients had eaten salted fish."

Alick's nose wrinkles. "Fine. One more round."

An explosion goes off behind us. We both startle and bump into each other. As I right myself, I trip over his foot and fall against the gunwale. My rib cage hits the rail, and my ticker pounds a flash of pain. I close my eyes to collect myself, and when I reopen them, Alick is beside me.

"A warning next time!" he calls to the cannon crew, then skims me for injury. "Are you hurt?" His gaze lands on my collarbone and his brows bend together. My chest scar has peeked out of my shirt. I adjust my neckline, covering myself again.

Laverick runs up to us. "I'm sorry! I thought you saw us practicing."

Alick has gone still, his expression pondering. I dismiss them both with a wave and hobble off to my cabin, clutching my aching side.

As I go inside, Radella pokes her head out from between two books. She confirms I'm not an intruder and tucks herself away again. My ticker pounds against my ribs. What does it matter if Alick saw my scar? I don't owe him an explanation. As far as I could tell, he didn't hear or see my clock heart, so I can pretend he didn't see anything.

A rap comes at the door.

"Everley?" says Laverick. "I have something for you."

A long silence expands between us. Maybe if I don't answer, she'll go away.

"I'll leave this outside the door. Let's hope none of the other crewmen catch sight of it, or they may want it for themselves." Another pause. "I'm going now. I won't bother you again. I hope you're all right . . ."

Unable to withstand another second of awkwardness, I yank open the door. Laverick holds out a short sword with a thick brass hilt and a thin blade.

"This is for you."

My fist curls around the hilt. The craftsmanship is decent, and the weapon's weight and balance are closer to my sword than a sailor's standard-issue rapier, but it still feels like putting on an ill-fitting glove.

"Claret and I found this on the ship," Laverick explains. "Not as lovely as your sword, but we thought you might like to have a weapon of your own again. You seem to really miss yours."

"You 'found' this lying around?" Often what the Fox and the Cat find is actually stolen. I start to hand the short sword back, but she pulls away.

"We want you to have a weapon of your own again. I asked everyone on board if this one belonged to them, and no one claimed it. I intended to give it to you sooner, but Claret said we should sharpen the blade. Wasn't that thoughtful of her?"

"Very thoughtful." Laverick's voice got strangely nervous when she mentioned Claret, her best friend, and I cannot figure out why. This whole conversation is odd. Since when does Laverick care about stealing?

A boom sounds overhead, strident as cannon fire.

"That wasn't me," Laverick says.

"Of course it wasn't." I push past her, stepping out onto the main deck. Thunderheads blot out the sunset sky, a thick and ominous shield. I scale the steps to the upper deck and join Vevina at the helm. "Are we on the storm?"

"We will be soon." She points behind us. "And we aren't the only ones."

Our shadow ship has come even closer.

Lightning flashes, crooked daggers of brightness chased by cracks of thunder. On the vessel's main mast, they fly the Realm of Wyeth's blue-and-green flag.

"Good sin," I breathe, "that's one of ours. How did they find us?"

"Maybe our queen is a seer after all," Vevina mumbles to herself, and then adds louder, "I had to slow our speed to take on the bigger waves, but we'll stay ahead of them."

Captain Vevina steers directly into the storm, and I charge down the stairs to the main deck. Alick waits for me at the bottom, blocking the path to my quarters.

"Everley, I beg a word with you in private."

"Not now, Alick. Our storm has arrived. Find Quinn and do as we discussed."

"The lass isn't my immediate concern." His attention falls to the location of my concealed scar. "I'm educated in the severity of wounds, Evie. The placement of your scar would have been caused by a traumatic event. How are your symptoms now? Is there anything I can do?"

I stare him in the eye. "You can follow the plan."

His lips press into a firm line, and he steps aside. "I'll care for Quinn. You needn't worry about the lass."

"As long as she's with you, I won't. Thank you."

I leave him and dash into my cabin. My satchel is packed and standing by. Though I prepared for this days ago, I still inventory the contents and then wrap my pistol in my spare cloak and shove it into the bag. Next, I slide the tin whistle and velvet pouch full of pixie dust that Father Time gave me into my trouser pocket and grab my sword.

Radella flies down and hovers near my head.

"It's time," I say. "All will go according to plan."

She narrows her eyes at me, her stare withering.

"We've been over this, Radella. Nothing will go wrong." I sound less confident than I would like. Between the storm, our pursuers, and the monstrous whale, anything could happen.

17

I take a bottle of oil that the sailors use on sails to repel water and slather it over my chest, giving special attention to the healed area around my clock heart. Keeping water completely out is impossible, but this should add another layer of protection.

Thunder grumbles overhead. Radella dives into the interior pocket of my satchel, stashing herself away. I put on my tricorn hat and sprinkle fruit flies into Cleon's bowl. Quinn will feed him and look after Jamison while we're gone.

"Stay hidden," I tell the pixie, and then I push out into the gales.

Raindrops stain the planks and speckle my cloak. Crewmen dart about, lighting the lanterns and manning their stations. The ship heaves over the waves, careening up whitecapped peaks and sliding down dips. I weave across the slippery deck to the port side where Claret and a pair of sailors prepare a longboat for departure. The Cat's eyes are alight, her countenance glowing. She flourishes when the risks are high.

Vevina relinquishes the helm to a sailor and joins us on the main deck. She peers through her spyglass, scouring the turbulent waters. Laverick stands between two cannons with her crew. An expert with black-powder mechanisms, she reconfigured the cannons to shoot harpoons as a precaution in case Dorcha attacks.

The second ship has breached the storm, and since we have slowed our speed to ride the deepening waves, the other vessel is gaining on us. Salt spray dampens my cloak, but my ticker is safe under my layered clothing. I toss my pack into the longboat and help Claret and the others maneuver the twelve-man vessel over the gunwale to lower it into the water. High in the crow's nest, the watchman bellows into the squall.

"Whale off the port side!"

Every soul on deck surveys the white-ridged waves. Massive thunderheads obscure the twilight, limiting our view beyond the lanterns. Gales blast at us, cuffing the sails, and the rains thicken to a swarm of wet slaps.

"There!" Laverick shouts.

A great hump ascends out of the water. The whale's sleek back is pockmarked with harpoon scars. Dorcha has terrorized the seas for decades, plunging back and forth between our world and the seas beyond. Mariners have sought to slaughter him and win the praise of his defeat, but he has always eluded his assailants.

Dorcha's arrival delivers a blow of urgency to the crew. Sailors tie off the lines of the longboat and man their stations. I tug out a tin whistle from my pocket while replaying Radella's instructions in my mind. At first, her directions for addressing the whale seemed strange. Now, in the throes of roaring waves, they feel inexcusably foolish.

Placing the tin whistle between my lips, I blow four times, long and loud, to cut through the winds. Radella insisted this noise is the closest sound to a whale call that a human can make. If she were not my ambassador from the Everwoods, I would not listen to her.

Dorcha races at us, the booms of thunder and lightning strikes coming nearer, as though he's towing the storm. Thick as the ship and half its length, the whale swims up to and alongside our port side. Rain pours down his shiny back. Amid his white scars, enormous barnacles cling to his fluke and chin.

"Why do you disturb Dorcha, Time Bearer?"

The whale's voice could itself be thunder, the booming rumble vibrating my insides. In addition to that voice, he emits a long, low-frequency call, unlike any whistle I have heard. Vevina and Claret join me at the gunwale.

"What's he doing?" Claret asks.

"I think he's trying to speak to us," Vevina answers.

"He spoke to me," I say. They both draw back in surprise. "You didn't hear him?"

"*You* did?" Claret challenges.

Neither seems to have heard the whale's gut-shaking voice. Radella warned me Dorcha is selective with whom he communicates, and that should he speak to me, his contact would be private. I understand her meaning now, even though I have no concept of how it's done.

The whale expels another loud, low call that translates to words inside my mind. *"Dorcha has been pestered by your hammering clock, human. The incessant ticktock grows tiresome. What do you want?"*

His voice rings inside my head, whereas I respond aloud. "I need you to lead me to Prince Killian Markham."

Vevina shouts over the wind. "What is he saying?"

I raise a palm to silence her.

"Dorcha will require compensation," says the whale, swimming alongside the ship. He lifts his head, his small, glassy eye staring at us.

"I have your payment." I pull out the velvet pouch. "Two handfuls of pixie dust." Radella insisted that the whale would covet the treasure. Pixies do not live in the Land Under the Wave. In Dorcha's world, such dust is rare and highly prized, and he would use it to disappear his pesky barnacles. "Will you show us the way?"

"Dorcha's world was not made for humans. Your timepieces shout at you and order you about. Our days and nights flow along seamlessly, a gentle current like the sands of time. If you go there, you must surrender to our tides."

Father Time must know my ticker can withstand the change, or he would not have suggested that I follow Markham. "Take me and a small party to the prince and let me worry about my heart."

"You're bold, Time Bearer. Bring the pixie dust and Dorcha will take you, but you must swear that the two-legged vermin with you will let Dorcha pass."

"You have my word."

"Your word on what?" Vevina asks.

"Dorcha will take us through the portal."

Vevina snatches the pouch of pixie dust from my grasp and tucks it behind her. I gape as she shouts over the wind. "I'm sorry, Everley. I can't let you do that."

"But . . . but Dorcha said he'll guide us to the Otherworld."

"We aren't going."

Claret and a second sailor grasp my wrists and yank them back, restraining me. Down the way, Laverick and her gun teams position the cannons with harpoons along the rail.

"Vevina, don't do this," I say, trying to wrench free. "I made a bargain with Dorcha. You have to call off the harpoons."

"I can't, Everley. I can't risk my crew. Magic cannot be trusted."

My clock heart thuds faster. "But what about your treasure?"

"The Terrible Dorcha is a big enough prize." Vevina holds on to her hat before a gust can lift it away. "I have to consider the good of all the crew, including you. We're safer in this world where we belong."

Laverick lights the fuses.

"No!" I stomp on Claret's foot and elbow my other captor in the nose. Twisting from their grip, I skid across the deck for the cannons.

Boom!

Boom!

The guns fire, ricocheting back, their rear ropes catching their powerful recoils. Roaring fills my head, punctuated by an angry whistle. I duck down and cover my ringing ears.

"Traitorous land vermin!" Dorcha howls, shooting air out his blowhole.

Waves slosh onto the deck through the gaps in the gunwale. As Dorcha yowls, I crawl through the receding waters and peer through an opening in the rail. Both harpoons found their target; one embedded in his back and the other deeper in his side.

The monstrous whale rolls toward the ship, pushing a wave at us. I scramble to my feet, and the water soaks me from the waist down.

"Intruders off the starboard!" the watchman warns.

Our pursuers have caught up to us, just minutes from our flank. Though the second-rate bark is a smaller vessel, she carries approximately the same number of guns. Sailors in gray uniforms man their top decks and arm their cannons. Unlike our crew of convicts and renegade sailors, they are well trained.

Dorcha rolls toward our ship, crashing against the hull and toppling Vevina and me to our knees. A bolt of lightning strikes the foremast, igniting the wood and canvas in a shower of sparks. In seconds, the sails burn bright and smoke pours into the heavens.

So much has gone wrong I cannot decide which disaster deserves the bulk of my horror. Whether luck or fate has interfered, this feels like sabotage.

Claret hugs the rail as another surge washes over her. Drenched from crown to foot, she looks like a drowned kitten.

"Captain," she cries, "we're taking on water."

Cracking noises carry up through the floorboards. Laverick's teams rush to rearm the harpoon cannons. The naval ship pulls back from entering our firing range and avoids colliding with us in the swells.

The pouch of pixie dust hangs from Vevina's hand. I snatch it from her and lurch to the gunwale. Dorcha has broken off the top harpoon, but the pole in his side is jammed in our hull. His fluke slaps the surface as he struggles to unpin himself, splashing the cannons and their teams.

Dorcha dives, pulling the port side down and tipping the burning mast toward the water. Gripping the rail, I sense the beat of my ticker weakening. I glance down the front of my shirt at the minute hand spinning clockwise. My ticker did this when I was near the gate to the Everwoods, at the edge of our world. We must be close to the portal.

The longboat we moved near the gunwale swings in the wind. Maybe if I can get down into the water with the whale, I can reason with him. I catch the lines, and the dangling boat nearly pitches me overboard. The lines are too taut and the boat too heavy for me to lower myself.

The whale bashes the hull, opening a wider hole. Raging waters rush into the lower decks near the bow, where Jamison's cabin is located.

I swerve across the slanted deck, evading raining embers, and clamber belowdecks. Water pours down the ladder, covering the floor to my ankles.

"Everley," Harlow calls from the main hold, tugging at her chains. "Let me out!"

I slog past her down the corridor as the floor steadily tilts to the port side. Jamison's cabin door hangs open, the entry unguarded. He wrenches on his chains and tries to pull the iron peg from the wall. I slosh into the now shin-high water, careful not to fall in.

"Evie?" he says in surprise. "You shouldn't be here."

"Someday when I come to visit you, you're going to be happy to see me. Where did your guard go?"

"He left as soon as the hull was breached."

The bastard ran with the hammer we need to release the peg from its manacles.

I grab his chain. Jamison braces a foot against the wall for leverage, and I lean back with my total weight. We pull together, but the peg stays in.

Jamison bends over his knees, winded. "Next time you come to save me, perhaps you could bring the right tools."

He should be grateful I don't have them or I might knock him over the head with one.

"It wasn't foremost on my mind. Things up top aren't going as planned."

"Yes, well, that seems to be our luck."

The ship jolts and the boards in the hull break open. Splinters fly and gushing water showers us in debris. We huddle together, Jamison's body leaning over mine. A whale fin fills the hole and then rips out again.

Salt water pours inside the gap, the water level rising to my knees. I pull out my carving knife and Jamison holds out his wrists. I use the blade to pry the peg out of the manacles and remove them.

"Another navy ship has found us," I say. "Radella is waiting with our longboat."

"Is the ship heavily armed?"

"Yes. Why?"

"We need to get to that longboat," he replies, urging me forward.

I pause to go back for his violin case floating across the room. "Your violin—"

"Leave it. There isn't time."

We wade into the corridor against the current, bracing against each other so we aren't swept away. Crew members run past and shove their way onto the ladder. One man pushes aside a woman, knocking her down. I help her up while Jamison grabs the back of the sailor's shirt and hauls him to the floor.

"Wait your turn," he orders.

We send the woman up first, then let the man follow.

"Lieutenant Callahan," Harlow calls from across the main hold, in direct sight of the ladder. "You cannot leave me!"

The other prisoners have escaped their confines or the guards have let them loose. I understand why they left her locked up. Everyone on board knows Harlow is Markham's consort and spy.

Jamison and I are next in line for the ladder. The ship lurches again, spilling more water down the open hatch. I sidestep the waterfall, and Jamison hesitates.

"She doesn't deserve it," I say. "Harlow would leave us and never look back."

"We aren't her."

He extends his hand to me. I reluctantly slap the handle of my carving knife into his palm. He wades to Harlow and unlocks her.

We follow her up the ladder and stagger onto the main deck, arriving in the middle of so much chaos I can scarcely believe that not long ago we were sailing calm seas. The three of us grip a line for safety while Jamison and Harlow take in the bombardment of disasters.

Though the rain has begun to extinguish the high flames, the foremast still burns and the topsails are scorched. Dorcha wails and thrashes alongside us, slowly sinking the ship on the port side, where my longboat is tethered.

Vevina and the Fox and the Cat have sought shelter from the fire by the stairway to the upper deck. Captain Vevina attempts to climb to the helm, but the ship's violent rocking sends her back down the stairs again.

The second-rate ship rides the mountainous waves beside us, its cannons aimed at our deck. Its captain, distinguished by his dark jacket, tan trousers, and wide-brimmed hat, stands on the upper deck beside the helm. Next to him, a man dressed in court finery peers at us through a spyglass. Jamison ducks his head and turns his back to them.

"Who is that?" I ask.

"The queen's secretary of state, Secretary Winters."

I calculate the timing of their voyage. "To be here, the ship would have to have left Dorestand soon after we voyaged to the isle. That was months ago."

"Queen Aislinn must have suspected Markham wasn't wholly honest with her," Jamison says. "They'll ask us to surrender. Where's Quinn?"

"She's with Alick. We've discussed what to do if they're captured."

"Good. Lead the way to the longboat."

We cross the deck, and like a human barnacle, Harlow follows. The three of us skid down the sloped planks, hanging on to lines and rigging to slow our descent. The ship is so tilted the longboat hangs over the gunwale, above open water.

The vessel shudders, plunging to its lowest point on the port side. Then the world swings as the entire ship flings in the opposite direction. The sudden propulsion ripples across the deck, a rapid-fire avalanche of toppling people and sliding bodies. We duck below our boat, and it swings wildly overhead.

Dorcha has broken free. His grumbly voice sounds inside my head. *"Time Bearer, you deceived Dorcha!"*

"I didn't betray you! My partners had second thoughts." My clock heart spins faster around and around. "Our bargain stands. I still have the pixie dust. It's yours, just as we agreed."

"You try Dorcha's patience."

"Father Time has ordered me to go to your world. You must take me."

"Dorcha must do nothing." The whale discharges air out of his blowhole again. *"But because you're his Time Bearer, Dorcha will honor our bargain."*

The whale dives into the base of an incoming tidal wave. I hold on to a line as the ship rides the slope up and races down the other side. A sailor mans our helm, but maintaining control over the damaged vessel in these seas is perilous.

The second ship barrels after us, steering masterfully up and down the huge wall of water. We reach the bottom of the wave, and before climbing the next, Jamison untangles the lines of the longboat.

"Get in!" he says.

I pull myself up and into the bottom. Radella's head pops out from the pocket of my bag, gets splattered by rain, and ducks inside again. Harlow starts to hoist herself up into the boat.

"What are you doing?" I ask.

She points my carving knife at me, which she must have pinched from Jamison. "I'm going with you."

I could draw my short sword on her and force her out, but Dorcha is waiting.

"Fine," I say, and she slides in.

As our ship scales another tall wave, Jamison starts to lower the longboat over the side of the gunwale, dangling us over the sea. Before we lose sight of the deck, I see Vevina, Claret, and Laverick scrambling after us.

"We're coming!" Laverick calls.

Now they want to follow the plan?

They climb onto the rail to jump down. The vessel pursuing us stays off our starboard bow as we mount another wave. The angled pitch of our ship unsteadies the women. Laverick falls forward and lands in the boat on top of Harlow. Vevina manages to hold on, but Claret falls off as well and plummets through the gap between the longboat and the hull. She screams as she drops and then goes silent when she hits the water.

"Claret!" Laverick cries, peering over the edge.

Vevina and Jamison watch with us from above as Claret resurfaces and drifts into the wake of the ship.

Captain Vevina shoves at Jamison. "Go get her, Lieutenant."

He carefully leaps down into the boat with us. Together, we swiftly lower our watercraft into the stormy sea.

As we release ourselves to the sweeping currents, a wave whams us and tosses Harlow overboard. I grasp at my drenched cloak and blink to clear my vision. Jamison reaches for Harlow, but the rippling surges sweep her farther out, toward Claret.

A mountain of seawater rises steadily before us, taller and taller until it surpasses the height of the ship. Jamison and I row quickly to escape the path of the colossal wave, but our oars are worthless against the rollers.

Waves heave Claret and Harlow about, thwarting their efforts to swim for our boat. A dark shape rises in the sea behind them. Claret flails and kicks harder, but the Terrible Dorcha speeds up and opens his huge mouth. She flows inside his gullet with the rushing waters.

The huge whale swims at us, the wave looming higher, on the crest of crashing down. He swallows Harlow next, gobbling her right down, and then his gruff voice booms through my mind.

"Dorcha warned you, Time Bearer."

Just as the tidal wave starts to fall on us, our longboat pours into the whale's cavernous mouth, deep into a storybook abyss.

Chapter Three

Jamison's grip on my elbow is so tight it almost hurts. Our surroundings have dimmed and hushed, the raging storm and sea far away. The tepid air smells of rotten fish. Its noxious stench makes me gag.

Over the sloshing water, the sound of breathing resonates all around us. My disbelief renders me speechless. We are inside the whale.

When I asked the Terrible Dorcha to take us to the Land Under the Wave, this was *not* what I expected.

Something near my foot starts to glow, growing brighter until I distinguish Radella. The pixie is the same blue as the heart of a flame. I haven't seen her glow for some time. I had nearly forgotten her luminescence.

Our boat sits in a sludge of water that gleams with slicks of oil. Dead fish and shellfish bob in the slop. The water is deep enough for our boat to float despite Jamison, Laverick, and I weighing it down. Dorcha's mouth is located at our backs, his teeth reflecting Radella's blue light, but her radiance is too faint to peel back the darkness before us.

My clock heart spins and spins. The sail oil I slathered across my chest has outlasted the rain and salt water, but the slippery thickness has diminished. I cannot find the pouch of pixie dust. I must have lost it when we were swallowed.

"Help," says a faint voice.

Radella darts out over the water, expanding our view. The dark-red innards of the whale are ribbed and slimy. His belly arches from one side to the other, a cavernous wall. Radella stops above Harlow, who is floating at the surface. Harlow rouses when she sees the pixie and swims after her to the boat in wide strokes. Jamison extends our single remaining oar to her. She grasps it and he pulls her in. Harlow clutches the side of the boat, her face pasty.

"Claret?" Laverick calls. "Claret!"

Harlow shouts another name. "Killian, are you out there?"

The whale grumbles loudly, the deafening noise echoing all around us. The women quiet.

Jamison fists the back of Harlow's dress and pulls. The weight of her soaked dress and petticoats drags her down, so I grip a fistful as well. The cloth is slick and reeks of fish oil. Together we haul her out of the water and into the bottom of the boat.

She lies on her back, panting, and stares up at us. "Do you see Killian?"

"Who cares about the prince?" Laverick replies. "Where's Claret?"

Radella flies out over the water again. She circles the boat, moving farther away from us with each lap. The pixie stops near the outer wall and flits around excitedly. She has found something. Jamison takes up our single oar and rows us out to the pixie.

Harlow sits on a bench and leans over the side of the boat. "Is it Killian?"

Part of me hopes he has been stuck in this cesspool, mostly because that means my sword would be here somewhere. But as we approach the light, I spot a woman.

"Claret!" Laverick perches on the side of the boat, sending us swaying. I pull her back before she tips us over.

Claret floats on her back with her eyes closed. Laverick and I heave her out of the water and lay her in the bottom of the longboat. Claret is missing both her shoes and one of her stockings. Laverick shakes the Cat, but she's unresponsive.

I place my hands over her chest like I've seen Dr. Huxley do with his patients. Finding her heartbeat, I exclaim, "She's alive."

Laverick pats her cheeks. "Wake up, Claret. Wake up."

Radella flies straight up above us, taking the light with her. All of us gaze up at the pixie in question and watch her dive at the boat. She speeds past us and lands, driving into Claret's abdomen.

The Cat jolts and coughs up water, gradually coming awake.

"Well done, Radella," Jamison says.

The pixie lands on his shoulder and preens.

Laverick strokes her friend's sopping hair, both women silhouettes in the dimness. "I'm sorry," says the Fox. "We should have never followed Vevina's plan."

"Why did you?" I ask.

"Vevina didn't want to leave our world," Laverick explains dully. "We didn't want to lie to you, but we thought once we conquered Dorcha and gave you the short sword, you would forget about your other sword and the prince."

Her voice warbles with fear. I rub my chilled arms and breathe through my mouth to lessen the nauseating reek in the air. I understand her trepidation about where we are and where we're going, but I wish they had been forthright with me about their intentions.

Claret lays her head against her best friend's. "We'll be all right, Lavey. We have each other."

The two of them huddle together for comfort. By comparison, the gap between Jamison and me on the bench feels monumental. I know he did not intend to come along, but just his presence eases the worst of my apprehension.

He faces the inky pit of the whale's middle. "Do you hear that?"

Air stirs deep within the whale, a hollow rustling that unnerves me. A sudden drop sends everyone scrambling to hang on. Water sloshes over the edge of the boat, splashing my boots. Radella dives into Jamison's breast pocket, and I grip the bench harder.

We sit, frozen, waiting.

The water slopes and pitches us backward in our seats. Our boat slides forward, deeper into Dorcha's belly. Laverick and Claret scream as we fall farther into the murkiness. Before we enter the recesses of the whale's bowels, a tremendous draft of air pushes us forward again.

We hang on while we speed toward the whale's clamped teeth. His mouth opens, and sunlight blinds us as our boat soars out of his mouth and splashes into the water. We dip low and then bob up again.

Waves surround us every which way, their peaks glistening the colors of diamonds and sapphires, reflecting the flawless sky.

"Look out!" Harlow cries.

A wave pushes us off-balance and the boat tips down on one side. As I start to slide toward the edge, I grab for Jamison, but my fingers slip through his and I topple into the sea.

I flail toward the surface, and then another wave piles me. My hand presses down on my ticker to seal out the salt water. I kick up and break the surface again.

Our boat is pulled away by the rolling crests, my friends veering out of sight. I swim after them, but a large wave slams into me and drags me under mountainous, sun-drenched waters.

A dripping noise floods my mind. The patter is not unlike the ticktock of a clock—consistent, niggling, unrelenting.

I sit up in bed. My dim bedroom window is cracked open, rain leaking in and collecting on the floor. I rise to shut it and crush something under my foot.

A daisy.

Father Time's symbol sends a prickle of awareness across my skin. He leaves me daisies when he's close by or when magic is afoot.

I tiptoe out of my room. The chairs in the sitting area are empty, and a fire crackles in the hearth. Uncle Holden's steaming cup of whisky tea rests on the table untouched. Rain beads down the kitchen window that looks into the alley. Wet footprints puddle on the floor, tracks leading from the back door to his workshop.

Another daisy rests in front of the partially ajar door. I creep up to the workshop and pick up the second flower. My uncle's voice carries out.

"What would you have me do, Brogan?"

Brogan . . . ?

"Stash it here a few days," replies a familiar voice. "I'll return before I leave for the isle. Ellowyn won't allow this weapon under the same roof as the children. Your shop is the only other place the blade will be protected. Killian won't think to look here."

A roar fills my ears, like the ticking of a thousand clocks. Ellowyn was my mother. And the second man's voice . . .

I pad to the door, toward the scent of fresh wood shavings, and peek through the opening. My father stands with his back to me. I would recognize his tall, top-heavy stature at any angle. His shoulders, torso, and arms are thick compared to his lanky legs. He wears his riding outfit, his breeches and boots mud stained.

I blink fast to clear my eyes. Father is alive?

"You shouldn't go back there," says Uncle Holden. He's seated on his stool at his workbench, the sword of Avelyn lying before him. He looks so *young*. After my family died, he seemed to age overnight. "Ellowyn and the children need you, Brogan."

"All the more reason why I must finish this," answers Father. "Worlds will be destroyed if he gets this."

"I know." Uncle Holden stares across his workshop at a sandglass, an object I haven't seen since I was a little girl. After my uncle took me in, he put the sandglass away and I never saw it again.

"Don't let him find the sword, Holden. I trust you to protect the relic."

"The sword is safe here. I swear."

My father grasps his shoulder. "Will we see you on Ellowyn's birthday?"

"I'll ride up in the evening. I bought her the red gloves you suggested."

I clutch the daisy in my hands, which are clad in my mother's gloves. She died on her birthday before my uncle could give them to her.

My father starts for the door, and my heart vaults into my throat. From his hooked nose to his russet eyes surrounded by smile crinkles, straight down to his pronounced throat knob, his face is home. I often combed back his straight hair, slicking down the front pieces that would stick out when he took off his tricorn hat. Those unruly strands poke out now and point down over his troubled eyes.

"Papa?" I whisper.

Without any acknowledgment, he puts on his damp hat and strides to the back door. I hurry into the alleyway after him.

"Papa, wait!"

He untethers his horse from a post. I maneuver in front of him and grab for his sleeve. My hand passes through him, sliding like a ghost through a wall. I gape at my fingers. They feel and look solid, and yet . . .

My father raises his gaze in my direction.

"Papa, it's me, Evie." I imagine he will grab me up and nuzzle his whiskers against my neck as he used to do. But he lifts his hand and waves to Uncle Holden, who is standing in the kitchen doorway.

Father vaults into the saddle, then snaps the reins and his horse trots off. I dash after him, calling his name. He turns on to the main road and rides out of view.

I bend over my knees, my head reeling. Why can't he see or hear me?

While bent over, I catch sight of my reflection in a puddle. My boots are not wet nor my clothes damp. I straighten and stare up into the rain clouds, waiting for the drizzle to dampen my face. I feel nothing, smell nothing. No rain, no soggy chill—no ticktock of my heart.

Jerking down the neckline of my shirt, I see the minute hand is motionless.

I drop the daisy and run down the alley. My footsteps make no splashes. I am here, yet I'm not.

Something strange like this happened once before. On the isle, when my ticker became waterlogged, my spirit floated out of my body and soared to far-off places. I saw things that still resurface in my nightmares—the battlefield with the warrior giants and Markham as master over my enslaved friends. Father Time let me see the future as a warning for what's to come if we don't stop Markham. Could this be a warning too? But how could it be when this is the past?

Uncle Holden closes the back door. I grab for the latch, and my fingers pass through it. I squeeze my eyes shut and step through the door into the kitchen.

My uncle stands at the hearth, sipping his whisky tea.

"Uncle Holden?" I ask, drawing nearer.

He glowers into the crackling fire. The sword of Avelyn is propped against the stone hearth. I reach for the hilt, and my touch goes straight through. My uncle sets down his teacup and picks up my sword. He walks past me to the staircase and starts upward.

"Uncle Holden. Uncle Holden, please!"

I scurry after him up to his loft. He kneels in front of his cedar chest and wraps my sword in a quilt. That's where the blade was when he first showed it to me.

My ticker clunks in my chest, then a fast ticktock sounds as the minute hand winds forward. Before I can figure out what's happening, the room spins. When the spinning stops, so does my ticker, and another daisy has appeared in my hand.

I'm still in the loft, but the scenery has changed. Moonlight floods through the dingy window onto the dusty floor, and Uncle Holden sits at the edge of his bed beside a girl.

She's *me*.

My raven hair is short like a boy's. This must be soon after my parents died, as that's the last time my hair was this length. Markham set fire to our house to conceal their murders. My uncle pulled me out in time, but it took nearly three years to grow out my burned hair.

"Let's go over this once more," says my uncle. He looks older than he did moments ago, as though he lost years off of his life in a matter of months. "What's your name?"

"Everley Donovan—oof, I squelched it again." The younger me pushes out her chin. "Give me another chance. I can do it."

"Of course you can. Take your time."

His kindness sends a current of affection through me. Good sin, I miss him.

"I'm Everley O'Shea," says younger me, "apprentice to Holden O'Shea, the clockmaker. Mr. O'Shea took me in off the streets. My father abandoned me—" She makes a sour face. "Do I have to say that?"

"It's the furthest from the truth, so yes." At her hesitancy, Uncle Holden pats her arm. "Have you heard of a distraction?"

"Carlin would accuse me of distracting him while he was practicing his flute."

My brother Carlin always let me know when I was getting on his nerves. Most of the time, I deserved his irritation. I would hum a different tune while he practiced to mess him up.

"Precisely," replies my uncle. "When you tell our customers or neighbors that your parents are gone, you will distract them from the truth."

Younger Everley rubs her palms over her knees. "Why can't we tell them what really happened?"

"Because it's our secret. Sometimes a secret hurts people less than the truth would. People believe you aren't with us any longer, that you've passed on with your mother, father, and siblings. Finding out you are here with me would make them curious." My uncle fixes the neckline of the lass's dress, concealing her scar. "Then they might find out how special you are."

"I don't feel special."

I feel her words weigh heavy in my own mouth, remembering how unpleasant they tasted. The lies—the necessary falsities—left traces, like grime on a glass windowpane. No amount of time will ever wash them clean.

Uncle Holden hugs her to his side. "No one who is special feels they are. What makes you different isn't shameful, Evie. You aren't hiding because you did something wrong. People fear what they don't understand. Now, you did well, except you left out one part."

The lass's expression scrunches in contemplation. "I'm Everley O'Shea, apprentice *and adopted daughter* to Holden O'Shea, the clockmaker."

He added the part about him so I wouldn't feel alone. My uncle never attempted to replace my parents. Yet late at night, when nightmares of big flames and deafening gunshots woke me, I would stare at the ceiling and recite this practiced speech. At times, the lies felt so real I wanted them to be true. I wanted to have never known my parents and my uncle to be my only family. Though I felt guilty for wishing something so selfish, living the lie lessened my heartache.

My uncle wraps his arm around her shoulders. "That's enough for today. We'll do this again tomorrow. Well done, Evie."

"You shouldn't call me that anymore." Her little voice holds resignation. "The lie must distract from the truth. I can't be Evie Donovan. I have to be Everley O'Shea."

"You must be Everley O'Shea around everyone else, but with me, you will always be Evie."

"No," she replies tightly. "The Donovan family is gone, and so is your niece."

Uncle Holden gathers the lass closer. Her head rests against his shoulder, so she doesn't see the tears trickling down his face. "Would you like to visit their graves?" he asks, tears absent of his voice.

"You said someone could see me."

"We'll go early in the day, and we won't stay long."

She gives no immediate reply, but I remember the battle raging inside her. My desire to see my family's headstones was intense, yet I thought this was a test of how well I could maintain my new identity. Ultimately, my decision came down to the truth that my family's remains were not in the cemetery for me to visit. Their ashes were shoveled away with the crumbled debris of our leveled manor. Their gravestones marked nothing but dirt.

"No, thank you, Uncle Holden," she answers softly, her head still against his shoulder and her gaze on the floor.

Her polite refusal unleashes more tears in him that I never saw. I wish he would have shown me them, even once, so I could have revealed my own without feeling weak or ungrateful.

My ticker begins to spin, faster and faster. An invisible force seizes me, and I float off the rug toward the ceiling. Alarmed, I drop the daisy and it vanishes in midair.

"I cannot go yet, Father Time," I say. "I want to stay home with my uncle."

The force holding me ignores my plea. I fly up through the ceiling into the night and the force suspends me over our rooftop. The city of Dorestand extends beneath me, a sprawling array of pitched roofs, smoking chimneys, brick buildings, and wet cobblestone roads brightened by lampposts and softly lit windows.

My clock heart spins continuously as I float again, higher and higher above the clouds and into a soft quilt of stars. Their radiance intensifies, flooding my vision with piercing light.

Whoosh.

Whoosh.

Whoosh.

Are those . . . waves?

I peel open an eyelid and peer into the sun. Scrunching my eyes shut again, I rub sand from my lips and roll off my back onto my hands and knees. My body feels hollowed out, the middle of me cored straight through.

Something tugs my hair. Radella hovers beside me, hands on her hips. I look around at the clear sky and scorching sun warming the pale sand. Huge rolling waves barrel in from the sea and slam into the beach. Beyond the breakwater, there are no boats or whales in sight. No debris from a boat wreck litters the shoreline, and I spot no tracks or footprints from other survivors. I crane my neck to view the coastline behind me and see nothing but sand dunes. Not a single tree or scrub brush is in view.

"Have you seen the others, Radella?"

She shakes her head solemnly.

Brushing my stringy hair back, I sit up. The tide has gone out, leaving a slope of wet sand between us and the surf. Gone are my pack, cloak, and short sword. I must have washed ashore, but my clock heart isn't waterlogged. Each beat sends a pang to the back of my teeth.

"How is my ticker not broken?"

Radella points at herself.

"You fixed it?"

She makes a motion like she's fluttering her wings and raining down dust.

"You disappeared the water?"

The pixie nods several times. Radella has already taught me the rules of pixie dust—it must touch something to make it disappear, and it cannot vanish anything made of creation power, only inanimate objects—apart from iron. She could have disappeared the water, but wouldn't she have vanished my ticker too?

I rub at the aching spot between my eyes, trying to remember what happened after I fell in. I recall visiting the past, something I had no idea one could do. But if Father Time can send me forward to the future, then it's reasonable to think that he could send me back to my childhood. He has the power to do so, yet why he showed me those moments is lost on me.

"Where are we, Radella?" I ask.

She puffs out her cheeks and draws a wave symbol with a mountain underneath it.

"We're in the Land Under the Wave?"

She claps for me, her expression mocking. Evidently, I should have realized where we were, but nothing about this place seems immediately different than my world. And I didn't anticipate a world covered with seas would have land.

I rise on rickety legs, my boots and stockings squishy with water. As I turn in a circle to evaluate the barren beach, I spot the moon, so large it outsizes the sun. I have never seen a moon this close, with craters bigger and darker and more definable.

Gooseflesh flocks up my arms. We *are* in an Otherworld.

"Do you think everyone else made it to shore?"

Radella shrugs, worry lines creasing her forehead.

"We'll look for them. But first, we need to find somewhere less out in the open."

The tide line is no place to linger. Since I woke, the water has rushed closer to us. Although we must go, my knees are locked. Father Time warned me that the Land Under the Wave is a haven for outlaws. Anything or anyone could be on the other side of the sand dunes.

One step, just a single step, and I can build momentum.

Why is the first step always the hardest?

Radella flies ahead, her azure wings bleeding into the sky.

Oh, quit being an infant, I tell myself. *Markham wasn't in the whale, so he must be here somewhere.*

If that entitled bastard can face this world, I can too.

I draw a steadying breath, shriveling my fear to a sizeable opponent, and start up the sand dune.

Chapter Four

Waves of heat shimmer off the sandy peaks and haze the horizon. I trudge upward, squinting and panting. A layer of grit coats my mouth, but I haven't enough spit to wash it out. My thirst is cruel, especially given the accessibility of the sea. All that water and not a drop to drink.

Radella pauses often to rest, hovering in the air. Her wings steadily wilt, until she finally sits on my shoulder. By the time we crest the dune, my boots are full of sand.

The ridge we stand on runs parallel to the water, like a long, sinuous spine. I rotate in a circle, seeking a landmark or sign of civilization. More of the shoreline is visible, yet there's still no sign of our comrades or longboat. I don't see much besides waves of both sand and water.

"Any guesses which way to go?"

Radella sinks forward, resting her elbows on her knees glumly.

"Me either."

I plunk down and empty the sand from my boots. Sweat trickles down my back, my neck baking. While I tie my waistcoat on my head as a sunshade, Radella takes off along the dune peaks.

"Where are you going?" I shove on my boots and stumble after her. "Radella, wait!"

She stops and points up the coast. I see nothing, but she gestures more urgently.

I shield my eyes from the sun and squint harder. A tall, thin shadow protrudes from the land.

"Is that a tree?"

She tilts her head from side to side. If it's a tree, it could provide us shelter and perhaps even food.

We set off in earnest for the lone landmark, Radella riding on my shoulder. While my clock heart stamps out a patient but quiet march, my tired mind drags me back to my worries about Jamison and the others. Radella made it to shore, so they might have too. Assuming anything else may cripple me to the point where I sit down right here and never get up.

Hiking out to the shadow leads us back to the water's edge. As I tread across the hard-packed sand, a fogbank creeps in from the sea, hedging in the beach and dimming the light. We approach the landmark, and what we thought was a tree transforms into the mast of a ship.

The shipwreck is half sunken in the dune. Radella tugs on my hair to gain my attention and frowns. She does not want to investigate. I agree that the wreckage is off-putting, but we cannot pass up the opportunity to scavenge for food or water.

"We might find supplies," I say. "We'll be careful."

Her wings droop. I feel how she looks—exhausted, hungry, thirsty.

We trudge up the dune. The fogbank has crept closer to the shoreline, almost concealing the surf. Up here, the wind is louder than the crashing waves.

The vessel must be about one hundred barrels in length. Two of its masts have pitched over in a permanent state of falling, and its third has cracked in two like a snapped twig. Countless sails are torn or missing. On the lower tipped side, the ship's deck is lodged in the sand. Its uneven planks, pockmarked by dents and holes, would be hazardous to climb on.

"Hello?" I call out. "Is anyone there?"

All the staterooms and cabins appear abandoned, but one of the doors has less sand in front, as though it has been cleared away.

The sensation that someone is watching us wriggles under my skin.

"Hello?" I call again.

Radella flies off my shoulder and lands on a scrap of canvas half buried in the sand. I dust it off and uncover a section of a flag. The symbol on it is unfamiliar—a crown of ivy wreathing a red apple.

A swift wind barrels past us, jerking the canvas from my grasp and flinging it into the sky. The piece whirls away, drawing my gaze farther up the coastline. I trudge past the sunken bow and halt, mired in astonishment.

More mammoth ships are scattered across the sand dunes, countless wrecks littering the shoreline. The ships have been tossed on their sides and stranded aground. They lie on battered hulls, their rigging snarled, anchors severed, and masts decapitated.

Radella quakes against my shoulder, her wings tucked in and her head down. I could remark on her cowardice, but my own insides have clenched into a fist. I open my breast pocket, and she dives inside, trembling next to my clock heart.

We investigate the next vessel. Although weather-beaten and land-locked, the standard fishing trawler is a common sight in our rivers back home. Its tangled nets are strewn over the gunwale on the port side, and the Realm of Wyeth's blue-and-green flag is wrapped around the main mast. My throat feels strangled, as though the flag has wound itself around me.

"Hello?" I say.

Again, no answer.

I continue to sense that someone is watching us. Still, the only movements come from the pouncing sand fleas, and we have not seen a single seabird or scavenger.

As the fogbank obscures the coastline, we venture from one ship-wreck to the next. A smaller vessel has been tipped upside down, its topside decks submerged in sand. Another, a flat-bottomed boat with a single mast and pontoons on either side, is the most peculiar watercraft here. On it are markings in a foreign language.

None of the grounded ships are small enough to be our longboat, and no other footprints can be seen in or around the wrecks.

This graveyard of ships tells endless stories. Each one began its life voyaging the seas, and, through tragedy, landed here. I have heard rumors of great storms sweeping ships away to the Otherworlds, and considering the number of mostly intact ships here, they must be true. Many of them are too big to fit through Dorcha's mouth or inside his belly. Where are their crews? No sign of survivors is evident, nor can I see graves or bodily remains.

The thickening fog dims the fading daylight. We will be lost in the murkiness soon, so I start back to the first ship, choosing the vessel to serve as our landmark in this empty sameness.

Radella glows to brighten our darkening surroundings. As the ship reappears in the gloom, she chirps at me.

"I don't like this place either, but this is the closest to where we came ashore, and it's better than sleeping out here."

She crosses her arms, her expression dubious.

I climb aboard and maneuver over the rotted planks to the nearest door. It teeters on a single attached hinge as I push inside. Radella's glowing light pours across the cabin. The furniture is overturned and water damaged, broken glass strewn across the slanted floorboards. She flies to the porthole to stand watch. My muscles ache and my ticker thrums quietly in exhaustion, but the possibility of finding food or water fuels me to look for salvageable supplies.

In one corner, I discover a compass with the needle stuck pointing northwest, a dry oil lantern, and a moldy straw mattress. A shiny gold coin on the floor catches my attention. One side has an apple encircled by an ivy crown, and on the reverse, a teardrop leaf. The inscription around the edge is in a language I don't recognize. I show the coin to Radella.

"Do you know where this came from?"

She points at a picture tipped on its side against the wall. The portrait has been damaged by water. The subjects of the painting are blurred, but I make out a man, a woman, an older girl, a boy. I cannot locate a caption.

"Who are they?" I ask. "What do they have to do with the coin?"

The pixie's eyes grow wide, then she zips across the cabin and hides in my hair.

"Radella, what in the worlds are you—?"

Then I hear something coming from outside the ship.

Singing.

Chapter Five

I run to the porthole and peer out at the foggy night. The singer is female, and although her lyrics are in a language I don't know, her music is enchanting. Her song comes from the direction of the sea. I start outside, but Radella yanks hard on my hair.

"Ow! What is it?"

She covers her ears and glares at me until I emulate her, which I do only to stop her from pulling my hair again.

The woman's lovely singing seeps past my fingers. Her voice is the purest call of life I have ever heard, a sign that creation power dwells in every living creature. I start to lower my hands, and Radella tugs on my hair again.

"Will you stop it? You cannot torment people into—"

"Jamison, come back!"

Is that Laverick? Her voice comes from outside, over the singing. I look out the porthole again, yet I see no one in the fog.

"We have to find him," says Laverick.

"Why?" Harlow retorts. "Let him go."

"We're not losing Jamison too. Listen. He's going that way."

I still cannot see them, so I call out, "Laverick, over here!"

Neither woman responds.

I march out the door. Radella flies after me and lands on my shoulder to ride along. I drop over the side of the ship into the sand, and we set out into the fog.

The woman's singing and the crashing waves grow closer. Oddly, the two rhythms complement each other, as though the singer set her tempo to match the sea's.

I travel in the direction I last heard Laverick and come upon the water. Moonlight filters through the fog, expanding my view of the roaring waves raking across the sand. Some fool is swimming offshore. I squint in the dimness and make out Jamison's blond hair. He's the person in the water, and he isn't alone.

A woman approaches him from out in the sea. Her thick evergreen tresses and pale-green skin are startling, but more so is her voice. She's the woman singing.

The stranger slides up to Jamison and pulls him close, running her fingers across his shoulders and up his neck. He's passive in her clutches, her touch roaming long enough for heat to rise in my cheeks. As she begins to pull him out to sea, Radella speeds off toward them.

I run into the shallows, cold water pouring into my boots. "Jamison!"

The singing woman jerks her head toward me. Her eyes are blank and soulless like a shark's. Her low brows and high hairline create a disproportionately large forehead compared to her other features.

Radella circles her head and snatches at her hair. The woman swats at the pixie, missing her, and then pushes Jamison's head underwater. He slides down into the sea without resistance. Radella grabs more of the singer's hair and pulls. The woman shrieks and splashes her with something I did not expect—a fish tail.

She's a merrow, fish on the bottom and human on the top. I should have seen it before. Her big lips protrude out over her small chin and are puckered like a fish's, and her large ears taper down to gills partially hidden by her voluminous hair. Ridges of spurs stick out from her upper spine, sharp bones pointed at the ends.

Radella does not let go of her hair, the merrow screeching instead of singing. In her struggling, she releases Jamison, and he resurfaces, sputtering up water.

I wave my arms big and wide. "Over here!"

He kicks for shore, traveling the same path as the waves. The merrow hits Radella with a bigger splash, sending her pinwheeling, and begins her melody again. Jamison halts his retreat, still too far offshore for me to reach.

The merrow glides toward him, her expression murderous.

"Jamison!" I splash into the water up to my knees. Clock heart or not, I won't stand by while he's drowned.

A man runs past me into the water, swinging a rope over his head. He releases the rope, and it unfurls into a net that lands over Jamison and the merrow.

She shrieks and thrashes, splashing so rowdily I lose sight of them in the spray. The commotion quiets, and the empty net floats to the surface. Jamison slowly swims for the beach. The merrow has disappeared and taken her song with her.

Prince Killian Markham tromps out of the water, muttering under his breath. "I almost had her."

I stare at him, my jaw slackening. *Markham* threw the net?

Jamison crawls from the shallows. I lug him up the embankment, and he lies in the sand on his back, rubbing his head and blinking blearily.

"Everley, you're alive?"

I dust sand off his cheek and try not to let our lackluster reunion bother me. He nearly drowned, after all.

Radella stares daggers at Markham as he reels in the fishing net. The immortal prince has not changed; his face is still unfittingly handsome for his rotten heart. My curiosity for where he came from and how long he's been here is less important than what brought me here. He doesn't appear to carry a weapon under or over his wet clothes. I charge up to him, sticking my nose next to his.

"Where's my sword?"

Markham pats his hip and pretends to search for it. "I'm afraid it's not on me at the moment."

I shove him in the chest. "Where is it?"

"Does harassing people often result in your getting what you want?" he asks lightly and then taps Jamison's leg. "Remove your feet from the water, Lieutenant. The merrow's enchantment will linger inside you as long as you're touching the sea."

"Don't tell him what to do," I say, hitting Markham again for good measure.

The prince's wolfish eyes flash. "Then let him swim to his death."

This moment is going terribly wrong. I imagined when Markham and I next met, I'd shoot him and take back my sword. Not only do I not have a pistol, or any weapon at all, but he doesn't have the sword of Avelyn.

Farther up the beach, Harlow emerges from the fog, pauses to view our party, and then runs at us. Markham drops his net and soon catches her in midair. Her legs go around his waist, and I cannot tell which one kisses the other first, but in an instant, their lips are merged. I look away, disgusted, and envious that Harlow received a warm greeting while all I got was puzzlement from Jamison over the fact that I'm not dead.

Laverick breaks out of the fog next and wraps me in a hug. "I knew you'd make it to shore. Is Claret here?"

"Last I saw, she was in the boat with you."

"We capsized." Laverick's voice hitches. "The three of us managed to flip the boat over and climb back in, but Claret was swept away." Her attention fastens on Markham and Harlow still embracing. "Is that Prince Killian?"

"One and the same," I grumble.

Out in the waves, the merrow starts her melody again, drilling a shiver straight through me. Jamison's bloodshot gaze starts to wander in her direction. I grab his hand, startling him, and lace our fingers together. In our world, merrows are storybook antagonists. Apparently, the tales about them luring men under the sea to their deaths are true.

"Here." Markham offers Jamison pieces of beeswax. "Put these in your ears to soften the sound. Resisting the merrow's song can be torturous, like your teeth are rattling out of your head."

"Why aren't your ears plugged?" I question.

"Younger men are more susceptible to the merrow's summons." Markham's lips quirk upward. "Don't fret, Countess. I won't let your husband drown."

I nearly shove him again, just to wipe away his smirk. He would let any one of us drown if it suited him. He pretends he's a hero when, in truth, he cast the net to try to capture the merrow. Jamison's hand squeezes down on mine as her singing grows more insistent.

"We must go," Markham says, lugging his net. "More merrows may join her song, and then their summons will be too strong for any of us to resist."

He and Harlow trudge up the sandy embankment into thicker fog. The rest of us stay where we are, except for Radella, who lands on Jamison's shoulder. Now that they're reunited, he has resumed his role as her favorite.

"Well?" Laverick asks. "Do we leave?"

A cringe deepens Jamison's brow. He's so tense about the merrow I doubt he heard the Fox's question. We need to move away from the seashore, and I still need to find my sword.

"Let's see where this leads," I say.

We catch up to Harlow and Markham and follow the prince into the boneyard of ships.

Markham does not waver from cutting a path through the shipwrecks. How long has he been here? Where *is* here? And what did he do with my sword?

To my surprise, he guides us to the same vessel that Radella and I chose to take shelter in, only he goes inside a cabin three doors down from ours and lights an oil lantern as we file into the small quarters. Broken deck planks cover the portholes, sealing in the lantern light. Four chairs and a wardrobe cabinet are toppled and strewn about, and a desk has slid across the slanted floor to the far corner.

The merrow's song has finally stopped. Jamison releases my hand and removes the wax from his ears while I skim the cabin for the sword of Avelyn.

Harlow finds a mismatched collection of bottles piled under the desk. She uncorks one and drinks all the water herself. Markham hands a second bottle to me.

"Drink up, Evie."

"Don't call me that." I begrudgingly accept the bottle, drink my portion, and pass it on. "How long have you been here, Markham?"

"Long enough for the merrow's singing to interfere with my sleep. By netting her, I thought I could quiet the wretch."

Laverick passes the bottle to Jamison. He pours water in a tarnished silver spoon he found on the floor and lifts it for Radella. After she drinks, he takes a swig for himself.

Markham opens a tin box of hard biscuits and sets it out for us. "How much time has passed in the Land of the Living?" he asks. "Time moves differently here."

"You left with Dorcha two months ago," I reply, uncertain what he means. My clock heart beats more softly than usual, but no differently than before we left my world.

"'Left,'" he says, quoting me. "I was not swallowed by a whale by choice." Harlow slides him a sly glance, and he laughs. "You weren't taken here by Dorcha on purpose, were you?"

"Everley was frantic to follow you," Harlow replies, kissing his cheek. "All I did was sit back and wait."

"I wasn't following *him*," I mutter. Harlow didn't inform Captain Vevina about my ticker because she correctly assumed that my hunt for my sword would lead her to Markham. She's as irritating as he is, and together, with all the touching and kissing, they're insufferable.

"Did you see anyone else on the beach?" Laverick asks.

"Just the lot of you." The prince runs a suggestive finger down Harlow's hip. "The merrows lure the surviving crewmen of these shipwrecks into the sea until they're all gone. No one survives the Skeleton Coast for long."

The Skeleton Coast must be what this graveyard is called. An eerie name for an eerie place. "For someone who hasn't been in this world long, you seem to know a lot about it," I note.

Markham uncorks an amber bottle of grog, a mixture of rum and water. "You forget I've walked the worlds a long time."

I haven't forgotten he tricked time and gained immortality. At over 350 years old, he has seen more days than he deserves. "If you have so much experience, why are you here on this deserted coastline? Why did Dorcha bring you to this world?"

Markham chuckles. "I've missed your bluntness, Evie. Did you know you have something on your chin?" He peels his lips back over even white teeth, amused with himself for pointing out the most recent scar he gave me.

"Where's my sword?" I snap.

"Where's my heartwood?"

"It's gone." At his appalled look, I explain, "You saw me throw it overboard."

"I didn't think you would let it float away! Heartwood is the most precious, most powerful element in all the worlds."

"Then you shouldn't have let me take it from you." His habit of redirecting attention from himself to others incenses me. He animated an army of wooden soldiers with the heartwood of an ancient elderwood tree. I tossed the heartwood overboard to remove it from his reach, thus ending his control over the arcane army. "I'll ask one more time. What did you do with the sword?"

"You can ask me as many times as you'd like. I still don't have it."

"You were holding it when Dorcha took you," says Jamison.

"Dorcha was hired to bring me to this world so I could repay a debt. The sword was seized soon after my arrival, and I was marooned here on the coast."

"Seized?" I ask, my voice pitching higher.

Jamison gestures at me to quiet down and addresses the prince calmly. "Killian, who has the sword?"

"I had an outstanding payment with a pirate captain for a few barrels of rum. He stole the sword as payment."

I inhale sharply. "You let the hallowed sword of Avelyn be taken by *a pirate*? To pay *for your rum*?"

"The pirates took it, so I don't know why you're badgering me," Markham replies, setting his bottle of grog down with a clunk. "I've already explained I don't have the sword, but you insist on not listening."

I take a charged step forward to show him just how well I heard him. Jamison slips between us. "Remember what you came for, Evie."

He isn't protecting Markham from me, but me from myself. Though I could beat the prince for his carelessness and disrespect, I'm not here for him. Hearing my father and uncle's conversation reinforced the importance of my task. Though I often say the sword is mine, Father Time is its appointed keeper. The sword of Avelyn does not belong in Markham's custody, and it certainly shouldn't be in the possession of a pirate. The prince probably relinquished the treasure at the first hint of opposition, the bloody coward.

"What do we do?" Laverick asks, chewing the inside of her cheek. "How do we find the sword and Claret?"

"You don't." Markham shoves a biscuit into his mouth and speaks as he chews. "Your companion should have washed ashore by now. If she doesn't surface soon, she has either drowned or been taken captive by pirates or merrows."

Laverick blanches. "You said women aren't enchanted by the merrows' song."

"I said young men are more receptive to their summons. Women are not immune." He brushes crumbs from his fingers. "You should abandon your cause and return to your world. There's nothing for you here."

His dismissiveness incenses me, yet my main concern is for Laverick. I extend a hand to let her know I do not share his opinion. She balls her quivering fingers into fists and storms outside, slamming the door so hard a plank falls from a porthole.

"She's pleasant company," Markham remarks dryly.

He cares nothing for Claret, and I'm beginning to question how invested he is in the sword. But Markham is an exceptional liar. He hid his identity as the lost prince of *The Legend of Princess Amadara* for centuries. He's so gifted that not only did he rise through the ranks of the royal navy to admiral but Queen Aislinn appointed him governor over her penal colony. I don't believe for one second that he doesn't know the exact location of the sacred sword.

Harlow wraps her arms around his neck and presses her bosom against his chest. He entangles his hands in the ends of her loose blond hair.

"I've missed you," she purrs.

"And I've missed you, honeysuckle. We have lost time to make up for." He takes her by the hand and leads her into an adjoining cabin, probably the officer's quarters, and closes the door.

"Honeysuckle?" I say to Jamison.

"Would you like a nickname?"

"Only if I can give you one too," I reply. He stares at the floor, his attention wandering elsewhere. "Jamison, are you all right?"

He shakes his head, his focus returning. "I'm fine."

"The merrow can't get you in here."

"Of course not." His gaze probes into mine. "How did you survive falling into the water? Your clock heart—?"

"Radella repaired it," I say, though a piece of what happened still feels missing.

He touches his fingertips lightly against mine. "I thought you were gone."

He doesn't say he missed me. He doesn't need to. I feel his worry. "How did you make it to land?"

"The current carried us to shore, and then the surf destroyed the longboat. We tried to find you and Radella, but we couldn't see through the fog. Then I heard singing. Next thing I remember, I was in the sea, swimming toward you and Killian."

"Markham is too at ease," I say, frowning. "Can you distract him tomorrow while I search the ship? He may be lying about the pirates."

Jamison's slight grip on my hand falls away. "Everley, my coming here wasn't on purpose. I went down into the water to help Claret. My opinion about your obsession hasn't changed."

"My obsession? I don't want to be here any more than you do."

"I'm not sure I believe that." He turns away to gaze out the port-hole. A thick silence expands between us, and I exchange frowns with Radella. She appears no more certain about how to address his moodi-ness than me.

"I'm going to check on Laverick," I mutter, then slip outside.

Laverick sits on the gunwale, her feet dangling over the side of the ship. Patches of the fog float away, offering glimpses of a silver moon and icy stars. I prop my hip against the wooden rail beside the Fox.

Despite the wind and sand and sea, the details of the vessel's craftsmanship have weathered well. If only my clock heart were so resilient.

"Don't pay any attention to Markham," I say. "He wouldn't know the truth if it landed on his head."

Laverick stops swinging her feet. "Claret said everything would be fine as long as we stayed together. I tried. We both did, but she was already tired from falling into the water the first time. Her hand slipped through mine, and then the waves came . . ."

"You did everything you could."

Laverick's stricken gaze slides to me. "Have you ever had a secret you couldn't tell because it could ruin everything, but holding it inside you is like trying to trap a giant in a hatbox? The thing's so immense you don't know how long you can stuff it away?"

My ticker skips three beats in a row. Does Laverick know? "No, but I can imagine that would be difficult."

"It is."

My concern that she has guessed my secret slowly dissolves. She's too immersed in her own emotions to grapple with mine.

Jamison comes out on deck, and his arrival instantly shifts the mood. A strained pause stretches between the three of us, tightening and tightening until Laverick hops down from the rail. She bids us good night and goes inside.

"I'll stand watch tonight," Jamison says, joining me at the rail, "and tomorrow I'll distract Killian for you."

"But you said—"

"I know what I said, but I also know Killian. He has more patience than the Creator, and no one can force him to do anything against his will. I don't know what he's after, but his coming to the Land Under the Wave was not to settle a debt over stolen rum."

My intuition says the same, but not understanding what Markham is after only frustrates me more.

Jamison kicks at a sand pile. "I don't want to contend with you, Everley, but I must be clear: My priority is to find a portal back to our world. I've been away from home far too long."

"Home . . . You mean Dorestand."

He studies the dark spots on the moon. "The man we saw on the ship is the queen's secretary of state and a friend of my father's. When I first enlisted in the navy, my father said if he ever needed me, he would send Secretary Winters. After my sister died, the secretary tracked me down and advised me to return to Wyeth."

I'm loath to consider what news could have sent the secretary of state to find him this time. "Are you certain he came to deliver a message to you?"

"That was my first instinct. My second instinct was to run." Jamison bows his head in regret. Clearly, he wishes he had stayed in the Land of the Living. "My father is an old man. Our last words to each other were of anger. I cannot let that be our final memory together."

I envy his chance to make amends with his father. It was late autumn the night my parents died. The first hard freeze was collecting on the field outside. Our manor was like an elderly woman with a chill in her bones, so my entire family had gathered around the fireplace in the study. *Put another log on the fire,* I said, my final words to my father. Directly after, Markham knocked on the door and Father left to answer it. My brother Carlin threw another log in the hearth for us. My last words to him were less polite. Carlin had played a musical number on his flute as a birthday gift for Mother. I told him his song was dull. Whenever I hear a flute, I think of how contemptible I was to him.

I have carried these regrets alongside others—little things my uncle did that I didn't appreciate, times I didn't say "I love you" to my parents, and patience I didn't have with my siblings. If I can, I will spare Jamison the anguish of similar regrets.

"We'll find a way home," I say. "I promise."

Chapter Six

My grumbling stomach wakes me well before dawn. The biscuits have all been eaten, including the crumbs, so I slip past where Radella is asleep and sneak outside into the early morning mist. The fog has skulked in, closing in around the shipwreck like a vise. I wrap my cloak tighter around me to offset the gloomy cold.

Jamison sits against the gunwale and rubs his bad knee. He was too spooked by the merrow to sleep before, but exhaustion should remedy that now.

I smooth hair from his tired eyes. "Go to bed, honeysuckle."

One corner of his mouth curls up. "I will, darling dearest." He hands me the sharp end of a broken broomstick, my defense against intruders, and lumbers off.

In the predawn quiet, the sounds of the sea are richer. The melodic waves drum a rhythm not unlike my ticker. As dawn burns through the fog, I lay my hand over my clockwork heart. The ticktock is still muted, perhaps even more so, but its beat is unmistakable.

Radella flies out on deck and plunks down in a pile of sand beside me.

"Did I imagine last night?" I ask. "Or did the monster who murdered my parents invite us aboard this ship?"

Radella holds her hands up and out.

"That's what I thought. Radella, how did my clock heart survive me falling into the sea? It should have been waterlogged. Even if you vanished the water, it still would have stopped."

The pixie draws a circle in the sand and adds half circles around it. She steps back to show me the daisy—the emblem of Father Time and our other two deities. Mother Madrona and the Creator are of one heart and one mind, but I have an inkling they're not who preserved me. Father Time can grow daisies spontaneously, transforming thorns into flowers. His regenerative power must have preserved my ticker.

Harlow comes outside from the cabin she shares with Markham and pads over to us in her bare feet, smoking a tobacco pipe. A man's dressing robe is wrapped about her, and a silver necklace hangs around her slim throat. They appear to be all she's wearing.

"We've run out of food," she says. "Everley, you and I will search another shipwreck for more."

"Why don't you take Markham along?"

"He's still asleep, and I want to go and be back before the day heats up."

I had intended to hunt for my sword, but this way, Jamison can sleep too. When we return, he can distract Markham while I check the ship. "Fine. I'm ready when you are."

"I'll get dressed." Harlow sneers at the pixie. "Your flying rat isn't invited."

Radella sticks out her tongue at her.

As Harlow goes, Laverick steps on deck wearing men's attire and dragging a fishing net. "I'm going to the sea to catch a merrow," she declares.

"Does Markham know you have his net?" I ask.

"I didn't steal it." Her color rises. "I'm borrowing it."

"I didn't mean to imply otherwise."

Laverick shrugs, though I think I've hurt her feelings. "The merrows might know where we can find Claret. I'm going to hide the net in the water. When they see me, they may come closer to investigate, and I'll catch them."

I hope the stories about merrows having poor eyesight are true. Laverick may have shoved her hair into a floppy hat and put on men's clothes to resemble a fisherman, but her facial features are distinctly female. Even so, this gives her something useful to do and makes her feel proactive. As she plods into the fog, I say to Radella, "Maybe you should go with her."

The pixie nods and zips off after the Fox.

Harlow returns fully dressed, carrying an empty sack and bottles of water. She drops over the gunwale into the sand and sets off.

"Where are we going?" I ask, jumping down after her.

"To a wreck up the coast." As she consults a crudely drawn map, her sleeve slides up her arm, revealing bruises along her wrist. She catches me staring and covers them again.

Golden daylight melts away the sea haze, revealing a vivid sky and shimmering coastline. We cannot have walked for more than fifteen minutes when Harlow stops at a strange wooden post sticking out of the sand. As she circles it, I notice the fine workmanship.

"What is it?" I ask.

"A mast."

This must be the very top. We sidestep down the dune to an exposed section of the ship's hull. The majority of the vessel is buried in sand.

Harlow discovers a hole leading inside the vessel and scoops more sand away from the opening. A strong gust rains granules down on us that I brush off my shoulders. Dunes migrate, their mounds toppled by the wind and rebuilt again. Soon, the entire ship will be covered.

"Is it safe to go in?" I ask.

"Are you scared?"

She's provoking me, just like the old days when we dueled in swordplay. She tucks her necklace under her shirt and crawls inside.

I go in after her. The only light within the ship comes through the hole we entered. The interior is massive, the corridors at least ten feet tall. We stroll past a chair twice the size of any I have ever seen and a hook on the wall as big as my head.

"Harlow, whose ship is this?"

"Why are you whispering? The crew is long dead."

She leads us down a very tall corridor, over broken planks and sandy deposits. As we turn a corner into the hold, we lose most of our visibility. I stay back while Harlow slides down the sloped floor inside.

Huge barrels have toppled over and lie strewn across the ground. A large rack stacked to the ceiling with more barrels hangs forward, partially tied to the wall with taut ropes. Sand trickles in through fist-size holes in the hull where the ship was damaged when it ran aground. Harlow pries open a barrel that has tipped on its side, standing very close to the tilted rack. She holds up a handful of dried apricots and throws me one. I turn it over in my hands. The fruit is three times the size of ours back home. She stuffs the sack with more while snacking on one. When she doesn't immediately keel over from sickness or poison, I nibble a bite. The apricots may be large, but they taste the same as I'm used to.

She scoots past me into the corridor and sets the half-full sack at my feet. "Finish gathering the food," she says. "I'll be back."

"Where are you going?"

"Just get the food."

She disappears up the corridor. Picking up the sack, I pad carefully into the hold and past the wall rack. A stiff wind could probably snap the ropes and bring it all tumbling down. I side-foot away over broken planks and trip. My hands go out to catch me, and my palms scrape against the sandy ground. I tripped over a string . . . no, a lace. I follow it to the largest boot I have ever seen. My nerves crackle with unease. Whoever it belonged to must have been enormous.

Harlow reappears in the doorway with a carnyx, a long, thin battle horn taller than her. The bronze bell at the bottom is fashioned into the shape of an openmouthed bear. Carnyxes were used in warfare long ago. Blowing through the mouthpiece resulted in a piercing roar that could be heard across a battlefield to rally the courage of allies and quiver the bellies of enemies.

She places the mouthpiece against her lips and blows. The noise that emerges is horrible, a banshee howl that forces me to cover my ears. The blare is so loud it could probably be heard in another world.

"What did you do that for?" I demand.

"I wanted to see if it still works."

"Now that you've woken the dead, can we go?"

"You're the one just standing around. You didn't even finish getting the food."

She and I shove handfuls of apricots into the sack. As we work, the barrel lightens and becomes unbalanced. I jump back as it rolls past the rack and bangs into the hull. One of the ropes snaps and the whole rack falls forward. I shut my eyes, waiting for the impact, but the last rope holds and restrains the rack.

Sand trickles faster through the holes in the hull.

I exhale sharply. "I want to go."

The ship groans as if in response, then the last rope breaks. Harlow and I jump from the path of the falling rack, barrels and shelves crashing into the floor. We lie on our sides as the dribbling sand widens to streams. More boards break where the fallen rack tore from the hull, letting loose a deluge.

We scramble to our feet, her with the carnyx and me with the food sack, and run for the door. A wave of sand bursts through the walls, chasing us into the corridor. Ahead, our exit slowly fills up, steadily trapping us. I dive into the shrinking opening and paw to the surface.

Outside of the ship, I roll to a stop. Harlow digs and wriggles her way out beside me. The hole fills in behind her, and the sand under us pours into the collapsing ship, sucking us toward the opening. We scurry up and dash away from the sinkhole, slipping and sliding, and somersault down the embankment to the other side. The ship is going under. Harlow scoops up the carnyx, I grab the food sack, and we run until the sand no longer threatens to drag us down.

We pause and stare at the cloud of dust blemishing the sky. I drop the sack and bend forward to recover and rest my ticker. Though I am winded, my clock heart isn't beating more quickly. I can scarcely feel its drumming.

"Let's head back," Harlow pants.

"I need another moment."

She hoists the sack of food over her shoulder with a huff, and then her eyes bulge. "Where's my necklace?" She spins in a circle, checking the sandy ground.

"It must have come off."

"I have to find it. My father gave that necklace to my mother."

We check around us and find nothing. The necklace could have fallen off in the ship or while we were running, which would mean it's buried under several feet of sand. As Harlow's chin begins to quiver, something drops out of her shirt. I scoop it up and see a glass-vial pendant dangling on the chain. Something little and black is at the bottom of the vial.

She rips the necklace from my grasp. "You had it all along!"

"It fell out of your shirt. What's inside the vial?"

"Something more valuable than your wormy life."

She marches off with the sack of food and carnyx across her back. I let her pull ahead to avoid another tongue-lashing.

Before long, Harlow crests the last rise and peers at the waters along the coast. I shade my eyes to see what's caught her attention and spot a ship. The watercraft is massive, larger than the royal navy's first-rate vessels. Its exterior is stained dark walnut, and it displays a black flag with white symbols, a sandglass over a skull and crossbones. I give a little shudder. I have read enough storybooks to recognize a pirate flag when I see one.

Harlow rushes down the dune to our wreck. Laverick sits on the gunwale of the lopsided deck, tying closed a hole in a fishing net.

"Killian!" Harlow calls. "They're here!"

Markham throws open the door to his cabin and marches out with a spyglass to view the ship. Laverick and I squint at the vessel off the coast and see a longboat rowing to shore.

"Who are they?" Laverick asks.

"That's the *Undertow*." Markham snaps the spyglass closed. "The Skeleton Coast lies within their territorial boundaries. Prepare to depart."

I rush inside the cabin to wake Jamison. He lies on his back, Radella stretched out on top of him. "Both of you get up. We have to go."

He rouses and rises quickly. Radella hovers in the air, stretching like a lazy cat.

"What's the trouble?" Jamison asks, pulling on a shirt.

"Pirates are rowing to shore. Our tracks are all over the beach."

Radella flies to the porthole to see for herself. Jamison leaves the hem of his shirt untucked and his sleeves unbuttoned and picks up the broken broomstick, our only defense besides the pixie's dust. Radella lands on his shoulder, and we all exit the cabin.

Markham has slung the carnyx over his shoulder and packed a bag of supplies. The longboat has landed and the pirates are disembarking. Even from afar, I observe that one of them is double the size of the others. Markham hops down off the deck into the sand. We jump down after him and duck around the hull for cover. The prince strides out into the open.

"Markham," I hiss. "Get down!"

He lifts the carnyx to his lips and blows. The horn blares a gut-shaking roar, drowning out the wind. Down the beach, the pirates halt and head in our direction.

"What are you doing?" I gasp. "You told us we were leaving."

He lifts his arms above his head and waves at the pirates. "We are."

Chapter Seven

Jamison and I stare in horror at the pirates lumbering up the sand dune. The largest one, who I distinguished by his immense size, leads their march. I don't require a closer inspection to figure out that he's too big to be a man. That pirate is a giant.

"Killian, what have you done?" Jamison asks.

"Everley wants the sword. This is how we'll track it down." Markham still waves at the approaching pirates, welcoming them onward.

Jamison fists the broken broomstick like a sword. "We're leaving."

"And where will you go?" Markham questions. "The Skeleton Coast will bury you in a sandy grave if the pirates don't find you first."

I wish Radella had the power to disappear a whole person or even parts of the body. Markham would be more bearable without his head.

Harlow takes the carnyx from him and kisses his cheek, rewarding him for a reason I am too staggered to inquire about. As the pirates crest the dune, Laverick comes forward out of the ship's shadow with us.

The giant treads to the top first, a mace dangling from his meaty hand. He must be nine feet tall, his neck, biceps, and thighs all wider than my waist. Rich-brown hair hangs about his shoulders and his bulbous cheekbones sit high and wide on his square face, offset by a hooked nose that extends like a beak over his mustache and thin lips. Disproportionate to his other features are his huge ears that stand equal with the top of his head. His clothes are refined, an ivory shirt with a ruffled collar and cuffs under a fitted jacket with red silk lining.

My uncle read me grisly stories about giants kidnapping and eating humans. This giant appears more sophisticated than the bloodthirsty images born from those tales, but his tremendous size is petrifying. He towers over us, swallowing us in his shadow.

His buccaneers flank him on both sides. The eight of them are our height and build, except they have oddly elongated faces and upturned noses. They, too, are dressed in formfitting quality wool, white cotton shirts tucked into gray trousers, and fine leather vests and belts. I catch sight of their pointed ears beneath their head scarves and understand why they look like overgrown pixies. They're elves.

All three groups of the triad are here—giants and elves and humans—all born from Mother Madrona's power under the direction of the Creator. My parents were Children of Madrona, worshippers of her as the Mother of All. They taught me to believe humans were members of the triad, but until now, I wasn't convinced such stories were true.

Every elf aims a cutlass at us. Radella stands on Jamison's shoulder and holds her wings taut, ready to race at them and disappear their weapons with her dust.

The giant's brown eyes, his smallest feature, take us in like he's found mice in his bedchamber. "Prince Killian, you've gained comrades. Were they the cause for the battle cry?" He glances from side to side, overexaggerating his survey. "You must have been confused, as I see no battlefield."

Markham extends the carnyx between them, presenting it to the pirate. "My apologies for disturbing your day, Captain Redmond. This was my only method of summoning you."

"The purpose of marooning you was so we wouldn't have to hear from you again," replies a sneering elf. Even darkened by anger, his features are handsomer than the prince's. He has deep-brown skin and a stern expression that is both audacious and alert.

Markham's charming exterior slips, revealing a venomous undertone. "You should know by now that I'm not easy to get rid of, Osric." He offers the carnyx to the captain. "We obtained this from a wreck."

The giant accepts the battle horn, and Markham smiles at Harlow. Our trek up the coastline to scavenge for food was a ruse. She didn't care about apricots. She wanted the battle horn so she could call the pirates.

"You summoned us here to give me an old horn?" asks Captain Redmond.

"You know me better than that," Markham says, cavalier despite the many blades aimed at him. "Do you, by chance, still have my sword?"

Captain Redmond peers down his droopy nose at him. "Do I still have the sword of Avelyn, you ask?" The prince's gaze turns stony. "Aye, I knew what weapon you carried. Why do you think I took it as payment for your debt? As I am certain you know, that sword is a highly sought-after relic. A ruler might give away his throne for it."

Markham's smirk wavers. "I'm certain we could work out a fair bargain."

"Oh, I doubt that. In any case, I no longer have the sword in my possession."

My ticker stumbles and then speeds up.

"How much did you fetch in exchange for the blade?" Markham asks, calmer than I am about this news.

The pirate captain fluffs his lacy sleeves. "King Dorian offered us unrestricted port access to Merrow Lagoon for four hundred tides. His taxes have become excessive. Few profiteers can afford to make berth for more than a day. First Mate Osric and I couldn't refuse."

Jamison glowers in consternation. He must have the same questions I do: Who is King Dorian? Where is Merrow Lagoon? Are tides a form of currency in this world? But none of these unknowns are more pressing than my greatest question. *Where is my sword?*

Markham's forehead wrinkles, the only indication that he is displeased. "Would you consider a trade for transportation to Merrow Lagoon?"

The giant arches a brow, intensifying his apparent distaste for dealing with the prince. "What could you possibly possess that I would want?"

"Her," Markham says, pointing at me.

Before I can blink, Jamison steps in front of me.

"Absolutely not. Everley is not a commodity to be traded. Killian, have you lost your ever-sinking mind?"

"The girl won't fetch a worthwhile price on her own," Captain Redmond says to Markham, ignoring Jamison's outburst. "I'll take all four humans and the pixie."

"The girl isn't for you to trade," Markham explains. "She's for your collection."

Their negotiating moves so fast I cannot keep up, but when Markham reaches for me, Jamison swings the broken broomstick at him in warning.

"Enough of that." Captain Redmond jabs Jamison in the chest with his finger and knocks him on his backside.

Radella flies at the giant. He swats her aside, sending her spinning into the sand. Laverick kicks an elf in the shin, but another elf points his cutlass at her gullet. At the same time, Markham grabs the front of my shirt and yanks. The top buttons come undone, widening my neckline to reveal an indecent amount of flesh—and my clock heart.

"What is that?" Captain Redmond bends closer for a view.

I clutch my shirt closed. "Back off, you brute."

He snaps his fingers, and three of his elven crew surround me. First Mate Osric wrenches my arms behind my back. I wriggle and thrash, kicking up sand. He twists my arm into an unnatural angle, and immobilizing pain shoots down my side.

Captain Redmond leans over me again, and his big fingers reopen my neckline. My every instinct screams at me to fight them off. I slam Osric in the shin with my boot heel and arch my head back, whamming him in the face. Both strikes land hard, yet the elf's hold on me does not falter.

I writhe and yell, thrashing with all my might. The captain finishes opening my shirt, and the wind pours across my skin, sending prickles down my hot throat.

"A clock heart," he breathes.

I hang forward, limp and rasping. The first mate takes on more of my weight, holding me upright. I wish he would let me go. I want to sink into the sand and disappear forever. Another part of me still rages for a fight, but I am paralyzed.

Never before have so many eyes beheld my biggest secret.

The elves whisper their disbelief. Above them I hear Laverick mutter her shock. I doubt she intends to slight me, but her reaction scalds.

Jamison rises, and an elf shoves him right back down.

"Everley's clockwork heart animates her," Markham explains.

Captain Redmond's eyes spread wider, and he turns his head toward my chest, so I can see the wiry hairs growing out of his ears. He listens to several dull ticktocks and shifts back, his sour breaths streaming across my exposed skin. He traces my chest scar and then presses his fingertip over my ticker.

I fasten my gaze to the ground and resist the urge to cry. Uncle Holden taught me that if I were discovered, I was to send my captors to him to answer their questions. But he is a world away.

"How does your ticker work?" asks the giant.

"I don't know," I reply hoarsely. My uncle believes Father Time spared my life with this miraculous invention, but when I asked Father Time, he was vague.

Captain Redmond tips my chin up. "Why have you come to the Land Under the Wave?"

"Father Time sent me. I'm here to retrieve the sword of Avelyn." I hear my reason, and now that I'm here, and the pirates have me, it feels like the stupidest reason in all the worlds to risk myself and my friends.

The captain's eyes narrow. My association to Father Time has not impressed him.

The beat of my ticker is fainter, my voice weak. "Please let me go."

Markham speaks right over me. "Everley will be the crowning achievement of your clock collection."

Captain Redmond listens to my heart again. The soft beat is nearly undetectable, my vision growing hazy. I feel more than see him open my shirt wider. In between the white dots zooming across my sight, I watch him shift back. "Prince Killian, you're bold to offer me a defective timepiece."

My gaze flickers to Jamison. Defective? He appears as alarmed as me.

"She's in good condition," Markham argues. "Look at her. The clock gives her life."

"Not for long," Captain Redmond says matter-of-factly. "Her clock heart isn't functioning at capacity. She's broken."

I hunch farther forward, my stomach cranking.

Harlow snorts, as though she knew all along that I was worthless. Markham grabs her wrist and pushes pain into her eyes, letting the pressure of his fingertips reprimand her.

"Mundy," he says, verging on desperation, "the girl has a clockwork heart. Her ticker must be of value for trading. If not Merrow Lagoon, then take us somewhere closer, Skull Reef or Hangman's Spit."

"Prince Killian, you're too clever not to know when you've lost." Captain Redmond snatches Radella from the sand, trapping her in his fist, and then signals his men. "Bring them."

The elves round us up and march us toward their longboat. I stumble down the dune, my head and shoulders sunk forward and my open shirt flapping. Markham blathers on about the captain making a mistake, but I hardly hear him. The sword is at the bottom of the sea, and with it my chance to finish my father's mission. Buried under my disappointment lies something deeper and uglier. I want to shut it out, but my mind booms with two words that confirm every doubt I've ever had about myself.

She's broken.

Chapter Eight

Captain Redmond sits in the middle of the bench, steadying the long-boat with his heavy weight. My shirt is still open at the top, the buttons broken, my scar and ticker exposed. Everyone takes turns peeking at my ticker. Even Laverick cannot contain her interest. My uncle cautioned me that the moment others learned about my clock heart, at a minimum, I would become a spectacle, an anomaly to gawk at. This scarring mortification is worse than he described.

Jamison casts worried glances at me and glares at our captors. His anger may be outmatched by Radella's, whose fury has changed her normal bright-azure color to the same purplish shade as a bruise. The captain still holds the pixie tightly in his fist. Before loading us into the boat, the pirates gagged and bound Markham. If only the prince were always muzzled. Unfortunately, they did not gag Harlow, not that she's speaking. No, it's her smirk that I would prefer to see covered.

We row out to the *Undertow* and up to her port. The massive ship is longer, taller, and wider than any I have ever seen, nearly double the size of our navy's intimidating first-rate vessels. Crewmen above toss down a rope ladder for us.

"Up with you, Ticker," says Captain Redmond.

I have never been comfortable on the water, and I don't enjoy heights, but I force myself to follow his command.

Grabbing the rope ladder, I climb to the top of the gunwale and hop onto the deck. A saltwater crocodile growls at me from where it lies a few strides away. I scramble away and flatten my back against the rail. From tail to snout, the croc is longer than a man is tall. I fully intend to scurry back down the ladder to get away, but the croc meanders off, tail sliding from side to side as it goes.

Once the crocodile is a safe distance away, I notice the crewmen standing at attention. There must be fifty of them, each one handsome, exquisitely so. They are impeccably dressed in a crisp uniform of gray trousers, a clean ivory shirt, and a head scarf that bears the symbols of their flag—a sandglass over a skull and crossbones.

All are elves, except for a second giant standing off to the side. His shoulders are rolled forward in a permanent hunch, but he is still larger than anyone else on board. He's brutish in girth, and his hair and mustache are gray and his face is thin like an old man's. His long nose hangs so low it nearly touches his upper lip.

The giant stares at me in puzzlement. I quickly grip my shirt closed.

Jamison steps aboard next, with First Mate Osric right behind him, and then Laverick. My husband watches me with such tender concern I am afraid tears might come to my eyes, so I direct my attention to Laverick. She scans the main deck, probably in search of a weapon for defense. The crewmen aren't carrying pistols, and I don't see a single cannon on the expansive deck. What kind of a pirate ship has no guns? My assumption that the pirates would be slovenly, disorganized, and unregimented also appears misguided. Their deck is in impeccable condition and order. The *Undertow* could easily sail for the royal navy and fit right in.

Harlow steps on deck and then helps Markham down beside her. The pirates unbound his hands but left him gagged. The first mate and captain must have warned Markham not to remove it.

"Prince Killian," Osric says, binding the prince's wrists again, "I have never felt this fondly toward you." Having thought the same of his gag, I scoff under my breath. The elf aims his severe stare in my direction. "Do you have a grievance with the prince, woman?"

"You could say so. He murdered my family and stabbed me through the chest as a child."

Osric grunts. "He's done worse."

Captain Redmond climbs aboard, Radella still captured in his hand. The huge ship accommodates the addition of his weight without any creaking or swaying.

The crocodile reappears and slinks toward us. Laverick gives a chirp of surprise as the large reptile slides past her to the captain. My upper lip curls as the giant strokes the croc's leathery head. The scaly beast goes very still and lets the giant touch him, not nipping or growling.

A crewman hurries forward with a birdcage, and Captain Redmond shoves Radella inside. The pixie flutters her wings, raining her dust to try to disappear the bars.

"Save your dust," says the captain. "The cage is iron."

Radella kicks and bangs against the bars, trilling furiously. The noise seems to irritate the crocodile, and it waddles down the deck again.

Captain Redmond chuckles. "Pixies are such expressive creatures. First Mate Osric, lead our guests to their accommodations."

"Happily, sir." Osric shoves Markham into a pair of elves, who grab his bound arms. "Take him to his cell and throw the others in the brig."

"I want to go with Killian," Harlow says loudly.

Osric smacks his lips in distaste. "You should reconsider your allegiance, woman. The prince is a dangerous fellow. He has betrayed many a lady companion, several of whom were far more beautiful than you."

Harlow holds on to her defiant glare, though her cheeks flush. Markham tries to say something, his expression scathing, but his gag muffles him.

Osric barks a dry laugh. "Look at you, Your Highness. You're a disgrace to your people and world."

"That's enough, Osric," says the captain, a gentle insertion. "The others will go below, but I want the girl with the clock heart in the day cabin."

Jamison wrenches from his guard's grasp. "Everley and I stay together."

The captain glares down at him. "Who are you?"

Jamison draws up to his full height. "I'm Lieutenant Jamison Callahan of the royal navy and the Earl of Walsh, a lord of the Realm of Wyeth. Everley is my wife. The countess and I will stay together."

"You're a mighty important human. He's impressive, isn't he, lads?" The captain snickers along with his crew. Then in the next second, he replaces his mirth with a sneer. "I own your wife now, Lord Human. She's part of my collection."

"Everley is a person, not a trinket," Jamison counters. His coldness is every inch that of a blue-blooded naval officer. If I had a heart of flesh and blood, it would swell.

Captain Redmond bends over Jamison, his massive size dwarfing him. To his everlasting credit, Jamison does not balk. "You speak on behalf of your wife as though she belongs to you, as though she's your possession. How does my ownership of her differ?"

Jamison cranks his jaw. "The difference is I care about her."

The giant smooths down Jamison's windswept hair, petting him as he did his crocodile. "Humans have so many emotions. We giants are taught to use our minds over our hearts. You must do the same if you hope to survive this world, Lord of the Humans." He swats Jamison on the back and knocks him into his guard, who detains him. "Take them below. The rest of you scrub the deck! I want to see my reflection in these planks!"

Crewmen scurry off, and the guards direct Jamison, Laverick, Harlow, and Markham to the hatch that leads belowdecks. Another pirate brings Radella along with them in her cage.

Osric prods me to a huge door off the main deck at the stern of the ship. I try yanking from his grasp, but he pushes me inside and locks me in.

"Let me out!" I bang my fists against the door. My torn shirt falls open, and my anger from the beach returns. "I said let me out, you two-bit elf! My name isn't Ticker! I'm Everley Donovan, and you're going to be sorry! I swear to the moon you will regret this!"

His laughter carries through the door.

I kick the door and my toe crunches. While I wait for my foot to quit hurting, I glance around at the day cabin. Windows line the far side, letting in ample daylight. A bunk and a workbench like the one in my uncle's workshop dominate the longest wall. Baskets of tools, cogs, gears, and balance wheels are piled beneath the bench. Scattered amid the furniture and set out on the floor are clocks—water clocks, pendulum clocks, watch clocks, cuckoo clocks, and a grandfather clock. Among them are even a couple sundials and sandglasses. The room must hold at least a hundred timepieces of various sizes, ages, and materials. Most are constructed out of fine wood, though some are brass inset with colorful jewels.

The absence of noise sends my hand to my chest. Other than the sound of my ticker, I hear no ticktocks from the timepieces, no swoosh of swinging pendulums or whir of spinning cogs. The noise in my uncle's shop wasn't uproarious, but one couldn't enter the presence of his dozens of merchandise clocks without the pieces welcoming them into the motion of time.

Pressing my ear to the side of the grandfather clock, I listen for life. More silence greets me. I inspect its mechanisms for bad gears or blockages and find nothing visibly wrong with the inner workings. The clockwork is so shiny I can see myself in the brass pendulum, and the gears are immaculate, as if the grandfather clock is brand new.

I go from clock to clock in search of a functioning mechanism. My hunt takes nearly an hour from start to finish. After I have inspected the last timepiece that has moving parts, I sit on the bunk and drop my face into my hands.

Every clock in the captain's collection except my own is dead.

Hours later, an elf brings me a pail of steaming water and a washcloth, then slips out again. I don't want to accept anything from these damn pirates, but sand has worked its way into hidden places, itching me and grating against my skin, and every time I scratch my scalp, thick grit collects beneath my fingernails.

I stare at the steaming-hot water until I cannot bear the itchiness any longer, then I strip down to my underclothes and wash my hair.

Someone clears their throat behind me.

The first mate entered the cabin while my head was in the bucket. My wet hair drips down my back as I cover my chest. My thin under-garments conceal most of me, but I am still apprehensive about one of my captors finding me in a state of undress.

"Have you any decency?" I ask.

"I'm a pirate," Osric responds, as though that is all the explanation I need. "Don't concern yourself with modesty, woman. Elves aren't attracted to humans. We mate only with our own kind. Humans are no more appealing to us than a dog or a rat."

I'm not seeking his approval, but his repulsion is a little more than I was prepared for. "You've stated your disgust well."

"Yet you still fear me."

"I do not."

"Your fingertips twitch toward your waist—where your sword must usually hang?—when you're distressed."

I clasp my hands in front of me. "I'm not afraid of you."

"Perhaps you should be." Osric begins to tour the room, examining the captain's vast clock collection. "Why did the prince wish for Captain Redmond to capture him and bring him aboard our ship?"

His phrasing perplexes me. "How do you know Markham wanted you to capture him? He protested quite loudly."

"Too loudly. Killian never knows when to shut his mouth, but he's no fool. He does nothing without a cause."

I wring out my damp hair. "How do you and Markham know each other?"

"We were friends once."

I'm surprised. His rancor for the prince is as plain as my own. I do not trust this elf, but I didn't lie when I said I was not afraid of him. Still, true to his word, Osric has shown no interest in my half-undressed body.

"We were friends ages ago," Osric explains. "I was young and precocious."

"How long ago was it?" I ask. Osric doesn't look much older than me, but elves live a long time, up to a thousand years, and Markham has the infuriating advantage of immortality, so for all I know they could have been friends decades, or even centuries, ago.

"We were friends long enough for me to see who he really is under all that charisma and bravado." Osric removes a small red apple from his pocket. He inspects the fruit for the right place to bite and then sinks his teeth in. I'm hungry from not eating all day, yet he offers me none and speaks between chews. "Before you dress, the captain has asked that the cabin boy take a close look at your ticker."

"No one meddles with my clock heart."

"You can trust Neely. His job is to fix things."

"He can't be very good at it or these clocks would be working."

"That's no fault of his. The tides rule the Land Under the Wave. Gear timepieces are easily corroded by the heavy air and salt water. Yours will be no exception if we don't act soon."

I clamp my mouth shut and quickly finish dressing. My clothes are dirty and my shirt is still torn, but I put them back on to stop the first mate from appearing as though he ate something rancid whenever he looks at me.

The door opens, and the stooped giant enters with a canvas bag, his bent head brushing the ceiling. "Good day, poppet. I've come to have a look at your clock heart."

I fold my arms across my chest and take in his big size and bushy gray hair. "You're the cabin boy?"

Neely's blue eyes dance. "Aye. I like when the crew calls me that. Makes me feel young again."

"How old *are* you?"

"It's rude to ask a giant's age," Osric says through a mouthful of apple. Then he adds in a poorly veiled murmur, "Humans are so ill mannered."

The hypocrisy of his statement, said with a mouthful of food, galls me so much that I cannot stop myself from tsk-tsking.

Neely sets down his bag. "I had my centennial birthday last year."

Giants don't live as long as elves, but they still outlast humans. Most humans would consider themselves fortunate to make it to their tenth decade.

The century-old giant strides to me, his attention fixated on the location of the clock heart under my shirt. "You needn't be shy, poppet. The captain said your clock isn't functioning properly. I've come to fix you up as good as new."

"Good as new" would mean a working heart of flesh and blood, something I gave up wishing and praying for when I was a child.

Neely towers over me and patiently waits for me to cooperate. Looking up at him brings on another bout of light-headedness. Despite my hope that my ticker will eventually improve on its own, it still beats faintly. The possibility that Neely may help encourages me to peel my arms away from my upper body.

The giant opens his tool bag. He doesn't tug down my shift—he is too polite—so I pull the neckline sideways to reveal my ticker. He removes a monocle from his shirt pocket and places it over his right eye. His small eye suddenly looks larger and more proportionate with his oversize features.

He leans over to study my clock heart up close. "How long has it been beating faintly?"

"Since before I left my world." I think back and hedge. "Actually, it started after I escaped the destruction of Markham's world, the Land of Youth."

"Prince Killian told you the Land of Youth was his world?" Osric asks, a chunk of apple bulging inside his cheek.

I nod, and the first mate grunts. I don't appreciate his interruption, so I finish answering Neely's question. "Not too long ago, my ticker was waterlogged, but Jamison fixed it and replaced the broken parts."

"Jamison? You're referring to the human lord who was disrespectful to Captain Redmond?" Neely asks. I remember their exchange quite differently, but I nod, and again, Osric grunts. "How long have you had your clock heart? The materials and workmanship are remarkable."

"My uncle is a clockmaker. He installed it almost ten years ago. He said Father Time directed him."

The giant's frown expands, multiplying the lines around his lips. He presses a fingertip against my ticker. The longer he seeks out the beat, the deeper the crease between his shaggy eyebrows grows.

Osric observes from across the cabin while he eats his apple. Could he chew any louder?

Neely finally sits back. "This is the finest clock I have ever seen. Regrettably, it isn't working at capacity."

I rub at the gooseflesh on my arms. "Can you repair it?"

"I will try, but I need to consult the captain before we go any further." The giant tucks his monocle away. "You and your clock heart truly are extraordinary."

My uncle often told me I was extraordinary too, but all I wanted was to be ordinary, to stand close to someone without worrying if they could hear the ticktock of my heart, to wear a flattering neckline instead of a collar buttoned up to my chin, to marry and have children someday and even grandchildren, and to live a long, full life in every sense.

"Extraordinary" really means missing out on the life that everyone else has.

Neely tries for an encouraging smile. "I'll return when I can, poppet."

The giant grabs his tool bag and hobbles out. Though I am relieved he won't tamper with my ticker without due consideration, I'm still anxious to figure out what's wrong with me.

Osric picks his teeth with the stem of his apple. He ate the rest of the fruit, including its seeds and core. He opens a trunk and removes a pile of clothes. "Captain Redmond is expecting you for dinner. Get dressed, and I'll be back soon."

In the wake of his departure, I dress swiftly. My movements are mechanical, my mind stuck on Neely's findings, or lack thereof. Osric left me a clean shirt, a leather vest, a belt, and trousers. The thick wool puts an end to my chilliness.

As I tug on my mother's red gloves, Osric returns. "Must you ruin your appearance with those dirty things?" he asks of my gloves.

"What do you care? You said humans repulse you." He grunts, which I'm coming to understand is his form of a chuckle. "Do you have any humans in your crew?"

"Off and on. Your kind don't survive long in the Land Under the Wave. Come along, Countess," he says, his use of my title mocking.

He grips my forearm and drags me outside. The moon nearly out-shines the waning sun, the sunset fading to dusk. I hardly get a glimpse of the happenings on deck as the first mate pulls me into the captain's cabin.

No one else is here. The galley must be on the deck below, because the scent of cooked meat is strong, yet no food is on the table.

My fingers start to quake. On the nights when my uncle read me tales about giants, I would lie awake, petrified that one would smash through our roof, scoop me from bed, and carry me away to its den. There, the giant would stuff me full of stewed apples cooked in pork fat, and when I was round and plump, it would drop me in a pot and boil me into a stew.

"Captain Redmond will be along shortly," Osric says.

"Are you joining us?" Elves don't eat humans, at least not in our legends. Osric's dinner attendance may be a sign that my childhood nightmare won't come true.

The first mate pulls another shiny red apple from his pocket. "I've other plans." He smiles thinly. "Enjoy your meal, my lady."

He takes a bite of his apple and saunters out, locking me in the giant's lair.

Chapter Nine

It is a well-known fact that a human who enters a giant's domain is likely to never again see their family or friends. I think of this caution, and of my chances of surviving and seeing my uncle or Jamison again, as I scan Captain Redmond's quarters.

In many ways, his cabin is furnished like any officer's, with a bunk, a table, and a desk, except everything is larger.

A leathery tail sticks out from under the bunk where the captain's crocodile sleeps. I stay across the cabin, far from the croc and near several carnyxes propped against the wall. Each battle horn has a bell on the bottom shaped in the form of an animal, including a bear, a crocodile, a serpent, and a wild boar. They all have dings and nicks, as though they spent time on the front line of a battlefield.

Colorful maps and globes on the captain's desk catch my attention. Seven globes are set in order, with the Land of the Living in the center and the six Otherworlds circling it, three on each side. They are the Land of Promise, the Other Land, the Land of Youth, the Plain of Delight, the Land Under the Wave, and finally the Silver-Clouded Plain. Although the flag of the Realm of Wyeth features the seven worlds, I've never noticed the layout resembles a round clockface, with the worlds in place of numbers.

Each globe has its own moon, with an individual symbol on the base. The Land of Promise, the elves' world, has an ivy crown wreathing an apple, the same mark I found on the torn flag and the coin while near that ship on the Skeleton Coast. Was the ship we took shelter in elven? Did Radella recognize the symbol?

My fingers brush over the Land of Youth, Markham's world. Seeing it again from a different perspective carves in me a deeper well of sorrow. I cannot fathom the total number of innocent lives lost and futures stolen. For a whole world to fall, the casualties . . .

Beneath the globes, a large map of the Land Under the Wave is spread across the desk. This world has one continent that, according to the scale, is the size of a large island. I locate the Skeleton Coast on the northwest end, and on the eastern side are Merrow Lagoon, Skull Reef, and Hangman's Spit. The village of Eventide, the only town on the land that's labeled, is right by the lagoon.

I commit the map to memory, relying on my experience drawing charts of my own. As I do, I notice another city far away from the continent, in the middle of the sea—the mythical underwater city of Everblue.

Seamen back home sing a chantey about the merrows' stronghold at the bottom of the sea. My father would sing it sometimes while he was combing or braiding my or my sister's hair. The lyrics flow off my lips.

> *Below the sun dance sapphire stars.*
> *The moon bleeds rubies to catch in a jar.*
> *The tides sing a song for the true,*
> *Ever strong, ever flowing, ever blue.*

"It's been ages since I've heard that tune," says a rumbly voice.

Captain Redmond enters his cabin, followed by two crewmen bearing utensils, bowls, and a large pot. The giant changed into an elegant burgundy velvet dinner jacket with black buttons and oiled down his mustache to frame his thin lips.

His crocodile slides out from under the bunk to greet his master.

"Tattler, come say hello to my new timepiece," he says.

I force myself to address the croc, something I couldn't do if I were merely a mechanism. "A pleasure to meet you, Tattler."

"I found him off Skull Reef when he was just a baby, chewing on a waterlogged clock. I knew straightaway we would be friends."

Tattler lies still as his master strokes his scaly head and back. The crewmen finish setting the table and leave us to our dinner. I stay near the desk, equally avoiding the giant and his pet, and waste no time addressing my foremost worry.

"Did you truly give the sword of Avelyn to the merrow king? Or was that said to misdirect Markham?"

The giant's lips slip up in amusement. "Are you usually this quick to call someone a liar?"

"My association with Markham has taught me to be thorough."

"The sword is indeed at the bottom of the sea, I presume in King Dorian's castle. No land dweller can survive the swim down to Everblue, so give up all thought of getting it back."

"But if you traded with the merrow king, there must be a way—"

"For you to take back the sword and return it to Father Time?" The giant laughs at my outlandish suggestion, the sound a cavernous rumble. "I think not, Ticker."

He must not believe I was sent here by Father Time. "But it's true. Father Time asked me to find the sword of Avelyn. You must—"

"I won't discuss this matter for another second. Remember that your husband's comfort aboard this ship depends on my generosity. Now, let's have a pleasant meal, shall we?" Captain Redmond lifts the lid of the pot and inhales the steam. "My cook boiled a piece of centicore backstrap that I traded for the last time we were at port. Meat is a rare treat in these waters. We don't get much wild game here."

I encountered a centicore while in the Thornwoods. The massive horned beast charged and tried to gore me to death. "The stew isn't also made with something else . . . ?"

"You mean the flesh of humans? No, I've never favored the flavor. You must be hungry. Osric said he hasn't fed you all day."

I squeeze out a small smile. "I would have some, but I don't eat meat."

Captain Redmond sets the lid down on the table. "Why not?"

"My parents worshipped Mother Madrona. They believed all life is blessed by her creation power."

The captain stirs the stew with the ladle. "Are you one of these so-called children?"

"I suppose so." Before I visited the Everwoods and met Father Time, I never thought of myself as one of the Children of Madrona. I had conformed to my family's beliefs for simplicity's sake, yet I have now come to accept that creation power exists in us all. "I was raised to believe giants and elves are legends; however, we accept the existence of the Otherworlds."

"Otherworlds," Captain Redmond scoffs. "The Creator crafted the seven worlds collectively. There is no 'other.' As a whole, the worlds have one name—Avelyn."

My clock heart ticks faster, its beat soft but purposeful. My sword was named after Avelyn, or perhaps Avelyn was named after the sword.

"The giants were the firstborns of Mother Madrona. We keep the histories of Avelyn straight and even named each of the seven worlds. Giants were Madrona's rightful inheritors of the Land of the Living, yet humankind inherited it."

I note his bitterness, though I cannot say if his opinion holds validity, as I have never heard this story. "How so?"

Captain Redmond lowers into his chair. "Humans truly are a forgetful lot."

"Giants are condescending."

He chuckles without humor. "Sit, Ticker, and I will tell you the story of the triad."

Obviously, my invitation to join him for supper was for his entertainment. If he wants to teach the ignorant human why she and her kind are thieves of his inheritance, then let him.

I slide onto the bench and kneel to see over the tall table. Before me are a regular-size spoon, bowl, and cup of water. He pours a ladle of stew into my bowl despite my declaration that I don't eat meat, and I notice ink markings on his forearm. The first mark is a sandglass with all the sand in the bottom and the second the face of a clock. I sip my water as he lifts the ladle to his mouth like a spoon, dining directly from the big pot. He does not slurp or shovel in his food, and he dabs his mouth with his napery. His manners are better than I presumed a giant's would be.

"When the ancient elderwood, Mother Madrona, created life, she bore giants from her bark, elves from her leaves, and humans—"

"From her acorns. Yes, yes. Humans know the origin story of the triad."

"Impatient," the captain mutters. "Humans are also impatient."

I press my lips together.

"For a time, the triad lived as brothers and sisters in the Land of the Living, but when they began to contend among themselves, Madrona sent the elves to the Land of Promise and sent the giants to the Silver-Clouded Plain, and then bestowed the Land of the Living, her first and most precious world, upon mankind." His meaty hand tightens around the ladle, his voice coarsening. "Giants live longer than humans, so we had ample time to fester over this injustice. As the first generation of humans died off, the giants began to plot an invasion to reclaim our birthright."

This story feels familiar, not sweet in the way my mother would recount *The Legend of Princess Amadara*. I recognize the tale from a deeper, hazier memory.

The captain blows across his steaming stew. "My ancestors strategized for forty years, and on the first full moon of the fortieth summer, they gathered their armies and snuck through a portal tunnel to the

Land of the Living. Their line of attack caught the humans unaware, and they commenced their slaughter."

I shift uncomfortably, even more certain now that I have heard this story, yet I still cannot remember where.

Captain Redmond swallows another bite of stew. I am not inclined to touch mine; the overly rich smell alone sours my belly. "The human armies were no match for the giants," he continues with no small amount of pride. "When the elves saw that the giants would prevail, they allied with the humans. And so the triad fought, brother against brother, sister against sister." He gestures at the rack of battle horns. "The giants' battle cries carried through the tunnels all the way to our home world. They were unstoppable with the ax and the spear."

The captain describes the war as though it happened yesterday. This story must be passed down by his ancestors the same way the Children of Madrona pass on traditions about the call of life and the sanctity of creation power.

"We were set to win until Father Time called the Creator to the battlefield." Captain Redmond's jawline hardens and his gaze flattens. "He showed her the future of Avelyn if the giants prevailed. Eiocha was sorrowful over the bloodshed, so she played a lullaby on her violin that put our army into a deep sleep. The elves aspired to slay them where they lay, but Eiocha would not abide more killing. She sent the elves back to their world and appointed them as overseers for the Land of the Living. Then she flung her violin into the sun, destroying it, and hid away the instrument's maker."

This is not the first time I have heard of Eiocha's music. It is said that after she cut the worlds from the cloth of the eternities with the sword of Avelyn, she sewed them high in the heavens with a song on her violin. Some say the true call of life is this song and that the melody can be heard in the first few moments of nighttime when the stars twinkle to life.

The captain's mouth twists grimly. "Over time, trees grew over the warrior giants, concealing them in the land. Humans forgot they were there, forgot their triad of brothers and sisters, forgot the violin and the Creator's song. Even today, your people travel through the forest where our warriors sleep, unaware how close their ancestors came to annihilation."

I recall this tale now . . . well, a portion of it. My father often said that giants lived in northern Wyeth. I wish I could remember what else he told me.

The captain's focus turns inward, his tone bleak. "As punishment for infiltrating another world, Eiocha sealed off the Silver-Clouded Plain with a curse, so that any giant who leaves our world is shut out. We can leave, but we cannot go back."

"The portals only work in one direction . . . so you're stuck here?"

"Aye. The village of Eventide is full of runaways and castaways, all banished or marooned from the seven worlds. The merrow king and his subjects tolerate our presence, but we are taxed mightily, and land-dweller resources are scarce. We steal and trade and hoard and scavenge to find beauty in this inhospitable world." He blots his lips clean with a napery, his manners a strange contrast to his morose mood. "I granted Neely permission to inspect your clock heart again, but I am not hopeful. He has been unsuccessful in keeping any of my clocks running."

My fingers tense on my water cup. Osric said the clocks were ruined by salt water or the damp air, but I think this world where the tides set the hour isn't made for human timepieces. Our clocks don't belong here and neither do I. I attempt to keep my voice light. "How long do the clocks run for before they stop?"

"Some last a day, others last weeks. It depends on the quality of the craftsmanship." Captain Redmond exhales a shallow sigh. "I didn't intend to become a collector. I'm searching for a certain clock, so I began by trading for timepieces sight unseen. I have yet to acquire the one I'm after, a silver pocket watch with clouds painted on its face. It belonged to my grandfather. That pocket watch was the only posses-sion on my person when I was banished from home." The giant rubs a hand against his heart as though it pains him to live without his watch. "Show me your ticker."

His command feels like icy water dumped over my head. He could reach across the table and reveal my clock heart by force, but I would loathe for him to touch me. Very slowly, I tug aside my shirt collar.

"It's still beating," he muses. "Perhaps you'll be my clock that survives, Ticker."

I cover myself again, my throat hot. "I have a clock for a heart, but that doesn't make me one."

"Doesn't it, though? We are what we carry in our heart."

The backs of my eyes burn. My ticker is made of cogs and gears, a balance wheel, and a torsion spring. It is crafted from wood and metal, materials that have no emotion. Perhaps that's all I am. Perhaps Markham cut out all the good parts of me and left nothing but emptiness.

Can I be more? Assisting Father Time gives me a defined purpose. Before this, my aim was to avenge my family. But neither accomplishment will change the past. What I want above all, what I've always wanted, is for the power that preserves me to become the power that changes me back into what I was. To make me whole, to help me out of the dark so I can stand in the light with nothing to fear about who I am. Secrets are a burden. The weight of mine has pressed down upon me for so long that sometimes I fear I will be crushed by it.

The captain glances around the dim room. "The sun has gone down. It's time for you to return to the day cabin."

"You have to let me go," I say, my stomach quivering. "I have a family and home."

He bangs his fists against the table, his outrage so sudden it takes me aback. "Everyone here had a life before they were cast away! What makes you more deserving of keeping it?"

"I'm not a castaway," I retort. "I came here to fulfill a task. Please, you'll kill me."

His face screws up in a nasty snarl. "Then that is your fate."

I push from my seat, wishing I had my sword. When I hold the sword of Avelyn, I feel more myself, less broken and more capable of confronting whatever comes my way. That blade was the only thing that survived Markham's decimation of my previous life. I won't let some dandy pirate tell me to accept this life without it.

Osric swings open the door and enters with a pail of fish. He takes in our aggressive stances, the captain bent over the table and me glaring him down. "Is there a problem, sir?"

"Aye, remove her from my cabin," Captain Redmond growls.

"Captain," I say as Osric pulls me from the table, "at least free my friends."

"They're too valuable a commodity to let them go. Everything in the Land Under the Wave is a precious treasure that can be bought or sold. Everything." The captain shoves pieces of beeswax into his big ears and then scoops a fish out of the pail and tosses it near his bunk. The last thing I see before Osric tugs me away is Tattler darting out and snapping up the fish.

"Let me go," I say, elbowing Osric in the side.

The first mate holds tight and hauls me back to the day cabin. "Don't make this difficult, Countess. The merrows will start singing soon. You're safer locked inside."

"I don't care."

"Go in or I will drag you."

I glower at him and try to determine if elves have special abilities besides their ridiculous beauty and extralong life spans. It is rumored that their hearing and eyesight are more advanced than humans', but I cannot tell if this is true just by looking at Osric, so I step into the cabin. Someone lit the lamps and closed the portholes, presumably in preparation for the arrival of the merrows.

"Does the captain wear wax in his ears every night?" I ask.

"He has to. Elves aren't tempted by a merrow's singing—we're of the same bloodline, a very, very obscure connection. However, giants can be enchanted."

What a terrible way to end each day, defending one's self against a rapturous call so strong that it could lead to your death. Not that I feel sorry for him.

"He deserves nightly torture," I say.

"Don't be so quick to pass judgment. Years ago, Mundy traded his most prized possession in exchange for rations to feed his crew. Neely was in especially poor shape—naturally, giants require more food to sustain them than someone smaller. Because of Captain Redmond, we didn't starve to death." Osric sets down clumps of wax. "Wear these or, at the very least, cover your ears."

"We wouldn't want one of the captain's precious clocks to jump overboard, would we?" I counter. "I thought you were different than Markham."

"Don't be a nidget. If it weren't for Prince Killian, you and your friends would still be stranded on the Skeleton Coast." Osric removes a small sack from his pocket and drops it on the table. "Your dinner, my lady."

I fling the sack at him as he closes the door. It bounces off the handle and strikes the grandfather clock. Inside the clock, the bell emits a low tone, like a person groaning after they've been struck. As the noise fades, somewhere outside the ship, in the waters, a merrow begins her song.

Chapter Ten

The merrow's singing goes on for hours. Even with my hands over my ears, the haunting melody plagues me. And if I am bothered and restless, I can only imagine how Jamison must be faring. He may be locked in the brig and unable to heed her call, but I don't want him to suffer.

I lay my head on the pillow, wishing he were here so I could see that he was all right.

That isn't entirely true. I want Jamison here so he can tell *me* that everything will be all right. I need assurance that we can escape, get the sword from the merrow king, find Claret, and go home. I bury my face in the pillow, daunted by the tasks ahead of me. How can I do even one of them when I am locked in this cabin?

By the time the merrow finally stops singing, the oil lantern has burned low and shadows dance across the walls. The silence of the clocks drills the fragility of my ticker into my mind. Sleep is a long way off.

Inside the sack Osric gave me, I find strips of seaweed and kelp pods, food that is considered inedible in my world. This won't be the first time since I left home that I've gone to bed hungry.

The sea winds bang at the door, a persistent drumming that I've almost managed to ignore, and then a gust shoves the door wide open. I scramble up to shut it before what I'm doing occurs to me.

Osric left the door unlocked.

This must be an accident, a serious mistake. But I won't squander the opportunity.

I creep out into the gusty sea air, the moon shedding a pale glow across the deck. High above, the pirate flag ripples in the wind. The skull and crossbones are a morbid threat, but equally so is the hourglass, a symbolic reminder that the sands of time run out for everyone.

An elf stands watch in the crow's nest. My movements remain cautious and my senses high. The ship has two hatches, the closest of which stands open. I pad down the ladder and duck behind it to get my bearings. The ceiling belowdecks is higher than usual to accommodate the giants. A main corridor runs the length of the ship like a backbone, and at the far end is the other ladder to the second hatch. The brig should be off this central corridor.

My ticker beats weakly, which is normal of late, but it has sped up to accommodate my nervousness, and now I'm light-headed. I wait until my head clears before setting out.

I pass closed doors and vacant cabins, searching one after another for the brig. Halfway down the corridor, I hear Markham's voice.

"You cannot keep me here."

"We won't detain you for long," Osric replies.

"You don't have many places left to maroon me. Where will it be this time? A sandbar in Skull Reef or a grotto off Hangman's Spit?"

"Nothing so civilized. You've lost the privilege of niceties."

Their voices carry out of an open door in front of me. I tiptoe closer and peer inside. Markham is tied to a chair. Osric stands before him, his arms flexed and his fists balled.

"You've hidden your heritage," says the elf. "Your sister would be ashamed of you."

"My sister wants what's easiest for herself and our people."

Osric backhands him across the face. "They're not your people! They no longer belong to you, nor you to them."

"Nor are they yours," Markham says, his voice strained with pain. He may be immortal, but he is not invulnerable to pain. "Alert the guard. Let them come."

The guard? Does he mean the pirate guards?

"You think they'd waste their time? No one's coming for you, Killian. No one cares about you anymore. Don't you see that by now? It's been four hundred years. No amount of time will heal what you've done."

I listen closely, cataloguing every word.

"We cannot go back to the way things were," Markham replies, "but that doesn't mean I don't harbor regrets. I still mourn your sister."

Osric grabs him by the throat. "Never speak of Brea."

"I loved her."

"Like you love that woman of yours who runs after you like a lost mongrel? Does she even know who you are?"

"Harlow loves me. I'll admit that the last few centuries haven't gone as intended, but we're nearing the end of our exile, Osric. I've found a way to go home."

The first mate shoves Markham so hard he tips over onto the floor. The prince groans as he lands on his side, still bound to the chair. "You have nothing," snarls the elf. "No name, no throne, no future."

"Nor do you. Why haven't you gone to the queen and begged for forgiveness? Why haven't you returned to your parents? You're still running too, old friend."

Osric kicks him in the side and then wrenches up his head, his fist full of the prince's hair. "Mundy has been too kind to you. I will be your reckoning. On my life, I swear you will pay." He lets go of Markham and starts for the door.

I duck into a shadowed doorway, my ticker thudding rapidly.

"Guards," he calls as he marches past me. Two men appear down the corridor. "Tomorrow at high tide, Prince Killian will walk the plank with millstones tied to his ankles. Make the arrangements."

"Yes, sir."

The guards start to return to the cabin they stepped out of.

"What are you doing?" Osric asks.

"Returning to our post at the brig, sir."

"You need to consult tomorrow's watch about my orders."

"And the prisoners?"

"I'll stay with them until you finish," answers the first mate.

The two sailors go down the ladder into the lower decks, where I assume the crewmen have their quarters. Osric strides to the cabin where the guards were on duty.

Alone again, I determine three things. First, Osric has gone to the brig. Second, elves do not have heightened hearing or eyesight or I would have been caught by now. And third, Markham has not been honest about his past. I dart across the corridor into his cabin. He still lies on the floor, tied to the chair.

"Everley, what fortunate timing. Would you please tip me upright?"

"I should kick you in the ribs."

"Osric already wounded that part. Perhaps try a less tender area?"

"Once I'm done with you, all of you will be tender."

"Oh, Everley, your temper is so predictable."

Crushing my teeth down on a growl, I heft Markham upright but leave him bound. His hair flops into his eyes. He blows it away, and a single lock sticks between his brows.

He puts on a mild smile. "Much better."

"Nothing will be better until you're gone from my life."

He clucks his tongue. "You were such a warmhearted child. Your clock heart has turned you cold."

I stroke the fallen lock of his hair from his face. "If that's true, do you think it's wise to antagonize me?" I grip a fistful of his hair and tug until I see ire in his eyes. "Who are the guards you spoke of? How can you return home? You destroyed your world."

Markham's lips slice upward. "You haven't deduced the answers on your own?"

"Don't put this on me." I shove his head down and let go of his hair. "I'm giving you the opportunity to be honest before you sink to an endless grave." Now that I think on it, I couldn't have designed a more fitting fate for him. As he cannot die, the millstones will weigh Markham down, and he will be stuck at the bottom of the sea, drowning endlessly.

"If I go to the bottom of the sea, so do all the answers you seek. Unbind me, and I will get us off this ship and help you find the sword."

He's dangling a juicy piece of bait, and I am tempted to leap for it, but Markham has never been forthright.

"Drown, then," I say, then revolve to go.

"Everley, I know the way to Everblue." Markham leans forward as far as his bindings allow. "Release me, and we can work together to retrieve the sword from King Dorian."

"Everblue is far away. No human can reach it."

"There are ways."

I should go, walk out and let him squirm. But, damn him, I have no other solution for getting to the sword. "Why would I partner with you? You led the pirates to us."

He spits at the floor. "That had a regrettable outcome, I assure you."

Some part of me enjoys standing over him while he's restrained. I'm not sure I want it to end. "I will bring the sword to Father Time. What do you hope to gain from this?"

"I've no interest in the sword. The king has other treasures worthy of my attention."

Markham never does anything for someone else that doesn't first serve him. He's probably lying right now to convince me to align with him. He must want the sword for himself, but he wants me to believe I can get it back so I will free him. He deceived me into helping him once. I won't make that mistake again.

"Find your own way out of here."

His voice pitches higher, his words tumbling off his tongue. "There's a portal for land dwellers. You won't find it without me."

"There's another portal?" I grab a fistful of his shirt. "Where is it?"

"If I offer to lead you there, will you go straight home or seek out the sword of Avelyn first? Maybe you need to consult with your husband before you answer."

I yank him forward. "Stop answering my questions with more questions and tell the truth for once in your infuriatingly long life."

His eyes glint as if he knows he has hooked me. "The portal is accessible by land dwellers; however, it's nowhere near the sword."

"Of course it isn't," I mutter, releasing him.

Returning home to Dorestand holds tremendous appeal. Just the prospect swamps me with homesickness. I miss the rain clouds that make my stocking drawers smell musty and my quilt slightly damp. I miss the scent of the bakery down the street baking fat loaves of soda bread. I miss the ring of the entry bell over my uncle's shop door when a customer arrives. I miss the horse-drawn carriages plodding over the cobblestones and the opposing rhythm of my uncle chiseling in his workshop. I miss turning the thin pages of my favorite book while I sit at the clerk's desk surrounded by ticktocking clocks. But I cannot return to Dorestand and leave the sword of Avelyn with the merrow king.

The sound of footsteps thuds down the corridor. I hurry to the doorway and see Osric going up the ladder through the hatch. Something feels odd about him forgetting to lock the day cabin, and now he has sent the guards away and left the brig unattended. Mistake or not, the guards are sure to return soon.

"I have to go," I say.

"Untie me first."

Markham looks so helpless bound to the chair, his hair a mess, his clothes disheveled. I stride to him and run the hard ridge of my nail across his chin, creating a faint line that will fade, unlike the scars he gave me. "I've often imagined what I would do to you if I ever had you to myself."

"Are you satisfied?"

"Not quite." I dig my nail in harder, wishing he could bleed.

"Unlike how you feel about me, I have never been disappointed by you." The prince's demeanor is so subdued, so earnest, for a moment, I almost believe he is harmless. No one should be allowed to have this much natural charm. "Everley, before you go, I have one tiny request. You will find a pearl in my jacket pocket. Take it and drop it out the porthole into the sea. The merrows favor shiny things. They will accept it as payment for their silence and leave us in peace."

"Are you hard of hearing? The merrows have already gone."

"They often return multiple times a night to wear down their prey. I would like to spend my last night above the surface not listening to their repetitive song."

Curious about this pearl, I fish my fingers in his pocket and take it out. By all appearances, it's just a jewel, except it's light blue, a rare color for a pearl. The ones my father brought home from his expeditions were ivory or pink.

"Go on," Markham says. "Drop it into the sea and protect Lieutenant Callahan. He's still susceptible to their summons."

Markham wants this too badly. Having fallen for his tricks before, I have learned that anything he begs for is something I should avoid. I slip the pearl into my pocket. "Enjoy your sleepless night, dear prince."

"Everley," he hisses, "don't leave me tied up. Everley!"

His pleading fades as I creep down the corridor. The brig is indeed in the last cabin. Radella's cage rests outside the cell, and within, Jamison sits hunched against the iron bars with his hands over his ears, while Harlow and Laverick sleep on the floor.

I tug at the cell door, but it's locked. Radella sits up from her sulk and motions at Jamison. He slowly lowers his hands from his ears.

"Evie?" he asks. "Did the merrows leave?"

"Yes. Where's the key?"

"The guards have it. How did you get out?"

"Luck, I hope." I kneel so I am eye level with Jamison. "How do you feel?"

"I'm better now that the merrow isn't singing. Markham said resisting their summons feels like your teeth are rattling out of your mouth, but I'd say it's more like maggots gnawing your flesh. When they locked us in here, I never thought I would be grateful for these metal bars." I wince at him trying to make light of what must have been torture. "Evie, what are you doing belowdecks? What if you're caught?"

"I came to see you. On my way here, I stopped to speak with Markham. He has a plan to retrieve the sword of Avelyn from the merrow king, and he wants us to align with him."

"I hope you told him to impale himself on the anchor."

"Essentially, yes."

"Good." Jamison slides his hand through the gap in the bars and threads my fingers through his. I grip him back, needing his company to steady myself. His expression creases with concern. "Is what the captain said about you true? Is your clock heart in trouble?"

"I have no idea. My ticker is still running and hasn't needed to be recalibrated since before you replaced the waterlogged parts." Truth mingled with omission tastes sour, but Jamison will react as my uncle would, worrying about me more than he already does if I tell him my clock heart has been functioning strangely for a while.

"Then why would the captain say that?" he presses.

"My heart is a mechanism, and mechanisms malfunction." I pause to rid the stiffness from my tone, and with great effort, I add matter-of-factly, "My ticker isn't a real heart like anyone else's."

"You have more heart than anyone I know." Jamison's thumb brushes over my knuckles. "You should consider Killian's offer."

"Have you gone mad?"

"Don't trust Killian—never, ever trust him—but he knows this world better than us. We can use him to escape and get the sword."

I blink rapidly in surprise. "What about going home?"

"You've been so preoccupied with the sword you haven't thought of the opportunity that finding Killian presents." Jamison's flinty gaze matches his determined tone. "We can convince him to help us, then imprison him, bring him home, and turn him in to the queen. Once Queen Aislinn has him, I'll persuade her to grant you a pardon for capturing him and turning him in."

His suggestion holds merit except for one part. "Markham will anticipate our duplicity."

"He petitioned *you* for an alliance. He must be willing to take the risk."

The prince is so arrogant he probably thinks we don't have the gumption to cross him. My mind turns Jamison's strategy over and over, searching for flaws, but the benefit of the queen pardoning me in exchange for Markham outweighs my reservations.

Jamison's grip on mine tightens. "Evie, we could go home and I could introduce you to my father."

I try to muster a smile. He hasn't thought much further ahead than my freedom. It hasn't occurred to him that he would still have to introduce his criminal wife to his father. I could never get too close to the marquess for fear that he may discover my clock heart. A pardon from the queen would absolve me of my remaining prison time, but I would still be myself. My dream that I might not always need this clock heart is too incredible a wish to attach to Jamison and me. I must be realistic. I'll need this heart to live until the day I die.

I rest my forehead against the bars. "Thank you for not treating me like I'm a spectacle."

Jamison's brows draw downward. "You shouldn't thank anyone for treating you with common decency."

My chest aches for wanting that to be true, but Captain Redmond and his men responded exactly how my uncle warned me outsiders would. He said that once people saw my ticker, they would forget the girl to whom it belongs. Jamison doesn't recognize how unusual he is.

Outside the ship, a merrow starts to sing. Almost immediately, another merrow lends her voice to the first's, and then another, and another, until several of them are serenading us. The merrow returned, and she brought reinforcements.

Jamison covers his ears as their singing grows louder. His eyes are already slightly glazed.

I have to get us off this ship. We cannot endure another night of this.

Voices outside the cabin carry up the ladder and into the corridor. The guards must be returning to the brig to finish their shift. I mouth a farewell to Jamison and spot Harlow staring at me, her hand clutching her vial necklace. How long has she been awake? And how much of our conversation did she overhear?

The sound of the guards' approach comes closer. I dash down the corridor and duck into Markham's cabin before I'm seen.

The prince blinks in astonishment. "Everley, have you reconsidered my proposal?"

"No—"

The merrows' singing drowns me out, coming from directly outside the hull. My fingers begin to tremble as a piece of my soul far down inside rattles. The vibration builds to a heady, raw throb. This must be their enchantment at work.

Markham narrows his eyes. "Do you have clock parts for a brain too? I told you to toss the pearl into the sea."

Even if what he says is true, I could toss the pearl overboard and send the merrows away tonight, but then what will I do when they return tomorrow? Or the night after that? Jamison said not to trust Markham, but the prince can be trusted to protect himself, and for once, we want the same thing. Moreover, the thought of leaving my friends caged below while I return topside to the cabin full of dead clocks is too much to bear unless it is temporary.

"You win this time," I say. "But you have to help us find Claret *and* the sword or we don't have an agreement."

"How can I work with you if you cannot do something as simple as throw a pearl overboard?"

I bend over him, lowering my face near his. "Did you understand my terms?"

"I'm to free your friends and recover your precious sword. You've made your demands very clear. Now I shall reiterate mine: cast off the pearl tonight, and tomorrow our hunt for the sword continues."

"How do you intend to get us off the ship?"

His lips purse. "I'm not a stranger to this world, as you're discovering. And I have no shortage of allies."

Could he have allies aboard this ship? I wait for him to enlighten me, but he discloses nothing more. I would walk out right now, except Markham always has lackeys at his disposal.

"We can wait until tomorrow, but no longer." The merrows' song still plays, jarring at my bones. "I have to go. I've been out of my cabin for too long."

"Part of our agreement was for you to untie me."

"Oh, I think not. I'll sleep better knowing you're locked belowdecks."

I expect him to chuckle, since most everything I say and do is laughable to him, but he tips his head to the side in thought, pondering me as he would an anomaly. "You didn't always find me contemptible."

He refers to the few times we met before he and my father departed on their explorations. I have successfully put those encounters out of my mind, for even then, the prince was too handsome, too charming, too quick witted.

"You were such a curious child," he muses. "I sensed your spirit for adventure straightaway."

"Stop," I snap.

He gives me an injured look. "You should have more respect for our history. How many people in your life have known you as long as I have? Doesn't time mean anything to you?"

"Tomorrow, Markham."

He sends me a saccharine smile. "Sweet dreams, Evie."

I dart out of the cabin, down the corridor, and up the ladder. The merrows' song is louder and bolder on the open deck. Everyone appears to have been chased inside by the singing, including the watchman in the crow's nest. I cross to the gunwale, my blood humming as though I am standing close to a pianoforte.

Overlooking the sea, I search for a glimpse of our tormentors, and a buzzing starts in my ears. The vibration grows faster and more intense as I arrive at the rail.

Several merrows float at the surface below, their green skin and hair lit by moonlight. The buzzing in my head increases, like an angry bee stuck in my ear.

Clutching the pearl in my fist, I climb onto the rail for a better view and hold on to the rigging. An inner warning tells me this is dangerous, but in addition to the buzzing, a message blares.

Come for a swim, child. Let us show you the many wonders hidden under the sea.

I lean forward over the water. Farther . . . farther . . .

"Everley!"

The call comes from behind me, from someone on deck. I blink fast and shift back. The buzzing in my head fades a little. Why am I on the rail?

I hop back down onto the planks, my clock heart fluttering swiftly and my chest pumping hard. The person who called for me is nowhere in sight. I toss the pearl overboard and flee into the day cabin.

My hands and knees tremble, the rattling in my head painfully insistent. I lie on the bunk and cover my ears with the pillow. Suddenly everything goes very quiet. I lift one corner of the pillow, braced for more pain. Nothing comes.

The merrows quit singing.

Moments pass while I wait expectantly for their return, but the throbbing in my head stops. I cannot determine which astonishes me more, that Markham told the truth or that his pearl has bought us peace.

I turn onto my back, exhausted and shaken, my mind swimming with a torrent of unknowns. The day has brought more questions than answers. What would have happened had I stayed on the rail any longer and someone hadn't called my name . . . ?

A shadow passes in front of the keyhole of the door, and then someone inserts the key and locks it. Osric must have remembered he left the door unlocked, or did he leave it open on purpose?

Peculiar things have happened all night, and Osric could be behind every one of them. He may have left the door unlocked to draw me out. Perhaps he knew I would speak with Markham, or maybe he's trying to uncover the prince's allies in the crew. But without understanding Markham and Osric's past, I am left with one conclusion.

Osric has laid a trap. Only I cannot decide if it is for Markham or me.

Chapter Eleven

By midmorning, with just hours to go until high tide, I am awake and waiting for Markham's escape plan. The door opens and the oversize cabin boy walks in.

"Good morning, poppet," says Neely, setting down his tool bag. "My apologies for interrupting your breakfast."

I'm finishing off the sack of dried seaweed and kelp pods from yesterday. My hunger finally made the fish food enticing enough to eat. I wash the briny taste from my mouth with the last swig of water from my cup and side-eye the giant. Could Markham have sent him?

Neely wanders over to the workbench, sets down his tool bag, and sorts through his instruments. "The captain asked me to take a closer look at your timepiece." He gestures at the bunk. "I need you to lie down."

After yesterday's dizzy spells, I feel more myself today. I don't want someone tampering with my ticker. "What if fiddling with the gearwork makes it worse?"

"I'll be careful. I was a mechanic in my home world."

I do want my ticker fixed, especially before I escape, so I shuffle toward the bunk. "What brought you here?"

"Giants are given a trade at birth that follows family lines. Butchers raise butchers, candlemakers raise candlemakers—"

"And mechanics raise mechanics."

"Aye," Neely says. "Back home, giants are trained to do one thing well. Mastering our trade shows appreciation to the Creator for our life. My father was a skilled mechanic, but his business was struggling. Our family was on our last meal when I was caught stealing grain from a farmer. My father was so ashamed of me he turned me in to our township officials. I was banished from my world the next day."

"How long ago was this?"

"Longer than you've been alive." Neely pats the bunk again for me to come over. "I could call for crewmen to force you down and restrain you, but that would be very unpleasant for everyone."

I agree, so I lie down.

The giant's fingers are too big to unbutton my shirt, so I undo it. Neely puts on his monocle and pulls the stool up to the bunk. He pries off the glass face from my ticker with the flat end of a chisel. "Close your eyes and relax."

"Do you know what you're looking for?"

"Anything that will reveal the impetus of your ticker. Understanding what animates it may provide me with a solution."

The inner workings of my ticker have been a mystery for years. I almost wish him good luck, but he may think I'm being sarcastic.

The wrinkles around Neely's eyes double as he concentrates. He must have eaten a peppermint after breakfast, because his breath is cool and sweet. He starts to hum to himself, causing me to jump.

"Sorry," he mumbles. "Habit I learned from working alongside my father."

My muscles tense as Neely hums some more. At one point, I hear a clink and then my gears start to turn faster. I breathe more deeply and relax my muscles, but I cannot make the ticking slow down. Dizziness grips me and whirls me around.

"Stop," I whisper.

Neely hums right over me. My strength to speak louder or push him away drains right out of me. Whatever he touched continues to knock me down a hole. I spiral further and further into that racing ticktock, plunging through a crack in my wooden heart.

I land on my feet. The falling sensation slowly empties away and my vision refocuses.

I'm at home in my uncle's workshop. He's here, at his workbench. Blood and ash cover the front of his good clothes, the evening attire he wears on holidays and birthdays. His face is buried in his hands and his shoulders quiver as he sobs.

"Uncle Holden?" I say.

As I go to him, my view of the table expands. I make out two small feet, one of them shoeless, and then the rest of the child comes into sight. She lies on her back, unconscious. Her hair is burned and her eyebrows singed. Soot covers her arms and legs. Her chest . . .

My knees give out. I stumble toward my uncle for support and float right through him. I am in a spirit form again, with no impact on my surroundings. Pulling back, I flee for the door, and there, in the threshold, stands Father Time.

His stately poise is as familiar as the swish of a pendulum on the first stroke of midnight. He wears all black, like the most distinguished of gentlemen. Eternally young and forever solemn, he has a daisy tucked into the lapel of his fitted jacket, an odd splash of brightness to pair with his dour apparel. He places his fingers to his lips, requesting my silence.

"Holden," he says, gliding to him.

My uncle drops to his knees and grabs the hem of his jacket. "Save her. Please save her."

"We don't have the power to bring her to life."

"You can give her more time." My uncle weeps against Father Time's leg. "She's just a child."

Father Time meets my gaze from across the workshop. I sense he wants me to look at the shell of a girl lying on the table, but I cannot. Not without also seeing the life I lost and the loved ones I buried.

"She's all I have left," says my uncle. "I couldn't . . . I couldn't help the others. Please do this."

"It will require a sacrifice of your time. An entire decade."

My uncle looks up at Father Time, his eyes shining with tears. "Whatever you require, I'll do it. She will have what she needs."

Father Time strides to the lass on the workbench, and I turn around and face the storefront. I can hear the clocks for sale ticktocking on the other side of the door.

"Do you know what this is?" Father Time asks, his voice a notch above a murmur. My uncle must not know, because Father Time answers his own question. "This is heartwood from an elderwood tree."

I whirl back around. In the palm of Father Time's hand is a piece of heartwood. Markham called the heartwood the most precious treasure in all the worlds.

"What do I do with it?" asks Uncle Holden.

"Bring us the sword and we will show you."

While my uncle thuds upstairs to his loft where he hid the sword, Father Time holds the heartwood over the girl.

I stare at my boots. "You can see me."

"We have seen your whole life," Father Time replies, "from birth to death. Do not fear what was or what will be."

My curiosity builds until I muster the courage to look up.

The lass—me at age seven—is so little. Back then, I still had all my baby teeth. I had never ridden horseback alone. Never gone for a swim in the sea or stayed up past midnight to dance. Never made a best friend or learned how to bake my father's special plum pudding recipe. I had barely begun to live, and there I am, limp and bloody in the ivory party dress that I wore for my mother's birthday.

I expect an emotional purge of hysteria or fury or mourning. But as I tread over to my younger self, I am engulfed by astonishment. How did Father Time and my uncle take this broken, battered body and make it whole again? They wrought a miracle.

My uncle returns with the sword of Avelyn, and Father Time sets to pulling aside the girl's tattered dress, revealing the gruesome mess of her chest.

"I can clean her up," says my uncle.

"We've no time. Please, hold out your hand."

Father Time takes up the sword. It should look strange, an old-fashioned gentleman with an ancient blade, but he is its master.

"Are you certain this is what you want, Holden? The years must come from you willingly."

"I'm certain."

Father Time cuts my uncle's palm and then presses the heartwood into his hand, over the cut. Next, he lowers the bloodied part of the sword to the girl's chest wound. I scrunch my eyes shut, too squeamish to watch, but I can hear him working. It sounds like a butcher sectioning apart a lamb. When the sawing stops, I open my eyes.

Father Time takes the heartwood from my uncle, the wood stained with his blood, and slides it into the cavity of the girl's chest. A glow starts in her chest and ripples out across her body to her head, fingertips, and toes. She does not wake or stir. The only difference, besides the fading light, is her chest rising and falling with unbidden breaths.

"She has reanimated with time," Father Time declares. He sets the sword beside her and strokes her pale cheek. The movement is so intimate and tender that I blush. "Carve the heartwood into a clock and disguise her heart. Although the clock will be powered by time, ultimately the heartwood, animated by your blood sacrifice, will preserve her. We will leave her and our other treasures in your care."

"Thank you," my uncle says, gripping his arm.

"Go to work before she wakes."

Uncle Holden gathers his tools and sets to carving the heartwood into a clock. I observe from the other side of the table, fascinated by how quickly he toils and the brilliancy of his artistry. Father Time steps out of the workshop into the storefront.

"Wait," I say, hurrying after him. "Is my clock heart permanent? Or can it be changed?"

"You wish to live without it, but you cannot."

My chest sinks, my spirit drooping. I've never told anyone my dream to become whole, yet I feel the future grow dimmer and drearier, hearing that I cannot live without my ticker. "You're Father Time. If you can give me a clock for a heart, can't you make me whole again?"

He scowls, offended. "The heartwood *has* made you better than whole."

"No." I shake my head over and over, refusing to think I'm better off this way.

"Your heart is crafted from the heartwood of an elderwood tree. Its creation power is not to be taken for granted."

The clock heart saved me, but the finicky mechanism is too demanding. "The pirate captain says my ticker is broken."

Father Time's expression becomes severe. "Your clock heart is more powerful than a world full of pirate captains. Holden gave you something infinitely valuable, an entire decade of his own life to prolong yours."

I hear the ticktocking of the clocks around us, all competing for the loudest boom in my head. I glance through the doorway at Uncle Holden bent over the lass. "I took time away from my uncle?"

"Time was necessary to stimulate the creation power within the heartwood. For time is love, and love cannot be forced upon another."

My throat and eyes burn with withheld tears. Standing in my uncle's storefront, each clock that he crafted with painstaking care and set out as merchandise signifies the sacrifices he made to take me in. I cannot change what was, but I can choose how to move forward. "You sent me to find the sword. It's at the bottom of the sea and I cannot retrieve it."

"Can't you?" Father Time removes the daisy from his lapel and then closes my gloved hands around the bloom. "The sword of Avelyn was always meant for you. Holden could have stopped you from learning swordplay, locked you in your room, and kept you from the world, but he knew you had a great purpose. Find the sword of Avelyn, and you will have all you need to bring Prince Killian to justice."

More vague promises. More indistinct directions. More faith I do not have. "But I stabbed Markham with the sword, and it did nothing."

Father Time sets a top hat on his head, his striking young face dismayed. "You proclaim what cannot be done too often. Everley, you are a Time Bearer, a protector of the worlds and a knight of Evermore. You must see with infinite eyes."

My legs grow weak. I need to sit down, but I cannot, or my spirit will drop straight through the chair. "What's Evermore?"

"Evermore is yesterday, today, and forever."

"I don't understand." He stares wordlessly, offering no other explanation. I groan in impatience. "Oh, it doesn't matter, because I don't want to be a knight. I don't want to be a Time Bearer. I want to go home!"

Father Time snaps his fingers. Every clock in the storefront stops, the silence deafening. He lowers his hand and they restart their march, all of them ticking and tocking sharply in perfect rhythm.

"Your purpose, and the gifts you were given to fulfill that purpose, would come to you sooner if you would open your heart," he says firmly. "You keep trying to change what was, when you should be concentrating on what will be. The past is out of your control."

He speaks of control, but I was given none over my own heart. The first nights after I woke to learn my family was gone were agony. In my darkest moment, I wished my uncle had not helped me survive. What happened in my past very much affects my present and future.

"Markham changed everything," I say. "You let him, and you continue to let him."

Father Time's voice softens, and with it, the ticking clocks around us gentle. "We replaced your heart with a timepiece, but the essence of who you are was not altered. You will find wholeness in accepting your place as Time Bearer. Do more than survive, Everley Donovan. Bloom." He waves his hand over the daisy in my grasp, and the flower blossoms fully, the yellow petals spreading wider.

He tips the brim of his hat at me and vanishes between the next tick and tock of the clocks.

The second he disappears, the clocks resume their rival tempos, a loud, disorganized mess of noise I associate with home. But I am not permitted to stay, because my spirit starts to float upward. I catch one more glimpse of my uncle in his workshop and then pass through the ceiling and into the rooftops.

Above the city, I pick up speed and zip into a blanket of stars. My spirit seems to have memorized the heavens' pattern, for I navigate them like a map and fly back into my body.

Neely is still on the stool and bent over me.

I sit up onto my elbows, my stomach queasy, as though I'm recovering from a sudden drop. My clock heart has been reassembled. "Are you finished?"

"I've been done for some time. You drifted off."

"Did you learn anything?" I ask, buttoning my shirt.

"The cogs and gears and balance wheel are in prime condition. Everything seems in working order." Neely shakes his head woefully. As he puts his stool away, I swipe his chisel and slide it beneath me. He regards me again. "I'm sorry I don't have better news, poppet. I will notify the captain."

The giant plods out with his tool bag. I wait until I hear the lock slide shut in the door and then tuck the chisel into my back pocket.

As I get up, my hand presses down on something under me. I pick up the daisy and twirl it in front of my nose. Father Time said I need the sword to stop Markham, but am I to use the blade against him or does the sword hold another power?

I feel wretched about leaving my uncle, as though I left him to care for an ailing child on his own. That horrifying night has long since passed, but the memories of the years in between are strong. He nursed me back to health and made his home mine. I ran to him when I lost my first tooth, and together we learned how to cook my father's plum pudding recipe. Uncle Holden was my best friend, my only friend, and he kept the secret of my clock heart from me. For so long, I felt as though I was living the years my family would not. I haven't been living their years but his.

A sense of panic grips me. The tenth anniversary of my family's death—of my clock heart—is soon. I don't know how time moves differently here from my world, so I cannot say today's date with certainty, but the time remaining until the anniversary was numbered in days when I left home. What happens when the ten years my uncle gave me are spent?

The ship begins to slow. I quit twirling the daisy and get up.

Osric throws open the door. "The captain requires your presence on deck."

"Why?" I ask, tucking the daisy under my pillow.

His attention snaps to the movements behind him outside, then back to me. "Come along, Countess."

I don't want his hands on me again, so I tug up my red gloves and follow him out.

The entire crew appears to have congregated on the main deck. Even Jamison, Laverick, and Harlow are here, their hands bound.

Radella too, though she's sulking in her cage. Harlow's head is down to hide her face behind the curtain of her hair.

Laverick's gaze flits across the crewmen, never settling on anything or anyone for long. She must be worrying about Claret, as am I. The longer we take to find our friend, the less likely it seems that we will.

A plank has been extended over the water and held in place with sandbags. Markham stands near it, his hands and feet tied. Bloody bones, it's high tide already. Neely was with me longer than I thought. Markham is going right up to the minute on this. I send him a look that says, *This is your very best?*

He lifts his hand loosely, palm up, in a *What can I do?* gesture.

Osric leads me to the other prisoners, leaving me between Harlow and Jamison. Jamison scours me for a sign that I have followed his advice and allied with Markham. I shake my head slightly, because I honestly have no idea what the prince has planned.

Captain Redmond marches out of his quarters. His crocodile sunbathes on the upper deck, its toothy mouth open wide and eyes glassy. The captain, once again dressed elegantly in velvet and satin, halts before Markham. The giant could crush the prince's neck with one hand. Perhaps he has already tried, in which case, I commiserate with his frustration.

"Let us begin," announces the captain. "Killian Markham, crown prince of the Land of Promise—"

My eyebrows shoot up, and I hear Jamison choke on his breath. The captain must have misspoken. Markham is from the Land of Youth, the world he destroyed, not the elves' world. Captain Redmond blusters on before I can correct him.

"You are hereby banished to the bottom of the sea for misusing a battle carnyx, attempting to trade a faulty clock"—I blanch at his reference to me—"and generally being a thorn in my side."

Osric clears his throat.

"And in my first mate's side," adds the captain. "String him up!"

While two men tie millstones to his ankles, one of the pirates yawns and another one gazes off at a cloud. It is odd to attend an execution where people are daydreaming. I suppose this is somewhat anticlimactic, considering the accused cannot perish.

Osric and two elves hoist Markham onto the gunwale. Now would be a good time for Markham to implement whatever plan he has devised.

"Are the sharks circling yet?" Osric asks.

Markham peeks over the edge of the ship. "It doesn't appear so, but there's time yet."

Osric shoves him forward. Markham shuffles out to the middle of the plank, his steps weighted by the millstones. Harlow has yet to lift her bowed head.

Captain Redmond's voice booms across the deck. "Will you regain a kernel of honor by jumping, Prince Killian? Or must we pull the plank?"

"I need no assistance." Markham tips his head at me. "Thank you for tossing in the pearl, Evie. Best of luck beating us to the sword."

Before I can stammer out a reply, Markham walks off the plank.

Chapter Twelve

No sooner do I hear the prince splash into the water than someone has me by the throat.

Harlow locks her bound wrists around my neck and digs a sharp metal nail under my chin that she must have pried from a floorboard. The crewmen around us draw their cutlasses.

"Stay back or I'll bleed the life out of your precious timepiece," Harlow says.

Captain Redmond waves at his pirates. "Pull back."

Harlow forces me to sidestep with her to the gunwale and peeks over the side. I cannot move my head to see what she's looking for.

"Let Everley go," Jamison says, his knees bent, ready to spring even with his hands tied.

"Stay out of this, Callahan." Harlow pushes the nail into my skin, and hot pain shoots out from the sharp prick. The chisel I swiped is in my back pocket, out of my grasp.

"You're a coward," I growl.

Harlow presses her lips against my ear. "Race you to the bottom of the sea."

She lifts her arms, sliding them up over my head. I duck down to avoid the sharp nail, and she climbs onto the rail and jumps overboard.

A dozen blades are suddenly in my face as pirates rush the gunwale. I rise as the sound of Harlow's splash carries upward. Jamison and

Laverick come up behind me, and everyone leans over the gunwale to see where she's gone.

Harlow surfaces, and she has company.

Markham treads water beside her, his bindings removed. He unties her, and they start to swim away, moving unusually fast against the current. The farther out they travel, the more the shadows underneath them become visible. They seem to be standing on something under the water that is carrying them away.

The captain takes a cannonball from a crewman—I missed where they came from—and presses it between his ear and his shoulder. Everyone stands back as the giant rotates in a wide circle and flings it over the rail. The cannonball arcs high in the sky and falls to the sea, landing remarkably close to the targets. The large splash slows Markham and Harlow down momentarily before they speed off again.

"Aren't you going to chase them?" I ask.

Osric exchanges a glance with his leader. "Another round, Captain?"

"Make it two for good measure."

Captain Redmond and Neely each pick up a cannonball and repeat the spin-and-throw maneuver, tossing them even farther than before. Neely is spry on his toes, and his cannonball gets more lift than the captain's. Though they both miss their target, it occurs to me that this is why they don't require cannons on board.

Markham and Harlow slow to a stop out on the water, and then several man-size fish surface around them. Even from a distance, the newcomers are frightening. Deep blue and scaly on their upper halves, the creatures have fins along the tops of their heads that trail down their backs. Their bottom halves are legs like ours, and their upper halves are aquatic.

The fish people stand while riding upon armored turtles. Their shells are as wide and long as wagon wheels. The turtles are harnessed for the ease of their riders, who each grip the reins with one fin and wield a golden trident in the other.

The largest of the fish people lifts a trident over its head in a triumphant salute or gesture of greeting, I cannot tell which.

Osric waves back, his voice mockingly cheerful. "Rot your eyes out, you filthy finperson."

I recall from stories about the Land Under the Wave that finfolk share these seas with the merrows. The two groups are age-old rivals, each with their own territories and leadership.

A turtle rises from beneath Harlow and Markham, so they are standing on its huge shell, and then they and the finfolk set off for the horizon.

"Let them go," Captain Redmond says. "We've put on a believable display."

"What do you mean?" I ask.

"This was our only course of action against him," Osric replies. "You dropped the blue pearl into the sea."

"I did that to stop the merrows from singing all night."

"Is that how Prince Killian persuaded you to assist him?" The first mate grunts, laughing at my stupidity.

Heat climbs up my face. Of course Markham was lying about the pearl.

Captain Redmond adjusts the sleeves of his velvet jacket, turning down his cuffs over the ink markings on his wrist. The marking of the clock has clouds on the face, just like the pocket watch he's searching for. "At least the prince didn't take all his human companions. The lot of you will fetch a bundle of gold from the traders, and you, Ticker, you are too precious to stow away in my collection. Novelties draw in considerable interest on the high seas. Osric, lock them in the day cabin. I want them close by."

"Are you certain you don't want them in the brig, sir?" asks the first mate. The brig must be easier for him to guard.

The captain regards him coolly. "Are you questioning me, Officer?"

"No, sir," replies Osric.

He rounds us up while more crewmen remove the sandbags and pull the plank back onto the ship. I pick up Radella's cage and carry her with us into the cabin. Once inside, Osric removes the bindings from Jamison and Laverick.

Jamison dabs the cut on my throat with his sleeve. "Does it hurt?"

"A little." In all the upheaval, I forgot I was bleeding.

"Hold this against it," he says, passing me a piece of canvas he found on the workbench. "The mark is shallow, but it may scar."

Another scar. Grand.

Osric drops more sacks of dried seaweed and chewy kelp pods onto the table. Another crewman brings a full pitcher of water and cups. Osric pours our drinks, his movements short and jerky.

"Would you please enlighten us as to what just happened?" Laverick asks.

"Isn't it clear to you by now?" Osric rejoins. "We needed to make the prince think he escaped so he would leave. Killian is a danger to everyone around him; trouble follows wherever he goes. When I saw Everley drop the pearl in the water last night, I knew this was our chance to get rid of him."

"You left my door unlocked on purpose," I say, my pride stinging. It hurts to have been manipulated once, but twice?

"It was only a matter of time before Killian maneuvered someone into giving him what he wanted," says Jamison. Since he encouraged me to align with Markham, he must also feel the burn of embarrassment.

"I still don't understand," Laverick interjects. "How did a pearl help the prince escape?"

"Dropping a blue pearl in the sea is Killian's personal call to the finfolk for aid," Osric replies. "Markham allied with them long ago. He told Everley the pearl would silence the merrows' singing, but the merrows only fled to avoid a skirmish with the finfolk. Recently, the two rivals have been quarreling over borders."

This goes beyond Markham's deception about the pearl. He led the pirates to our location, and when they seized us, he came aboard this ship with every intention of getting off without us. He's a monster who preys on the desperate and needy. I know that, I have always known that, yet I was so focused on escaping, I put my instincts aside.

"Why did the captain say Killian hails from the Land of Promise?" Jamison asks.

"Prince Killian is not as he seems." Osric removes an apple from his pocket and shines it on his chest. "Centuries ago, he had a glamour enchantment put on him by a powerful sorceress so he could pass between the worlds without being recognized. Before marrying Princess Amadara of the Land of Youth, he was Prince Killian of the Land of Promise, second in line for the elven throne."

"He's an *elf*?" says Laverick.

"The spell hides his elven features, thus he resembles a human."

I am so full of shock I am almost vibrating. Markham is a gifted deceiver, but the Land of Youth was his home, and he was wed to Princess Amadara . . . unless he was from the Land of Promise first?

Osric downs one of the cups of water that he poured for us himself. "Killian left our world long ago, after he was estranged from his family. He's been trying to find a way back ever since."

"Why doesn't he just go home?" I ask. "The portals are open between your world and the rest, aren't they?"

"It's much more complicated. Killian was banished for falling in love with someone beneath his station. When his sister, the queen, found out, he ran away with his companion and they were both declared deserters."

"Were you banished too?" Jamison asks.

Osric stares into the bottom of his empty cup. "Unofficially. Killian was in love with my younger sister, Brea. I discovered she was meeting him in secret, but I never thought he would forsake his throne for her." The first mate grinds his jaw. "My parents blamed me for introducing

Brea to the prince. Mother told me to find my sister and bring her back, and my father warned me not to return home without her. They thought if I could convince Brea to end her infatuation with Killian, our queen would welcome her home. I searched all over and finally found her and Killian holed up in the wreck on the Skeleton Coast."

The ship we took shelter in, the one Markham brought us to, did belong to the elves—the prince of the elves. "Radella, you knew about his upbringing. The family portrait we saw. Was that of him and his family?"

The pixie nods.

Suddenly, this no longer feels like some olden tale far removed from myself and my reality. I stagger to the table and sit down, my ticker pounding fast.

"Brea was heavy with child," says Osric, his tone despondent. "She had several weeks until her child's delivery, but the tides pulled at the water in her belly and started her labor early. While Killian was out looking for help, I remained with Brea. She and her unborn child died before he returned."

No one speaks.

Osric stares at the apple in his hand, at a loss for what to do with it. "Killian and I buried my sister and stayed on the coast to mourn her. A long while later—I lost track of how many months passed between—a ship bottomed out offshore. When the twilight hour arrived, so did the merrows. The crew jumped into the sea one after another to heed their summons. Killian and I saved only two of them—Redmond and Neely. Their ship, the *Undertow*, was damaged but salvageable. The four of us worked together to make her seaworthy again, living aboard the vessel and taking in other castaways as crewmates. Markham struggled to cooperate with the crew. He was a prince unaccustomed to hard work and didn't respect the hierarchy on the ship. He thought he deserved the position of captain and would not accept any disagreement. We marooned him, but he eventually came back, and Redmond took him in again. Over and over, Killian would overstep his authority, we would maroon him, and he would find a way back to us. The last time we forgave him, he stole our rum, sold it to traders, and bought passage out of this world. Then we heard tales that he had married a princess from the Land of Youth, but I didn't see him again until recently, when Dorcha brought him back to us with the sword."

"What did Markham plan to do with it?" Jamison asks.

"He never said." Osric turns the red apple in his hands like he's spinning a world. "But Prince Killian never bleeds a drop of blood that doesn't serve him."

I massage my temples to quiet my drumming headache. Jamison sits at the table beside me, our water and food in front of us untouched.

Osric finally bites into his apple and speaks around the chunk in his cheek. "None of you should feel ashamed. The prince has fooled many well-intentioned creatures. You aren't the first, nor will you be the last." He picks up a sandglass from a shelf and turns it over, triggering the sand inside to pour through the hourglass vessel. "It won't be long before the captain sells you to the traders. Enjoy the time you have left with us. Whoever purchases you may not be so kind."

The first mate sets the sandglass on the table and walks out.

Jamison has not moved from his chair. He stares at the hourglass as the sand filters from the top to the bottom of the vessel. When the time is spent, he turns the sandglass over again. He seems to be watching and waiting for something to happen. Maybe he thinks when the sand fills up the bottom enough times, he'll have an answer to our problems.

I released Radella from her cage right after Osric left. She perched on Jamison's shoulder and is still there. The two of them have been brooding for hours.

Laverick and I haven't been good company either. I sit at the bench overlooking the stern while she stretches out on the bunk. I'm loath to think of Captain Redmond selling me like a timepiece in my uncle's shop, and I dare not imagine what awfulness he has planned for my friends. I have said nothing to anyone because all I can offer my friends is an apology, and an apology is less than they deserve.

I hate Markham for making a fool out of me yet again.

I hate that he ruined our plan to turn him in to the queen and set me free.

I hate that, no matter what I do—fight against him or fight with him—he scars me.

As the sunset washes brilliant yellows and oranges across the sky, Laverick joins me by the window. "I think I prefer the brig," she says. "These silent clocks are eerie."

The dead timepieces aren't helping my mood. The pirates might as well have locked me in a tomb with corpses.

"I like your ticker, Evie."

I perk up a little. "You do? I thought you were repulsed by it."

"I was surprised, not repulsed. Why would I be? Everyone answers to time." She sighs to herself. "I asked Jamison about it while we were in the brig. He told me what Prince Killian did to you when you were a little girl. I wish you had said something."

My preference is still that no one besides my uncle knows about my clock heart, but that level of privacy is gone. "I'm sorry about this, and about Claret."

"Do you know how we came to get our nicknames?" Laverick asks, smiling to herself. "Most people think it's because I resemble a fox with my reddish hair and long nose, and Claret resembles a cat with her tapered eyes and fine grooming habits. But I earned my name because Vevina said I could sneak into a henhouse and steal the eggs right out from under the chickens without ruffling a feather. Claret earned her name because she's like a cat with nine lives, always landing on her feet. No matter what happened to her on the streets, she could always maneuver her way out of getting caught. If anyone can outlast this place, it's her."

Claret truly has a respectable resiliency, and it's charming just how much Laverick admires her friend.

"Can you keep a secret?" she asks more softly.

"Always."

"Claret and I have grown closer since we left Dorestand. We're close friends, but I want to become *closer*."

Her meaning soaks in, and tears well in my eyes. "Oh, Laverick."

"Well, creation," she says. "I didn't expect you to cry. Is it such an offensive thought?"

"Not at all! Now that I know how you feel, I'm even sadder Claret isn't here with us." Children of Madrona believe all love stems from the collective beauty of creation power. No one is whole without family, friendship, and love. Laverick falling in love with Claret should be celebrated the same as if she loved a man. "Why didn't you tell me how you felt about her?"

"No one wants to tell their secrets to someone who won't share theirs," she answers, leaving me with no defense. "On the ship, Claret and I tried to spend time with you. We weren't loitering outside your cabin to steal a glimpse of Radella. We were hoping you would let us in and introduce us to her."

I wish I could go back in time to invite the Fox and the Cat into my cabin and be friendlier, but I would also take back Captain Redmond exposing my ticker to everyone. I have never offered my secrets willingly, because I couldn't, and I'm not sorry for being careful.

"Do you think Claret wants to be closer to you too?" I ask.

"I haven't told her how I feel yet, but I think she does. We had a moment before we left our world . . ."

"A kiss?" I ask, my gaze sliding to Jamison. I have not kissed him since I locked him belowdecks on the *Cadeyrn of the Seas*. I made the decision to abstain from kissing so we can more easily return to our old lives when the time comes.

"Claret and I were interrupted by crewmen," Laverick says, "but it may have been for the best. Claret still relishes the life of a pickpocket, and she likes roving the seas with Vevina. I've been thinking about opening an ammunition shop outside Dorestand, a small place where I can tinker with my black-powder experiments, like how I rigged the cannon to shoot harpoons." Laverick quiets even more. "But I cannot picture my life without Claret. There was a moment when we were separated in the Thornwoods. Just a few minutes, but it felt like forever. And now this . . . I took my time with her for granted. I would give anything for another chance."

I slide another glance at Jamison. I couldn't have known I was bringing him or my friends into a world with which Markham was familiar. Had I known, I would have never done it, but there is no second chance for this.

"Well," Jamison says loudly, addressing the room, "we've wallowed long enough. Before we work together to form a plan, we need to decide what to do if—no, after—we get out of here. Obviously, we should prioritize the sword but keep an eye out for Claret."

Laverick's mouth bobs open and shut. "Obviously?"

Radella shoots in front of Jamison and wags her finger at him angrily.

"They have a point," I answer, rubbing at my aching temples. "Markham wants us to follow him. That never ends well."

Jamison raises his hands to the pixie in a bid for peace. She still scowls at him, so he collects parchment and ink from the workbench and then returns to the table. "Radella, why don't you write down your thoughts on the matter?"

He extends the quill to her and she takes it, dipping the end in the ink and then brushing the tip across the paper.

Laverick folds her arms across her chest and stews. After our discussion, finding the sword seems much less urgent than looking for Claret, but I don't see why we cannot do both.

"We're not giving up on her," I say.

Her frown lessens a little, just enough to let me know she believes I'm resolute, yet she's still reluctant to agree to Jamison's suggestion to put the sword first.

Radella finishes jotting down her formal complaint. She's acting quite cowardly, considering Father Time sent her as his representative from the Everwoods. She finishes her note, and Jamison silently reads what I am certain is a contemptuous monologue. He patiently lays the letter down and soothes her in a gentle voice, his words too low to make out.

Radella stomps her feet and trills angrily.

He raises his voice over hers. "No one here asked you to leave the Everwoods and come with us. For that matter, none of us is forcing you to stay. You can fly away if you want, and we'll do this without you."

Radella zips up to his nose, and the little scamp kicks the end of it. Her booting him probably hurt no more than a flick of a finger, yet Jamison flinches. She dashes to the top of the grandfather clock and perches out of sight.

I leave Laverick and go to the table. Jamison hesitates a moment and then pulls out a chair for me. We sit together and watch the internal trickle of the sandglass.

"My father is fascinated by timepieces," he says. "He's a great admirer of your uncle's work. His collection isn't as eclectic as the captain's, but he owns several hourglasses, and his favorite storybook tale is of the infinity sandglass."

I haven't heard this story in a long while. Setting my elbows on the table, I lean forward to listen.

"As the tale goes, the infinity sandglass is ancient, older than all the worlds combined. The glass vessel is made from the ash of a sun, the sand of a moon, and wood taken from the first-ever elderwood. Turning the sandglass ushers in the hours and keeps time across the seven worlds. The job belongs to Father Time's helmsman. Like a helmsman in charge of flipping an hourglass on a ship, he keeps the worlds on schedule."

"That would be a big responsibility," I say.

"Immense," Jamison answers. "My father would inspect every hourglass he came upon in hopes that it would be the infinity sandglass. I have always wondered how it would feel to hold the pulse of time in my grasp." He opens his hand and flexes it shut. "I underestimated Killian. Now that I know he was banished by his family and lost someone he loved, I understand very well his desperation to make it right. He will make more reckless decisions to redeem himself."

"The sword of Avelyn can stop him." Of all the secrets I hold dear about my clock heart, this one Jamison should know, if only to help me figure out the meaning. "Father Time said the sword will be Markham's undoing."

"Then we cannot leave this world without it."

Across the way, Laverick nods in agreement. Though she isn't as invested in finding Markham, she accepts that the sword cannot stay here. Even so, I feel guilty for uniting them in my cause and drawing them into more danger. I grip the base of the hourglass, seeking strength from time itself. "Maybe the three of you should look for Claret while I race Markham."

"I've had a lot of time to think about your sword." Jamison grabs the hourglass and drags it closer to us. "Before the sword of Avelyn was a blade, it was a star. After the star was broken, she could have faded away, but she fulfilled a new purpose and became the greatest sword in all the cosmos. I think Father Time asked you to retrieve the sword because the task would change you, change us, for the better."

His confidence in me is more reassuring than he knows, but whenever I think of the permanency of my ticker, I'm torn. I want to believe that its life-sustaining power is for my own good. But if I'm whole with a clock for a heart, does that mean I'm whole without Jamison, without love?

His morning-sky-blue eyes bore into mine. "You're not alone, Everley. We still have a chance to deliver Killian to the queen and purchase your freedom. I'm not giving up."

"Neither am I." Laverick smiles, a sincere albeit weak gesture of support. "And you never know. Maybe if I help you capture the prince and turn him in to the queen, she'll pardon me and Claret too."

I stop myself from launching across the cabin and grabbing her up in a hug. "I won't let you down."

"Now we just need Radella to come around," Jamison says with a pointed glance in her direction. High up on the grandfather clock, the pixie flutters her wings in discord. "My only real concern is whether Everley is well enough to continue."

My throat squeezes down on a swell of excuses. I wish I could tell Jamison, tell all my friends, what Father Time said about my clock heart and what my uncle did for me. But it is so unbelievable I don't know where to start. "My clock heart is always a gamble. This is no different." I remove the chisel from my back pocket and hold it up. "Let's make some trouble."

"Finally, something I'm good at." Laverick hops to her feet and begins to case the cabin. "The lack of cannons and guns is a fair indicator that there isn't any black powder on board, but that doesn't mean we can't make something else that goes boom."

Liking her line of thinking, I leave Laverick to plot up something devious. Markham assumes the pirates have taken us out of the race, so he's free to do whatever awfulness he intends next. He's been in control since we arrived in this world, but we're going to get what we're after, and then we're all going home.

Chapter Thirteen

We are ready for the pirates.

Though we assumed the captain would off-load us to a trader relatively quickly, it's taking longer than expected. Besides bringing us meals, the crew has sequestered us in the cabin for two days. Osric hasn't returned, and neither have the merrows. Their silence has been unnerving, as though they're storing up their resources for something more nefarious. We have been on guard constantly, and the wait is wearing on us all.

Laverick is curled up on the bench by the window, her back to us, her attention on the sea. Radella came out of hiding once, just long enough to disappear our cups. Jamison called her an imp for her spitefulness. She stuck out her tongue at him and flew back to the top of the grandfather clock. When the time comes to escape, she better do what we planned or we'll be in trouble.

Jamison and I sit on the bunk side by side, and he traces the lines of my palm. We have tried to fill our waiting time with less stressful topics and activities.

"This is your head line," he says. "The head line is associated with your beliefs, attitudes about life, and self-control. Your line is straight and unbroken, which means you have a strong sense of justice and injustice."

Palm reading is a parlor trick among nobility. The people hosting the party bring in an old woman who's supposedly a hag, and she entertains them with mystical projections about their wisdom and destiny. My parents invited one into our home once, but I was too young to remember much. Jamison comes from a higher circle in society—my father was only a baron—so he undoubtedly has more experience with charlatans. I feel ridiculous paying attention to such nonsense, yet I cannot quell my interest.

"Your fate line is unusual," he says. "You have one, when not many people do, and it's strongly marked."

My lips turn downward. "What does that mean?"

"It means you are strongly controlled by fate."

"Does it say what my fate is? Perhaps something about Evermore?"

"I don't know what that is."

"Never mind. Go on."

Jamison pulls my hand up to his face and inspects it closer. "This here is your heart line."

"You don't need to read that." I try to yank my hand away, but he holds on tightly and will not let go.

"The heart line is the most important part of the palm reading. It indicates your romantic life and your emotional stability." He traces the thick line that runs from one side of my palm to the other. "Look how strong it is. This is by far your longest and most identifiable line."

"Which means . . . ?"

"You love with your whole being," he says quietly. "It also means you are resilient. Regardless of what life thrusts upon you, you never give up on trying to set the world right."

I squint hard at him. "Is that really how that line is interpreted?"

He kisses the center of my palm and grins. "Are you questioning me, darling dearest?"

"I wouldn't dare, honeysuckle." I turn his left hand over to analyze his own palm lines. "It's my turn to read your lines."

"Oh? All right, Lady Callahan. What does my heart line say?"

All I know about palm reading I just learned from him, but I ponder on his emotional stability, about him wanting to return to his father, make amends, and win back his life. He must miss his huge estates, his servants doting on him, and the grand social life of a noble, yet he never speaks of such matters. He seems more comfortable serving aboard a navy ship, working among the other crewmen, but for how long? He joined the navy to escape his father, and now all he speaks about is going home.

"Everley?"

"I'm getting to it." I squint at his hand, pretending to divine his fortune. "Your line curves upward toward your index finger, which implies that your heart will change many times in your life, but the line is strong, so you will withstand any loss you endure."

He gazes into my eyes for so long I almost forget what we are talking about. "You have a talent for palm reading," he remarks at last.

"Are you saying I have a future doing parlor tricks?"

He laughs, and I am certain there isn't any better sound.

Laverick straightens and leans closer to the window. Radella flies over to look out the glass as well. Her wings flutter excitedly. We join them to see what has garnered their attention. The ship is sailing by a rocky spit. The sliver of land looks like a tail sticking out in the middle of the water and is made up of boulders all piled together. I see no vegetation, except, at the farthest point, there stands a single gnarled tree, its splayed branches barren of leaves or acorns or berries. A body hangs by a noose from a crooked bough, its bare feet dangling. Scales adorn its chest and a sack covers its head, the shape of which is too large to be human.

"It's a finperson," says Jamison.

"I wonder who strung him up?" Laverick asks dimly.

I wonder what he did to get here. Back home, Dorestand's execution yard is in a quad between the prison and the courthouse. My uncle and I would pass by it on our way to the lumberyard. On days of scheduled hangings or burnings, we took the long route to the yard to evade the crowds from the queen's self-made Progressive Ministry gathering to witness the deaths of those convicted for worshipping Mother Madrona. What crimes merit execution in this world?

We sail past the hanging tree, our path parallel to the skinny crag of rocks. The land builds in height to sheer limestone cliffs, and low sandy beaches stretch in the path of the treacherous tides. No other foliage grows alongside the rocky cliffs besides sparse clumps of crabgrass. The single tree at the end of the spit endured the winds and tides and saltwater spray, as though it's there exclusively for hangings.

According to the world map I saw in the captain's quarters, we are traveling alongside Hangman's Spit, sailing up the coast to Merrow Lagoon. East of the lagoon is Skull Reef, and directly out from the reef, far below the surface, lies Everblue.

We stay at the window, mesmerized as the terrain transitions again to sloping hills of loose dirt and scrubby seagrass. The ship approaches a large stone structure with an open top for a fire signal, and past it, we receive our first glimpse of Merrow Lagoon and the continent's only village, Eventide.

Eventide is nestled between the hills and cliffs at the base of an ashen mountain. A path winds up the side of the mountain to a structure of sorts, like a lookout. Along the bowl-shaped bay are clay buildings with terra-cotta tile roofs. The rock faces are white with a pearly sheen, and the shallower water of the lagoon gleams pale indigo. Docks extend into the waterway, where smaller watercraft are moored.

Cries carry in from outside as the crew lowers the anchor. The four of us scramble to our stations and wait.

The afternoon gives way to evening, but the pirates do not come for us. Eventually, Jamison leaves his position by the door to pass out supper. Laverick gnaws on a strip of seaweed, while Radella watches out the window as the lights of the village twinkle to life just ahead of the stars. Her little wings droop again. She could fly off without us, but for all her haranguing, she will stay.

Jamison devours five kelp pods in a row, shoving them down so fast that I doubt he tastes much. My nerves are too jumpy for me to choke down more than a few bites.

Radella perks up and points out the window. I run over and see one of our longboats rowing for the docks. A good-size party is aboard, including the unmistakable silhouette of Captain Redmond.

"Jamison, the captain is leaving with one, two, three . . . eight crewmen. Now's our time."

"Plan two it is, then." He sweeps his arms at the door while stepping aside. "Laverick, if you'll do us the honor."

She shoves the dulled chisel into the keyhole and then wriggles it until she springs the lock.

Jamison grabs the knob. "Ready?"

Radella nods with her whole body, zipping up and down. Laverick and I remove the wooden stakes from where we shoved them down our backs. I ripped the back wall panel off the grandfather clock and cut out makeshift weapons with Neely's chisel, using the flat end of the hourglass as a hammer. A third weapon, the largest carving I have ever crafted, is tucked into the waistline of my trousers.

Jamison opens the door. Directly outside, lying with its head and teeth facing us, is the captain's crocodile. Jamison shuts the door again.

"Damn. We're on to plan three. Radella, your turn."

The pixie picks up her wooden stake, a smaller version I made for her. Jamison opens the door and she zips out, flying right for Tattler. The croc lunges and snaps at her, but she whizzes through his open jaws, loops upward, and jabs him in the eye.

The crocodile growls and waddles off, his tail twitching.

"Go."

I slip out, followed by Laverick and then Jamison. The decks are quiet and unoccupied. We cut across the main deck, Radella ahead of us. She pulls up short, but we're too late. Neely is seated atop a group of barrels, reading. Behind him is the last longboat.

He lays his book down in his lap. "You shouldn't be out of your room. You're going to make trouble for yourselves. Go on, then. Go back to where you belong."

"Neely," I say, "we're leaving."

"You know I can't let you do that, poppet. The captain has gone to shore to meet the trader. Because of you, he'll finally be able to buy back his grandfather's pocket watch."

My mouth goes as dry as sand.

"I like you, poppet," Neely says, shutting his book. "I don't wish to hurt you or your friends."

"I don't want to hurt you either, Neely." I pull the carved pistol from my hip and aim it at him. "Let us pass."

"That pistol doesn't look real."

"Are you certain?" I ask, aiming it between his eyes. "Seems like a big mistake for you to make."

Neely hesitates, and in that beat of indecision, Jamison and Laverick rush past him for the longboat. Radella stays with me, and although her pixie dust is mightier than the fake pistol in my hand, I wish we were a more formidable team.

The giant releases a cavernous sigh and gradually stands. My hands are clammy, but my grip on the wooden pistol doesn't waver. He grabs the end of the pistol in his huge hand, squeezes down, and crushes the stock.

Jamison and Laverick pause from untying the boat, and we all gape as the broken wood pieces rain down on the deck. Having no fourth plan, I improvise.

"Radella," I say, "your turn."

The pixie flies at Neely and buzzes around his head. Jamison and Laverick go back to preparing the boat for the water, tugging the ropes and working the block and tackle. I try to slip past the giant while he's distracted. But Neely bats Radella hard, sending her spinning into a sail. He swings his arms to grab me, and I jump back and draw my stake.

"Poppet," Neely says gruffly, "stop this ruckus and return to your cabin with your friends, or I'll throw you in the brig and tell the captain what you've done."

Across the way, Jamison and Laverick work faster. Radella has recovered from her crash, her open wings ready to take flight.

I plant my feet before the giant. "You have to catch us first."

He swings his arms to catch me, and I raise my stake to jam it into him. Someone above us whistles, halting us both and drawing our attention upward.

A shadowed figure stands in the sails and releases a black ball. About the time I realize a cannonball is plunging at us, it strikes Neely in the head. A sickening crack echoes across the deck, and then the giant tips over and lands flat on his back.

"Holy elderwood," I say.

Neely's head is bleeding. He's unconscious but breathing.

Osric drops down from the rigging beside me. I aim the stake at him.

"No tricks, Everley," he says, his hands empty of his own weapon. "You're halfway to escaping. Don't let me get in your way."

I remain on guard, prepared to lunge. Jamison and Laverick are frozen in shock, and Radella peers down from the boom above, her stare incredulous.

"You're letting us go?" I ask.

"Setting Prince Killian free was the captain's idea, not mine. I want Killian gone for good. We can help each other, but you have to go. Mundy will trade you if you stay, and then it will be impossible for me to help you race Killian to the sword." When I don't move, Osric's voice pitches higher. "Didn't you hear me, woman? I said go!"

I keep my wooden stake tight in hand in case he changes his mind and run to the longboat.

"Go straight to shore," says Osric, following me, his step urgent and authoritative. "Tell the wharfman you need to find the Lazy Lizard Tavern. He'll direct you, but if you get lost, listen for the music. The barmaid will know my name, so sit and wait for me."

"How do we know we can trust you?" Jamison asks.

Osric draws his cutlass and lays it on the deck by his feet. "I swear by the Creator by whom my people swear. If I break my oath, may the land open to swallow me, the sea rise to drown me, and the moon fall upon me."

He steps away from the weapon. Jamison scoops up the blade and aims it at him. The first mate still has his short sword, but he doesn't draw it.

"All right," says Jamison, "but we get Killian. We need to deliver him to our queen."

"She cannot hold him."

"Let that be our problem."

"We can discuss what we'll do with Killian later." Osric steps around Jamison and begins maneuvering the ropes that secure the boat to lower it into the water. "Lord Callahan, I need your assistance."

Jamison slowly passes the cutlass to Laverick. She aims the blade at Osric while he and Jamison swing the boat out over the water. The Fox climbs in and I follow her.

"Once you reach the tavern, go inside and wait for me," Osric says. "Don't try to flee or you'll draw attention to yourselves. Humans aren't thought of very highly in Eventide and don't last long unattended. I need to tie up Neely and go belowdecks to ensure that the rest of the crew don't escape their locked cabins before I meet you."

Jamison pulls himself into the boat next to me. Osric need only lower us into the water, yet some of the rigging is snagging on the block and tackle lines. Radella flies over the loose ropes and sprinkles her pixie dust, disappearing the troublesome portion and distributing the weight to the free lines.

The first mate lowers us into the sea. "Find the Lazy Lizard. Stay together and blend in."

After we drop from his sight, Laverick says, "Everley, can we trust him?"

"I don't know what choice we have."

Jamison and I pick up the oars and row for the docks. No one chases us or sounds an alarm as we maintain a steady pace across the bigger waves into the glassy lagoon.

As the night sky yawns, thousands of little blue lights begin to glow below us. A few of them float by, and I see they are tiny shellfish. Shadows dart among them, some small, but many big as us. Jamison and I row faster, keeping an eye on the shore while Laverick observes the *Undertow*. When something bumps the boat, Radella dives into my pocket.

"You're her new favorite," Jamison notes of the pixie.

"That's because I don't call her names," I reply, and he arches a brow. "At least not so she can hear me."

We row up to the dock, and Laverick jumps off. Jamison tosses her the rope, and then we disembark while the Fox ties off the boat. We start down the dock for land. No one else is here, at least not any other land dwellers. Shadows swim below, and every so often, fins or fish tails break the surface. The glowing blue lights reveal sinuous bodies, yet none of them rise from the shallows to acknowledge us. A different world exists underwater, and we're not part of it.

The sandy shoreline is set back from the lagoon, and up a path from the beach and dock, the white clay buildings reflect the soft silver moonlight. Eventide is a quaint seaside village that, if in our world, families would visit and fishermen would hail from, but it seems deserted compared to the constant movements in the sea.

An elf hefts a pail of sea snails down the beach, and a giant pushes a wheelbarrow full of fish up the steep incline to the village. They are the only people in sight, and neither one appears to be the wharfman.

Jamison pauses to evaluate the path up the hill. "The tavern can't be far."

Though I would rather wait for directions from the wharfman, I do agree that, in most villages, the taverns, favored havens for sailors, aren't far from the docks.

Jamison puts on the tricorn hat that he found at the bottom of a chest in the day cabin, and I lower the hood of my cloak down over my forehead. Laverick ties on one of the pirate's red head scarves, turning it inside out to hide the image of the sandglass over the skull and crossbones. Radella peeks out of my pocket but doesn't come out. Together, we climb the path to the village.

Cool air pours in from the sea, wrapping itself around us in a chilly embrace. We crest the top and stop before a maze of roads that weave uphill. The roads are not cobblestone like they are at home but made up of crushed seashells and coral.

Everyone must have gone in for the night, because not a soul is in view. The structures closest to us are huts, too small to be public taverns. We all stay close and watchful, gripping our weapons, and start up the widest street.

Most of the homes and shops are shuttered so tightly that barely any candlelight shines through. About every third building has been boarded up and abandoned. The wind funnels down the closed-in roadway, tearing past us at wicked speeds. My ears roar so loudly that I don't immediately hear the music until after Jamison turns down a narrower road.

The melody leads us to a single-story building with a large outdoor terrace full of people. We duck down an alley across the road between two dim shacks and peek out at the lively outdoor gathering place.

Rigging has been strung above the terrace, resembling fine latticework. Candles burn on the mismatched tables made from trunks and barrels, and three fiddlers play in a corner, their song intermingling with the voices and laughter of patrons. Carved into an old set of oar paddles that make up the entry archway is the name, "The Blood Moon."

Except for a group of gnomes sitting on an old chicken crate, most of the creatures are elves or finfolk. I should have assumed the latter could live on land, since their bottom halves are anatomically like ours.

The crewmen from the pirate ship have clustered together for drinks. Opposite of them, Captain Redmond shares a table with two seedy characters—a burly giant that outsizes even Mundy and an elf wearing a white wig. They are in discussion with the captain. I assume they are the traders.

My back and hands grow hot and begin to perspire. Although Osric gave us directions to meet him at the tavern, I want to get as far away as possible. Mundy is telling more people about me, about my clock heart.

Jamison gently grasps my hand and rubs a circle across the back with his thumb. "Let's keep going," he says.

I set off at the front of the group, creeping past the tavern until the music fades out of range. We venture higher, through more shuttered houses, and our view expands of the blue-lit lagoon and the *Undertow* anchored in the harbor. Farther ahead, the road turns again and again in switchbacks up the mountain, perhaps even to the lookout.

Over the howling wind, I hear music coming from a two-level structure backed up to the hillside. The crooked sign near the boarded front window reads, "Lazy Lizard."

Radella dives into my pocket, and my neck tingles with a shiver. Even though I can hear the music playing inside and Osric said it was safe to go in, this place doesn't look habitable. Jamison and Laverick guard my back while I tread up to the main entrance and push inside.

Chapter Fourteen

The Lazy Lizard smells of stale seaweed and spilled grog. A stairway by the entrance leads to the upper level, the staircase unlit and uninviting. We follow the candlelight and the sultry music into the open dining area.

Tables are set in the center of the tavern. I locate one near the outskirts of the room and cross to it, evading eye contact with the bartender, barmaid, and seated patrons. Radella hisses in my pocket as we pass the bar, at what or whom I cannot tell.

The slower music switches to a swinging beat. Onstage, in a tub full of water, a female merrow sings a melody different from her peers' summons of enchantment. She lies on her back, gripping the sides of the tub with her slim green fingers and black nails. Her opaque tail fin drapes over the bottom of the tub, and her hair cascades over her shoulders and outside the basin. Her tresses are duller when dry, gray green like the northern hills of Wyeth, and the scales of her lower body glimmer from green to blue to indigo with an undertone of violet. Her ears stick out like fins, and her onyx eyes gaze emptily into the audience. Outside the tub, also on the small stage, two elves play a toe-tapping beat on drums.

Jamison has paused in the alcove. I go ahead of him, assuming he will follow, but he is stalled in the doorway, fixated on the merrow. Laverick pulls him along to the table. He slides onto my bench and she sits across from us. He hasn't removed his focus from the merrow. Her tune is different than the one the merrows sang to call us to the sea, and none of the other patrons appear influenced by her voice.

I raise my hood and set my hand on Jamison's knee. "Is she enchanting you?"

"No, but I've no trust that she won't." He grips my hand so hard his knuckles bleed of color.

At the next table, an elven gentleman in satin, the first elf I have seen with gray hair, keeps company with a lass in an olive gown. Other groups are scattered throughout the dining area, some in parties of three or four. As far as I can see, we are the only humans.

A barmaid arrives at our table to take our order. Radella hisses at her, and I sit back, startled by the girl's bare feet and shapeless burlap sheath. Her most stunning feature is her long silver hair that hangs to the floor. She squints her pale-gold eyes at us.

"Did you go out alone?" asks the barmaid. "We don't serve unattended humans."

"We're waiting for someone," I say. "First Mate Osric of the *Undertow*."

"Oh, Osric! He's so handsome, isn't he handsome? I'll bring you some whiskies. And what can I get your pixie friend?"

Radella hisses at her. The barmaid woofs gruffly like a dog in return and storms away.

"Did you hear her bark?" asks Laverick, her tone touched by amazement. "I think she might be a selkie."

She may be right. Selkies are seal people, men and women who change forms between a seal and a human depending on whether they're on land or at sea. Most sailors and seafarers have heard of them, though they are rarely seen in our world. According to myth, selkies shed their sealskins to become human. Whoever owns their skin owns them.

"I don't care what she is," I say. "Radella, you're being rude."

The pixie trills at me and juts out her chin.

The barmaid returns with three glasses of whisky and a thimble full of pink fluid. "Flower nectar for the pixie," she explains curtly before leaving to serve another patron.

I pour the entire cup of whisky down my throat in one go. It's flavorful, though a tad watered down. Radella flies from my pocket to the table and samples her drink. Her wings perk up at the first taste, and then she pretends to glower as she glugs the whole thimble.

The merrow's tune changes to a sea chantey, a story about a woman who left her lover for the land of the giants. The older elf and his companion near us get up to dance, as do more and more couples. Jamison swallows his whisky and bangs the glass down.

"Everley, come dance with me."

"But your knee—"

"Is fine." Jamison stands and offers me his hand. "Osric told us not to draw attention to ourselves, and most everyone is dancing, so we should try to fit in."

I look to Laverick for help.

She gives a one-shouldered shrug. "He did say not to stand out." She shoves at me. "Go on. Radella and I will keep an eye out for Osric."

I accept Jamison's outstretched hand. He leads me to the dance floor and pulls me in close. "We never danced on our wedding night," he remarks.

"That's because I wanted to throttle you."

He chuckles and tugs me closer, holding me close despite the lively music. We rock gently, hitting every other downbeat. After our escape from the ship, the slower pace is about all my tired clock heart can withstand.

His voice curls into my ear. "Did you ever imagine this day would end with us dancing?"

I never would have thought that I would accept his invitation, but we should maximize the time we have together before we return to our old lives.

"Did I say something wrong?" Jamison asks.

"Not at all." My clock heart beats faster, but still too softly. I rest my head against his shoulder. "You're a fine dancer, Lord Callahan."

"As are you, Lady Callahan."

I wince instinctually at his use of my title. He doesn't seem to notice. His ideas for what our lives will be like when we go home will be spoiled eventually. For now, let him have his dreams, and honestly, I am flattered they include me.

Osric enters the tavern and stops to speak to the bartender. The bartender points to us, and the first mate marches over.

"We have to go. Right now." He prods Jamison and me over to Radella and Laverick and drops a handful of coins with clamshells engraved on them onto the table.

"Osric, what's happening?" I say.

"The elven guard is coming."

Radella flies into my pocket, her wings trembling. Osric leads us across the dance floor, past the stage, and to the rear door.

"Who are the elven guard?" Jamison asks.

"They serve my queen. She must have received word that her brother is here."

My neck stretches in alarm. Markham is in Eventide?

Outside the back door of the tavern, Osric glances at the moon and then creeps around the tavern. There, he crouches low to the rocky ground, and we all hunch in the shadows.

Silence settles between us.

And then I hear it over the wind—*thud, thud, thud.*

A unit of five persons runs down the road from up the mountain, clad in all-black garments with light chain mail vests overtop. The group moves as one, purposeful and controlled, as dangerous as a pack of wolves. Moonlight reveals their pointed ears and chins and glints of the swords at their hips. Osric sinks lower, so the rest of us also flatten our bodies to the ground.

Following the guard, roaming from one side of the road to the next, pads a large black dog. The canine is the size of a small bear, with a rangier build and shaggier coat. The beast weaves down the road behind the elven guard and pauses periodically to sniff the ground.

I hold still as the elves march swiftly past. The dog lags behind and then trots toward us. It roves up to the front of the tavern and sniffs about. The guard rounds the bend in the road, and the big canine tears off after them.

"What was that?" Jamison whispers.

"A barghest," answers Osric. "A hound trained to hunt elves, or any other creature they've been directed to track down."

I start to get up, but Osric waves for me to stay low and quietly draws his short sword. Laverick gazes up at the roof of the tavern without lifting her chin and readies her wooden stake.

Someone is up there.

Osric rises and steps out into the open. "Come down from there, Killian, you coward."

At first, no one responds, and then two people hang down from the second floor and drop, landing on their feet before us. I push to standing, my gut bunching. Since we last saw them tearing off with the finfolk, Markham and Harlow have acquired breastplates and swords.

"You haven't lost your touch, Osric," says Markham.

"Why are you here?" The first mate paces out onto the road, and Markham follows.

"We needed something that would help us dive to Everblue. We're having a race, and as you know, I don't like to lose."

A banging noise draws my notice to a broken shutter on the second floor of the tavern. Markham and Harlow must have been above us while we were inside. Jamison confronts Harlow, both of their blades extended. My wooden stake feels ridiculous against their sharpened steel.

"The elven guard is after you," Osric says. "Your sister must have heard of your misdeeds. Surrender to them, Killian, or I'll whistle and the barghest will be on you faster than a bolt of lightning."

Markham laughs at him and then addresses me. "You must be desperate to have aligned with this simpleton. His threats alone are torment."

"You double-crossed me," I snap.

"I can see you're angry about that," he says, arching a brow to mock the wooden weapon in my grasp. "No hard feelings, my dear. But, truly, you made it impossible to align with you. Did you think I was unaware of what you intended? You hoped to turn me in to Queen Aislinn and clear your name. I knew better than to trust you, what with your awful temper."

"You're bold to mention untrustworthiness," Osric cuts in.

Markham speaks right over him. "Everley, you must admit you do hold a grudge." While I stammer at his astonishing thickheadedness, he asks, "Have you found a way to Everblue?"

"Do you truly expect me to give away my secrets?" I reply.

"You are a dreadful liar, Evie. It's the only thing I dislike about you." Markham pats the sack at his side. "We traded for our way there. You must use that pretty head of yours to find your means of travel, or this race will be mighty dull."

"How did you afford to trade for bubble tonic?" Osric asks, all color seeping out of his face.

"We didn't trade anything we couldn't spare."

Harlow grimaces and touches the bare base of her throat.

"Where's your mother's necklace?" I ask her.

"Mind your own business." She jabs her sword at me, revealing more bruises along her wrist than last time.

Harlow will never be my friend, but this is wrong. "Did he trade your necklace? Harlow, your father gave it to your mother."

She touches her bare throat again. Her parents are dead, and Harlow had little left of them other than that trinket.

"Markham doesn't care for you," I say. "He hurts you and gives away your precious things. That isn't love."

"This coming from the girl with the ticker for a heart," Markham says, tone scathing. "Everley, how *does* one love without a real heart?"

"You tell me," I retort.

"There's that temper again."

I lift my arm to hurl my stake at him, but Laverick restrains me.

"Don't give him the satisfaction," she says.

Markham finally acknowledges Osric. "We're finished here, old friend."

"Turn yourself in, Killian. Do something right for a change."

"Turn myself in, what an intriguing suggestion." Markham makes eye contact with Jamison and then tosses him his sword.

Jamison catches it as a reflex and stares down at the weapon in bewilderment.

"The barghest was trained to hunt down anything that's marked with their target's scent," Markham explains. "One thread of their target's hair on your jacket would lead them to you, and even touching something that belongs to them or picking up something they just held would transfer their scent. Lieutenant Callahan, which of us do you think is the faster runner?"

Jamison drops the sword. "You bastard."

"I'm guessing by your response you think it's me. Shall we find out?" Markham purses his lips and whistles, a loud, piercing call.

Almost immediately, a howl, like the lonely shriek of a banshee, fills the night.

Osric's pale face screws up in panic. "Move!"

The first mate takes off, abandoning the road for a trail that leads downhill through the houses. Jamison, Laverick, and I sprint after him into the gravelly hillside. Another howl rises as we barrel onto another road, cross it, and leap down the next slope. Radella zooms ahead of us, her glowing light speeding ahead.

A third howl sounds above us, followed by a woman's shriek. I slow down to look up the trail. Jamison skids to a stop ahead of me.

"Everley, come on!"

"I think that was Harlow."

"We can't help her now."

Radella flies from the front of the group back to Jamison and me and gestures for us to hurry. I start off again, falling into step beside Jamison. We catch up to the others and rush out into a road, just down from The Blood Moon. Osric's pace slows and he leads us off the path. We run from shadowed hut to hut, darting across dim alleyways. Radella flies into my pocket and hides her light as we come up to the tavern.

The terrace where all the patrons were sitting has quieted. The fiddlers have stopped and gone, and all the patrons have emptied the area, except for three.

"I don't know where they are," Captain Redmond bellows.

Osric pauses in the alley. We tuck ourselves against the wall, relying on the night for cover. The wig-wearing elf and the huge giant who were drinking with him earlier have pinned Captain Redmond to the ground. The burly giant has his legs locked around Mundy's chest and holds a cord of rope tight around his throat while the elf points a dagger at the captain's left eye. The crewmen who accompanied Mundy ashore lie strewn across the terrace, unconscious, some of them in piles of toppled chairs and overturned tables. In most cases, they're bleeding from what must have been a raucous brawl.

Captain Redmond goes on, his strangled voice raspy. "My first mate will bring them to you. Wait until you see the girl's ticker."

"You don't have a girl with a clock heart," snarls the elf, "and now the elven guard is in the village. You called them to disrupt our deal."

"No." Captain Redmond pulls against the throttling rope. The larger giant yanks harder on the confines, restraining the captain again.

Osric waves us across the alley. We sprint past the tavern one by one and down another slope. Radella leaves my pocket to fly, her bluish light casting an eerie glow over the road. Once we are far away from the noises of the captain begging, I ask Osric what they'll do to him.

"They won't kill him, but he may not be eating solid foods for a while."

I find myself more disappointed than I thought I would be about the captain's survival. I doubt I will ever forgive him for turning me into a novelty.

Another howl sounds behind us, still chillingly close yet farther away than before. Osric darts between two huts and sinks against a wall to get our bearings. We are almost to the overhang leading to the lagoon.

"It isn't safe to stay in the village," Osric says. "I know of a place out of the way. Follow me closely. The trail there is dodgy."

One after another, we scurry after him and out into the open. Radella sneaks into my pocket to lessen her glowing light. The cliff above the lagoon provides an unobstructed view of the harbor below. Merrows have left the blue-lit depths to lounge on rock pilings and lie out on the dock. Osric stays back from the steep edge and leads us down a gravel trail through crabgrass.

Sounds of the merrows' gaiety rise to us. Below the surface, the lagoon is still bustling with them and other creatures swimming about.

"What are they doing down there?" Laverick asks.

"That's their market," Osric replies. "They come to buy and sell goods."

I imagine their market is much like ours, with merchants and craftsmen and shoppers coming together to trade, only everyone has fins.

The farther we go, the more the lanterns of the city dim and the waves become more radiant. Lines of the soft-blue lights lead off into the open sea like underwater roadways. The *Undertow* is still anchored in the harbor, its stern lanterns unlit.

Our path narrows and cuts closer to the edge of the cliff. I focus my tired mind and body to prevent myself from slipping and falling. A headache gathers like a storm behind my eyes, and Jamison begins to limp. We finally reach the watchtower at the top of the cliff at the mouth of the bay. Osric pushes his way inside.

"No one else is here," he says. "The tower guard died long ago and no one replaced him."

All the walls of the watchtower are curved. The furniture is scant: a bedroll and a lantern on a stool. In the middle of the single room, a staircase leads to the rooftop platform where beacons are lit to warn away boats from the reef and mark the entrance to the lagoon.

Radella leaves my pocket and flies inside the cylindrical tower. She perches in a gap between two stones midway up the wall and lies down to rest. Clearly, she's had enough of everything and everyone.

We let Laverick take the bedroll, and Jamison and I trudge up the steps to the roof. The view is unhindered in every direction, providing a panorama of land and sea. Under my feet, the platform is singed from the signal fires that were once burned here. We sit on the cold, stained stone with our backs against the hatch and face the sea.

"I think the elven guard caught Harlow," I say. "I've never heard her scream like that before."

Neither of us debates whether Markham escaped the barghest. We know he probably did, because that's our luck.

Osric comes to sit with us on the roof. He stretches out his long legs and crosses his ankles, then he removes an apple from his pocket and stares at it as though he isn't hungry. I should probably thank him for helping us, but I have too many questions.

"You abandoned your captain and crew to set us loose," I state. "Do you really hate Markham so much?"

Osric rolls the apple in his lap, his expression hard. "I think of what Killian did to Brea every day. Before she ran away, I found bruises on her. She tried to convince me she had fallen, but I knew they had been inflicted by someone. I tried to get her to tell me where they came from, but she got defensive and quit talking to me. She ran away with Killian soon after. I made myself leave the matter alone. Every day I regret not trying harder to get through to her."

I'm still queasy about the bruises on Harlow. What occurred between the prince and Brea only adds fuel to my disgust.

"Where did the elven guard come from?" I ask.

"First you must understand that Eventide is a trading outpost. The population fluctuates depending on how many ships are at port. The *Undertow* is the only vessel currently here, but often there are up to half a dozen. Profiteers come from all over the seas to barter." Osric holds up his shiny red apple. "The land here is scarce and fallow. Our resources come from the sea or trade with other worlds."

Jamison straightens beside me. "How do the traders get here?"

"You may have seen a structure at the top of the mountain. It's a large staircase that leads to a portal in the sky."

All three of us give our attention to the mountain. Half of its face is frosted with moonlight, the other eclipsed in shadows. The structure that I thought was a lookout stands at the top. Knowing the portal is right there, and that we have a way to return home, sends me grasping for Jamison. He slides his arm through mine and watches the distance with me.

"King Dorian appointed a boggart to regulate the comings and goings of land dwellers to minimize access to that portal. The other portal is deep in the sea over Everblue and guarded by the king's soldiers. No one may travel through either portal without the merrow king knowing."

"The portal near Everblue must be the one the Terrible Dorcha travels through," Jamison says.

Osric nods. "On the morrow, we'll visit a friend of mine, a collector. She may have more of the bubble tonic Markham traded for.

Bubble tonic gives land dwellers the ability to breathe underwater for hours, but it's very hard to find."

"Wouldn't it be easier to ask the merrow king to come to us instead of trying to go to him?" Jamison asks.

"King Dorian rarely leaves his castle. Mundy had to petition him three times before he would send a guard to inspect the sword, and then he acquired it sight unseen."

"Why does he never leave his castle?" I ask. "Is it because of the finfolk?"

"Dorian spends most of his time with his daughters. He lost his wife a while ago, and now he rarely leaves their side. His children are his most precious treasure. The king dotes on them to no end. He even acquired the sword of Avelyn as a gift for his eldest daughter."

The thought of a merrow princess in possession of my sword is discouraging, but I push my reservations aside and cling to the positives. Today, we escaped the pirates and found the portal. I will hold on to the afterglow of our accomplishments for as long as I can, for tomorrow we continue the race.

Chapter Fifteen

Fog hangs over the green clearing like the smoky breath of a dragon. My ivory mare shifts nervously under me, both of us directed at the murk. The Black Forest, known for its coal-barked flora, fringes the field, and a battalion of armed soldiers flanks us, including Jamison and our allies.

Across the field, from within the dim, something marches in our direction. The unbroken, collective stomping quivers the evergreens' branches and dries out my throat. Through the slots in my helmet, I see the outline of the opposing army take shape, towering ghouls materializing in the gloom. I grip the reins to steady my horse, my clock heart ticking wildly.

The marching escalates to thunderheads colliding in my ears and then abruptly halts.

In the beat of silence, the whole of the world seems to cower from the army of giants. Their soldiers are massive, taller than the trees and thick as megaliths. Every one of them is adorned in heavy armor in a style of olden days, helmets with plumes, shields engraved with intricate skyscapes, and thick silver chain mail. They carry an array of sharpened arms: long swords, battle-axes, and maces.

I raise my own weapon, a lighter short sword, an ideal defense for a buccaneer swashbuckling in the tight quarters of a ship, not a sensible blade to brandish against a giant.

A horn blares from the other side of the field, the sound piercing. My horse spooks, rearing up and tossing me. I hit the ground, dropping my sword, and my mare tears off into the fog. As I rise, I notice my battalion has left me, either run off into the labyrinth of woods or spirited away into the mists.

The call of the horn concludes, and the giants charge.

I search for my short sword, but it's nowhere to be found. My enemy gains on me each second. I sprint for the trees to retreat, and something shiny catches my eye—the sword of Avelyn. My blade is nestled on a bed of seagrass. My fingers curl around the gold hilt, and the blade glows white.

The giants' strides eat up the land fast, crossing the clearing so that by the time I lift my sword, the first opponent has arrived.

Ropes of thick hair hang about his hulking shoulders, his expression mangled in a ferocious sneer. As he looms over me, his face transforms into Markham's. I raise my shining blade to the prince's true figure. At last, his outward appearance matches the monster in my mind.

He roars a bloodcurdling war cry and swings his long sword. Our weapons clash with a crackle of lightning. An arc of light bursts from our crossed blades, its force striking me like a blast and throwing me backward to the ground.

The clap of starlight fades to an endless vault of midnight. I sit up, my head pounding and my ticker tapping. The battlefield and army of brutal warriors are gone. Unfortunately, so is my sword. I am still atop the watchtower at the opening of the harbor. Jamison is asleep beside me, and Osric stands watch nearby, his attention on the sea.

Lying on my back again, I stare up at the icy stars, my mind ringing with Markham's horrible war cry from my dream and my hand aching to hold my sword.

As the first light of daybreak spills over the horizon, the *Undertow* hoists its anchor and voyages out to sea. Osric monitors the ship's departure while the rest of us stay in the watchtower and wait for the pirates to sail by.

Laverick and Radella found a barrel of stale water and more of my least favorite food—dried seaweed. I munch on my briny breakfast, bleary eyed and sore from yesterday's exploits. Radella found a fly to dine on, which I studiously do not watch her eat. I have seen her devour enough of them to recall that she takes off the fly's wings and eats the body first, saving the wings for last. Utterly disgusting, and yet, I wonder if the fly tastes better than this seaweed.

I slept little after my dream woke me. Though I have lived the events of that battlefield more than once in my nightmares, the scene varies. I always confront the army of giants with my sword, but this time, the giant's face shifted to Markham's. I never see who wins or loses. The sword of Avelyn always blinds me and I jerk awake.

Osric throws open the door. "They're gone."

We pack a sack with the last of the food and fill two water casks. Radella finally devours the wings of the fly.

"The grotto is half a day's walk from here," says the elf. "We should go."

I slog outside after him without a word. A marine haze hangs over the village and the lagoon. We turn away from the watchtower and shuffle down a footpath to the rocky beach, traveling westward along the steep crags that line the coast. Radella rides in my pocket next to my quiet ticker.

"Why are we on the beach?" Jamison asks. "Aren't we more visible down here?"

"Stone runs empty into the sea between here and the west end of the continent," Osric replies. "This will be faster than navigating inland around them."

The hard-packed sand littered with pebbles and shells resembles the beaches near my childhood home on the northern seashore of Wyeth. All that's missing are the logs that washed ashore that I would teeter across as fast as possible without falling. My brothers, Tavis and Carlin, made forts out of smaller driftwood, while my sister, Isleen, searched for shells. Off the coast of Wyeth, the seafoam would drift inland and soak the sand. Our parents told us not to step in the foam, for where the land and the water churned up a froth was where the Creator first took physical form as an ivory mare, wild and serene as the sea, strong and sturdy as the land.

The waves here do not churn into something more, something hopeful.

Our walk marches us into midday, the fog vanishing to reveal a sun flanked by the colossal moon. Radella pokes her head out of my pocket, glares at the sunny waves, and hides again. No amount of time in this world eases her contempt for the water.

Osric suggests that we eat and drink as we travel. Any depletion of my strength leads to faintness, so I devour the seaweed and stale water without protest. He keeps his endless supply of apples to himself. His lack of willingness to share chafes at me. A while later, when he takes out yet another perfectly round red fruit, I can no longer contain my irritation.

"Has no one ever told you that it's rude to eat in front of others?"

"We're hungry," Laverick adds miserably.

"Humans can't eat apples grown in an elven orchard," Osric explains. "They're cultivated from special seeds enchanted with creation power. When consumed, charm apples slow our aging, but for non-elves, they're poisonous." He takes another bite and talks with his mouth full. "An elf who eats a charm apple a day will live longer than one who does not. Regrettably, the older we are, the more we need for upkeep."

"Why haven't we heard of charm apples?" Laverick questions.

"They're only grown in the Land of Promise, and it's unlawful to remove the trees or fruit or seeds from my world."

"Then how do you get them here?" Jamison asks, joining our conversation.

"I buy them off traders. Years back, Prince Killian and I ran illegal shipments of charm-apple bushels from our world to the others. After we stopped, different runners took our place."

Laverick appraises him with respect for his success as a smuggler. "Did you ever get caught?"

"Once we were nearly decapitated by a gnome trader." Osric grunts to himself, a soft laugh. "I did it for the coin, whereas Prince Killian relished the danger and the opportunity to rebel. He has a history of infuriating his sister."

"Not just his sister," I mumble.

Osric proceeds down the trail, eating his magical apple. His friendship with Markham is long over, but the memories they made together will always exist.

The first time I met Markham, he and my father were embarking on a voyage. I was barely five years old. Markham, an admiral then, wore a gray naval uniform and shiny black boots. I remember how handsome he looked, how indomitable he appeared, seemingly untouched by misfortune or sorrow. He was everything a naval officer should be—the type of gentleman my parents may have hoped I would someday marry.

I don't recall much else about him, not that it matters. Nothing about the prince was genuine, then or now. Even his appearance has been altered by a spell.

The tide starts to creep closer, so we hike up the hillside and mount a tor to view our progress. To the west runs a long, narrow piece of land, and far off at the end of it, there's a crooked tree. We have returned to Hangman's Spit.

I lay a hand over my faint ticker and recover from the climb. Jamison observes me from the corner of his eye. I am monitoring my clock heart, and he is monitoring me.

"This way," Osric says.

We descend the other side of the hill to a stony inlet. Twin two-person skiffs are moored to the shore.

A gnome jumps out from behind a rock, wielding a small spike.

"It's me," says Osric, "and these are my human friends."

The gnome grumbles something indecipherable.

"No, I didn't steal them from a trader." Osric gestures at the boats. "May we take these to go see her?"

The gnome grumbles, and then he notices Radella sticking out of my pocket and growls. She trills at him so loudly I fear she may rattle my clock heart out of my chest. Gnomes and pixies coexist in the Everwoods, but that doesn't seem to make a difference to these two. I finally move away from him so she will stop.

"What's wrong with you?" I demand.

She trills again, less irritably than before.

"I don't care," I say. "We're all tired and sore, but you don't see me snapping at anyone."

"Certainly not," Osric drawls, one eyebrow lifted.

Radella chuckles against me.

"Oh, shut up," I tell her.

Osric steps into the first skiff. "Laverick, you come with me. Jamison and Everley, you take the other boat. We need to go quickly. High tide is coming in."

Jamison and I climb into our boat, facing each other on parallel benches, and the gnome unties us. We row out of the sheltered inlet into low waves.

Osric steers toward a group of sea stacks—vertical rock columns in the coastal waters—and rows straight for the largest stack. The white stone column is so tall its shadow blocks the sun. In the lower face of the stack is an archway. Osric's boat bobs up to the opening and slides through it into the rock structure. Jamison and I double our speed, wrestling against the currents, and row up and into the stack.

We pass through the arch and into a cavern. The water inside is glassy blue, and when reflected off the white rock of the low ceiling, it intensifies to a bold and dreamy cobalt. Waves slap against the boat as we look about for the other skiff, but they must have gone down one of the inner passages.

"Which way?" Jamison asks.

"I don't know," I say. "Radella, will you go find them?"

She shakes her head and folds her arms across her chest.

"Radella," I reply, "go look for our friends or I will never let you ride in my pocket or on my shoulder again."

She shoots up so fast her wings brush my nose and takes off down the nearest tunnel. I hold on to the side of the boat and take these few seconds of waiting to rest.

Jamison leans forward, entering more of my vision. "Everley, you've said you're well, but something is wrong. Is it your heart?"

"My ticker is functioning as it should," I say in all sincerity. My clock heart is spending the time I was given as it was made to do.

"I should still have a look at it." Jamison reaches for the buttons of my shirt, and I shift back.

"Neely looked at it twice. I told you, it's working as it should."

Jamison rubs at his bearded chin in frustration. "Do you remember what I asked of you the night of our wedding?"

"You asked for honesty, and I'm telling you the truth. Jamison, you cannot fix my clock heart." He doesn't need me to tell him that I'm living off borrowed time. His knowing will change nothing, except to spoil this time we have. Jamison and I have come a long way since our wedding day. I will not corrupt this easiness between us with doom and dismay.

"Please stop worrying," I say, cupping his jaw. "I don't need you to fix anything. Just be here with me."

He holds my wrist and leans into my hand. "Always."

His sentiment comes out naturally, softening the distance between us. We have a history together—a past and a present—and, at least for a little while longer, a future. Jamison's lips are so close to mine they tempt me to go against my previous decision to hold back on a kiss. I cannot stop myself from leaning into him, my lashes sinking closed, and my mouth—

"Hurry along, you two!" Osric calls. He and Laverick have rowed back to the opening of one of the inner channels.

Radella zips back to us and then flies ahead as we row toward our friends. The ceiling is closer, or, more accurately, the water is higher, the rising tide pushing us up. We maneuver through the narrow passage, following the other skiff. Our path is lit by sunshine pouring through gaps in the overhead rock face. The rising water continues to lift us nearer to the ceiling, so we hunch over and row, our strokes shorter due to our bent position.

We pass through an archway into a large cavern. A section of the ceiling has eroded, letting in daylight. Osric and Laverick row to the ledge and tie off their boat. We dock alongside them and climb out as water gushes through the passage, shortening the archway so it's no longer passable by boat.

A worn pathway lines half of the pool, and etchings cover the wall from the floor to high above. I can read some names and dates, all carved into the stone by different hands. The markings are so closely layered and clustered that I lose count of how many there are, but there must be hundreds.

"Look at this." Laverick taps an inscription. "This person signed their name over three hundred years ago."

"This one is four hundred years past," says Jamison.

His remark spurs a hunt for a signature and date that are even older. Radella locates another one from four hundred years ago, and then Osric points out a date five hundred years old.

"Who were these people?" Jamison asks.

"They were patrons of my friend's kindness." Osric brushes a fingertip over the one dated five hundred years ago. "They carve their names on her wall for her so she can better remember their stories."

Jamison and Laverick spread out to find more old names.

"Do you know any of these people?" I ask.

"This was my great-aunt," Osric replies, referring to the name he's touching. His voice brims with sadness whenever he speaks of his family or his home world. "She's probably passed on by now."

I feel his ache as my own. "Does missing them ever go away?"

"Not for me. Home will always call to me."

"Have you thought about going back?"

Osric drops his hand to his side. "Too much time has passed. The home I left is not the home I would return to."

We pace the wall, and I spot a big name at eye level—*Prince Killian Markham*, dated over three hundred years ago.

"How old is Markham?" I ask. "He told me he was not yet four hundred years old."

"He's almost as old as me. Around six hundred years."

My belly plummets to my knees. Markham tricked time and gained immortality 350 years ago. He walked the worlds almost that long before then. His age feels insurmountable. If people learn wisdom and gain knowledge through experiences over time, how can I outwit someone multiple centuries older than me?

"Carve your name next to his," Osric suggests.

"But your friend hasn't helped us yet."

"She'll forgive the anticipatory mark. Put your name above Killian's and make it bigger. Should he return here, the sight will vex him."

I take Osric's sword and carve my name above Markham's. After adding the date, I step back to view my handiwork. I have not carved something in a while, and doing so feels good.

Osric pats my shoulder. "It isn't much, but it helps a little."

I only wish the act helped lessen my anger. I would prefer to vandalize Markham's name on the wall, scratching it from existence. But that could upset Osric's friend, and we need to start off our meeting right to secure her help. I wonder about these people's stories. Their signatures and the dates are trophies of the collector's generosity. What did she do for Markham? What does Osric hope she will do for us?

"Osric," I say, "what does your friend collect?"

"I'll let Muriel tell you. Her powers are unique."

"Her powers?" Jamison asks from farther down the wall.

"Muriel is known in these parts as the sea hag. I wanted you to see this before I told you so you would know she's helped many people in dire circumstances."

His reassurance doesn't quell my unease. The only other sorceress we've met is the hag in the Thornwoods. She tried to poison us with apples and then use our bones to build her mongrel a place to sleep.

"I can sense you still have reservations. Perhaps this will persuade you." Osric stops near a slot in the stone that leads out of the pool cavern. On the wall near the exit is his own signature. "Muriel has helped me too."

Jamison and I glance at each other, both of us locked in uncertainty. Neither one of us moves or takes the first step; however, Radella flies to the slot in the wall, waves us forward, and darts in.

"The pixie is brave," Osric says.

Not really. Radella has been afraid of most everything in this world. Apparently, the sea hag is less intimidating than the selkie barmaid.

"Muriel is waiting," Osric says, and then he slips into the slot and disappears.

Laverick stares at the marking of his name and chews her inner cheek. "Do you think the sea hag can help us find Claret?"

"You should ask her," I say. "Look how many other people she's helped."

"But what will she ask for in return?" Jamison questions.

Laverick quits gnawing her cheek. "I don't care. I just want Claret to be safe." The Fox twists back her long auburn hair to prevent it from snagging on anything and slides into the slot.

I start to follow her, but Jamison blocks my way.

"You shouldn't get her hopes up," he says. "You don't know what the sea hag can do."

"And you don't know that she can't find Claret." My voice hitches on worries that I've repressed for Laverick's sake. For my sake too, if I'm being honest. I would rather concentrate on recovering my sword than Claret, because the sword cannot be drowned or enslaved, and the thought of either happening to Claret is too terrible to consider. "Until we hear otherwise, I will believe Claret can be found."

Jamison glances around the cavern, peering down the wall of names. "I don't like this. Osric should have told us he was bringing us to a sorceress."

"He wouldn't have brought us here if Muriel were dangerous." As soon as I say the words, I question how right they are. We barely know the first mate. Is his bitterness against his prince so great that he would put us at risk?

Jamison stays in front of me, locked in indecision.

I squeeze past him into the slot and then send him a conciliatory smile. "We should at least give Muriel a chance. We can't do this on our own. We need help."

He follows me, murmuring under his breath. It isn't until we are nearly through the opening that I make out what he said.

It isn't the help I question, it's the cost.

Chapter Sixteen

The sea hag's grotto is full of house cats.

Black cats with white bellies, calico cats, gray-striped cats with long fur, shaggy orange cats with ivory tips on their tails, and dusky-blue cats with huge golden eyes. Some of them meow while others yowl and prowl about or lie tucked in a ball. The cats crawl all over the furniture and laze in pools of sunshine. There must be three or four dozen of them living in this grotto in the middle of the sea. I'm so overwhelmed by their number I nearly overlook the young woman Osric is embracing.

"Muriel, you're looking well."

"Thank you, Osric, as are you. The apple bushels you left here are waiting for you in the kitchen. I saved them for your return." She waves us in from the entry. "Come in, come in. I've been expecting you."

I thought the sea hag would look more like an old woman, with bone jewelry dangling off of her, like the witch of the Thornwoods, or I thought that perhaps she would be a creature of the sea, with webbed toes, green hair, tentacles, and gills. But this woman—by all appearances, this *human*—has the most brilliant scarlet hair I've seen, wide-set silver eyes, and full crimson lips. I cannot place her age. She has a timelessness about her, and her pale skin has an inner glow, as though she drank the nectar of the moon.

She floats over to us in her blue linen dress, her feet wrapped in sandals. A long pearl necklace adorns her slim neck, and tied around her waist is a white apron with a silver hand mirror tucked into the front pocket.

"Dearest Laverick, I have a gift for you." Muriel presents her with a bundle of cannon fuses. "I thought they would bring you comfort."

Laverick accepts the fuses, goose quills filled with turpentine and fine powder, and clutches them to her chest. Her father, a cannon maker, kept geese on their farm and made his own. Though Laverick's upbringing was harsher than any child's should be, she often carries a bundle of fuses on her.

The sea hag moves on to Jamison. "Dearest Earl of Walsh, what an honor to have you in my company."

He bends at the waist, bowing gracefully. "Thank you for allowing us to intrude upon your day, Lady Muriel."

"Lady? Oh, I like that. You'll do well as a marquess."

Jamison nods in thanks and partly in puzzlement. She knows his title but not that he's been disinherited. It would be discourteous for him to correct her, nor would it be appropriate to bring that up upon first meeting, so he smiles.

Muriel's gaze flickers to me. "Everley Donovan, this is a union I've long awaited." She cups my gloved hand in hers. "Imagine my delight when I learned you were coming."

I paste on a smile. "How did you hear of our visit?"

"My good friend the boggart told me. He chats with the king's soldiers who guard the water portal, and they mentioned your imminent arrival." Muriel plucks at her pearl necklace and glances around. "Where is Radella? She must have found the jar of fruit flies in the kitchen. Radella? Radella, where did you go?"

The pixie flies in from what I assume is the kitchen, her cheeks stuffed with food. She lands on the sea hag's shoulder and finishes chewing. I have never seen Radella warm up this quickly to anyone, not even Jamison.

"Pardon my directness, Muriel, but are you human?" Jamison asks.

"As human as you are. People from the Land of the Living often think they're the only humans in all the worlds, but we can live anywhere." Muriel shoos the cats off a floral chair with crocheted armrests and sits down. A cat immediately jumps up into her lap.

Laverick dangles her cannon fuses so the cats can bat at them. More of them rub against us and meow for attention.

"Please forgive my feline friends," says the sea hag. "Five years ago, we had a terrible mice infestation. The traders brought in cats to eliminate the vermin, and the village became overrun. The villagers started trapping the cats to use as fish bait, so I took them in. I'm a soft touch for strays." She waves at the feline-covered sofa. "Please rest your feet. You've come a long way."

The furniture is what would be found in a cottage, sturdy traditional pieces upholstered with floral cloth in dusky-rose hues. Osric growls and the cats on the sofa beside him scatter. He plops down and then lifts the throw pillow behind him and pulls out a pistol.

"I forgot to warn you about the stashed firearms," says Muriel. "A woman living on her own can't be too careful."

"Is it loaded?" Osric asks.

"It wouldn't be much use to me if it weren't."

He passes her the loaded pistol, and she sets it beside her.

Laverick props herself against the armrest. Jamison stays standing, a white fluffy cat rubbing against his legs. I will not compete with the cats for a seat on the sofa, so I remain on my feet as well. My eye is drawn to the vase of daisies on a side table. The flowers are an unusual sight in a world where very little plant life grows. Radella perches on the footstool in front of the sea hag. The pixie leaves the cats alone, and they ignore her as well.

Muriel beams brightly at us. Her beauty is almost too radiant, like staring at the sun. "Radella, how are you enjoying your first assignment as ambassador of the Everwoods?"

Radella makes hand motions and little chirps.

The sea hag listens and watches intently until the pixie finishes, and then Muriel grins. "I can understand why that would try your patience."

"Do you know what Radella is saying?" asks Jamison.

"Of course. Everyone should be fluent in pixie. Radella and I are old friends."

Radella nods emphatically.

"She said that none of you listen to her. You really should consider her opinion more. You're hurting her feelings." Muriel scratches under Radella's chin with her pointer finger. The pixie leans into her touch and preens. "Pixies are the most delightful creatures, always trilling and spreading their magical dust, and they are unerringly loyal to the Everwoods and Father Time."

I gesture at the vase of daisies. "Was Father Time here?"

"I commune with him daily. He's here with us now."

I glance around, but all I see are cats, cats, and more cats.

"Not *here*. He's here." Muriel opens her arms wide. "Don't use your eyes. Listen."

All the cats quiet and still upon her command, no purring, yowling, or meowing. Their silence unnerves me too much to hear anything.

"I don't hear anything," says Laverick.

"Most creatures hear something like the soft patter of rain, while a select few hear music." Muriel sends Jamison a knowing smile. "You hear the Creator's everafter melody, don't you, Lord Callahan? I can tell you have a gift for song."

He stammers out a reply. "I play the violin—"

"You're too modest." Her gleaming eyes take him in, as though she's measuring him against her first impressions. "You recently lost your instrument, but it will be waiting for you when you return home. You will need the music for what's to come."

He turns speechless, and I, too, am taken aback. How could she know Jamison's violin was left behind on the *Cadeyrn of the Seas*? None of us told her, and Osric doesn't even know that Jamison plays.

Muriel expands her attention to the entirety of the group again. "Everyone can hear the sands of time, but they sound different in each world. In the Land of the Living, the clocks mask the sound, and here, the tides set the hour." Muriel presses a solemn hand over her heart. "It's a comfort to know Father Time watches over us."

Jamison and I swap looks that say, *Is she aware how peculiar she sounds?*

Osric smiles weakly. "Muriel and Father Time are friends."

Muriel waves a strict finger at him. "Father Time and Princess Amadara were friends. We will be more. From the minute I was born, I felt—"

"Pardon the interruption," I say, though I'm not sorry in the least. "You knew Princess Amadara, *the* princess from the legend? But she lived centuries ago."

"I feel as though we're sliding off course," says Jamison. He picks up the white cat rubbing at his feet, and it snuggles against him. "We've come for your help."

Muriel removes the silver hand mirror from her pocket and evaluates her reflection. "You seek the sword of Avelyn and your friend Claret."

"You know about Claret?" Laverick whispers.

Muriel tugs dissatisfiedly at the smile lines around her mouth. "You're in luck. Your friend and the sword are in the same place. She was taken by the merrows to serve as a maid in the king's castle. Humans make marvelous laborers—quiet, docile, obedient—especially when they're enchanted."

Laverick's eyes gape wider. "Claret has been in the undersea city, under the merrows' enchantment all this time?"

"Oh, stars yes. Otherwise she would have drowned."

"We need you to help us get to Everblue," Osric says. "Killian traded for a bubble tonic with an apple seed from the Land of Promise. He may be on his way to the castle now."

Harlow had an enchanted apple seed in her vial? That must have been what was so valuable about her necklace.

Muriel lowers the hand mirror. "I don't have any bubble tonic, nor do I have the ingredients to concoct it. The active element is grown only in the Silver-Clouded Plain, which, of course, is inaccessible to outsiders. I would request that the king come here to meet you, but Dorian and I aren't on speaking terms." The sea hag covers the ears of the feline in her lap. "His eldest daughter ate one of my cats."

His eldest daughter is the princess who has the sword. Nothing about this world should surprise me anymore, but a cat-eating merrow princess who has a fascination with blades sounds utterly dreadful.

"Didn't you steal a bag of the king's pearls?" Osric asks, his lips quirked into a smile.

The sea hag puts her nose in the air. "Dorian doesn't care about a handful of pearls. He's been on a rampage since his queen died last year." Muriel sets down the cat from her lap and rises. "Before we discuss any more matters, Everley Donovan and I must speak in private."

"Why?" I ask at the same time as Jamison.

"I have a message for her from Father Time."

I am reticent to be alone with someone so unpredictable, but a message from Father Time is reason enough to take that risk. Jamison sets down the fluffy white cat to come with us. The sea hag waves him back.

"The message is for Everley alone." Muriel sweeps her dress behind her and strides away, intending for me to follow.

Jamison steps beside me, slightly blocking my way. "Will you be all right?" he asks in a low voice.

I assumed he was going to try to talk me out of going off with Muriel alone, so his question takes me aback. "I think so."

"Call out if you need anything. I'll keep an ear out for you."

As he steps away, I wonder if I've known anyone who's trusted me to be myself more than he does. He doesn't just trust in what I say, but in what I do, my competency and capability to act of my own accord.

With Jamison watching, I square my shoulders and go to meet the sea hag.

Chapter Seventeen

On my way to the balcony, I pass the open doorway of a room full of junk. Piles rise to the ceiling, made up of random furnishings, dishes, artwork, linens, draperies, ropes, candles, boxes of ammunition, black powder, pistols, swords, and other odds and ends. The sea hag has an assortment of random things that she couldn't possibly use on her own. How many weapons does one woman need?

Continuing to the end of the passageway, I step out onto the sunny balcony high up the side of the sea stack. The sudden brightness blinds me, and when my vision clears, Muriel is in my way.

She taps my clock heart. "I sensed your ticker's presence immediately. Time is my favorite treasure." Her crimson lips curve downward. "But the time animating your clock heart is weakening. Do you know how much you have left?"

"No, can you tell me?"

She closes her eyes and brandishes her fingers over my ticker. Her eyes snap open again. "Do you fear death?"

A spike of dread drives into my gut. "No."

"Lucky lass." She waves a hand over her face, and her glamour falls away, revealing a much-older woman with shriveled lips, thin skin, and dull gray hair weaved with muddy browns. The sudden shift from vibrant young lady to wizened crone startles me speechless. Beneath her sultry facade is the real sea hag, a woman who has seen more years than I can fathom. Her wrinkles and gray tresses speak to a wisdom that shows in her silver eyes, the only feature that remains unchanged.

Her fingers flutter past my face, and then she lifts her hand mirror to show me my reflection. I feel no trace of her magic, but I hardly recognize myself. My blue eyes are unnaturally vivid, my cheeks have a fetching blush, and my raven hair shines like wet stone.

"Glamour can change beauty, but the best charms emphasize what is already there." Muriel throws up her own glamour again and, at the same time, removes mine. She puts away her hand mirror in her apron pocket. "I'm sorry I cannot repair your ticker. My glamour charms create a convincing illusion, but it's an illusion all the same. Even if beauty was what you seek, you couldn't afford to compensate me."

"What did you ask for in exchange for the glamour charm you gave Markham?"

Muriel removes a spyglass from her pocket and peers at the watery horizon. "My customers give me something much more precious than gold or silver. They give me time."

I grip the sides of my trousers with my clammy hands. "How?"

"I harness the creation power that exists inside us all."

Her explanation only complicates my understanding. "So if the names on your wall represent people who traded years off their life in exchange for your powers, what did you do for Osric?"

"Something much costlier than a glamour charm." Muriel snaps the spyglass closed and puts it away. "Any sorceress can do glamour. My real power, my gift and my curse, allows me to see through time. For a price, I can show my customers any moment of their choosing from the past, present, or future."

I think I understand now. "Muriel, you're a seer."

"A seer is a spinster with crooked teeth. My teeth are straight." She smiles wide to show me, but I am unsure if her teeth are real or another illusion. "I grew up in the Land of the Living, in a cottage near the woods. My father was a woodcutter, my mother a sorceress. They were poor but happy. One morning, when I was stacking firewood, I saw Princess Amadara sneak through a burrow under a tree. I waited there until she crawled back out that evening. She refused to tell me where she had gone, and I was too afraid to go myself. When she returned the next day, I waited by that tree for hours until I built the courage to follow her."

Muriel sweeps away to the balcony, and her gaze rises to the cloudless sky. "I only went once, but the Everwoods changed me forever. I inherited my mother's ability to see creation power in plants, and animals, and people, but after I returned home from the Everwoods, I began to envision things that once were or would be. When I foresaw the destruction of the Land of Youth, I was so afraid I fled my world and began to offer readings. At first, I asked for payments of gold and silver in exchange for my services. I soon realized my customers had a more precious commodity that I could take if they were willing."

"When did you meet Markham?"

Muriel twists her pearl necklace around her fingers, her silver eyes glassy. "Killian came to visit me a century later. He offered to sign away more years of his life to me than most humans ever see. Glamour charms are the illusion of beauty; they don't prevent aging. I was short on time, so I took his bargain. It wasn't until he left that I foresaw the tragic fate of Amadara and their unborn child."

"A child?" I ask. "There was no child in *The Legend of Princess Amadara*."

"You only know Killian's rendition of the tale. He didn't know Amadara was with child."

I grip the banister harder. "What really happened between him and Amadara?"

"Amadara was a Time Bearer, like you. You'll learn what that responsibility means soon, but for her, she was assigned to guard an ancient artifact so powerful that Father Time gave her the sword of Avelyn to protect it. Amadara always knew Killian was a monster. She couldn't see through his glamour, but she knew straightaway that he was evil. She married him to keep a closer eye on him, and he truly fell in love with her, but she, like many others, underestimated the prince."

Muriel's eyes go hard and flinty, tears gathering. "Soon after Amadara became with child, Killian discovered she was guarding the artifact and was furious with her for lying to him. She called upon the pixies of the Everwoods to take the artifact to safety, so Killian locked Amadara in a tower, took the sword of Avelyn, and gathered his army to storm the Everwoods. He intended to chop down elderwood trees to force Father Time to hand over the artifact. Amadara did the only thing she could to stop him—she tore a piece of time that Father Time had given her. Unfortunately, Killian had gone ahead of his army and was in the Everwoods when time was stopped in the Land of Youth. He escaped, but Amadara and her unborn child did not."

I'm flabbergasted by the discrepancies in Markham's story. I read the journals he kept during the decades after Father Time cast him out of the Everwoods. He loved Amadara, that part was true. He used that truth to distract from his other lies. "What was the artifact?"

"That's something Father Time should tell you."

I don't know if I want to speak with him about the matter. Father Time should have done more for Amadara, and he should do more to help me. "Why would he let Amadara tear time? Why didn't he stop her?"

"Because some sacrifices are so immense they change the course of the future. Father Time understood that, in order to defeat Killian, he had to let him prevail for a time."

"Have you seen any other visions, perhaps of giants going to battle?" I ask, recalling my dream.

Muriel's pupils narrow to pinpoints. "Have you seen something yet to come, Everley?"

"No," I answer quickly. "I mean, I don't think so. How could I? I'm not a seer."

"Time Bearers are able to navigate Evermore—the timeline of Avelyn." The sea hag drags her fingertip across my forehead, her attention turning inward. As she traces a line across my skin, my dream from last night flashes back in a series of pictures. "The seven worlds were cut from the cloth of the eternities. The Evermore timeline is the thread that stitches them together. Time Bearers can visit points in history bound to their own timeline, particularly moments appointed by fate."

Muriel withdraws her hand, leaving a wake of gooseflesh on my skin. These notions about the Evermore timeline and predestined moments are too massive to digest, so I set them aside. "You said Father Time sent me a message?"

"He wishes to tell you himself." Muriel extends a finger and taps my clock heart.

My spirit jumps from my body and hovers above us. The sea hag puts her hand in front of her lips and exhales, as if blowing a kiss. Her deep breath sends my spirit spinning into the sky, up into the clouds, into the heavens.

Just as quickly as I rise, I fall, plummeting so fast that I fear I will strike the ground like a bolt of lightning and scorch the world.

I land in a grassy field on a cliff overlooking a gray-blue sea. Thin clouds streak the sky, and on the hill above me, a large house faces the water. It's my childhood home, the one Markham burned to the ground.

Across the field, running toward me, comes a little child with raven hair and ruddy cheeks. Chasing after her is my mother.

"Evie! Don't go far!"

Her pursuit of the little lass is half-hearted. She lets the child romp through the high grass and pauses to stare out to sea, two fingers pressed to her mouth. I caught my mother daydreaming a thousand times. She would stand by the water's edge or at a window and seek the horizon for a glimpse of my father. I could tell she was thinking of him because she would rest two fingertips upon her lips.

Younger Everley toddles past me down the hill. She cannot be more than three. The girl runs with abandon, her tummy out and her feet like a puppy's, barely keeping up with her enthusiasm. She barrels past me, headlong for the cliff. I glance at my mother, but she's still preoccupied, so I hurry after the child.

Below on the rocky shoreline, foam has frothed in the sea, and the waves push it to the beach. An ivory mare sprints down the coast through the foam and water.

Younger me is nearing the drop-off. I grasp at her, and my spirit passes through her little arm. A larger hand darts out and pulls her back from the edge. Father Time is kneeling in the field, partially hidden by the grass.

"What have I told you about staying with your mother?" After gently reprimanding the child, he opens his hand and offers her a daisy. She scoops up the blossom and swings it about like a sword.

"Evie!" Mother calls from up the hill. "Evie, come to Mama!"

"Go on," Father Time says, patting the girl's back.

She toddles up the rise to Mother. Though I do not hear my mother's words, I can see her scolding expression. Younger me offers her the daisy, and I watch Mother's worry melt away.

"You have always been a daring spirit." Father Time rises and begins to walk along the cliff.

"I met Muriel," I say, following him. "She told me about Amadara and the artifact. What was worth her life and her child's life to save?"

"I was with Amadara for half a century before I told her what you now ask of me."

His statement opens the floodgate on my frustration. "But shouldn't I know what Markham is after? And why didn't you tell me I don't have long to live? What did you mean when you said I need the sword to defeat Markham?"

"You have many questions, and we do not have long." He peers over the cliff at the mare racing up the beach. Her movements are elegant, graceful. "Listen well, Everley. We have prolonged your life by harnessing the creation power of the heartwood and animating your clockwork heart with time given to you by your uncle. As you are aware, that time was not infinite. The sword is the key to unlocking more. You must find the blade and bring it to your uncle, so he may repeat the ceremony."

I balk at his suggestion. "I won't take more time from him."

"You may accept time from any willing individual, but you must have the sword to complete the ceremony."

"Muriel doesn't need the sword and she takes time from people."

"Her methods of sorcery exploit creation power and pillage time, but her donors are willing, so we cannot interfere. The cost of her manipulating time is high. Muriel exists in a state of half life, chased by death and decay. The purity of your heartwood ticker would be harmed by such invasive practices."

What I must do dawns on me with each step. Someone else will have to bleed time off their life to feed my ticker. I cannot ask someone to sacrifice themselves for me. Living day to day for years has taught me just how precious time can be. "Isn't there another way?"

"You could live in the Everwoods, but the moment you leave the forest, the time in your ticker will resume counting down." His alternative feels like a punishment, not a solution. "We have brought you to the past again and again, revealing more to you than we have to any other human, so that you may leave your past alone. You must quit looking back, wondering what could have been, and move forward in faith."

My clock heart spins and spins, free of the time it's bleeding. "But how can I know everything will turn out all right?"

"Trust your task. Find the sword of Avelyn and bring the blade to your uncle to perform the ritual, or you will perish and Prince Killian will prevail."

"Prevail in what?" I ask, still shaken by my dream of the battlefield. "What does he want?"

"He isn't after a 'what,' he's after a 'who.' When Prince Killian nearly stole the artifact from Amadara, we hid it far away. He has since deduced the whereabouts of the artifact and will find any way possible to get there. That is all we can say or we will compromise the timeline."

Influencing time may not be so terrible. I rather prefer this memory of my younger self over my niggling fear about what's to come. I want a promise of what the future holds.

Father Time's voice sounds close beside him, his attention fixated on the woman and child playing up the hill. "Do you know why mankind inherited the Land of the Living?"

"Not in the slightest." The elves and giants I've met so far seem much more capable and durable than humans.

"Mankind's limited time fuels an insatiable lust in them to live their fullest life. Humans value time more than any other creature. They are encouraged to better themselves each day and do something worthy of becoming a legend."

"I don't want praise or acclaim," I say, lifting my gaze to the sky for patience. "I want to go home to my uncle and for my friends to return home safely. I don't want to waste any more time racing Markham."

"You are already learning that time is love."

Father Time walks back toward where we started, and we plod up the field to my family's manor. While younger me twirls in the grass, my mother has once again given her attention to the sea and placed two fingertips over her lips. Her love for her husband is something that, as a child, I prayed was in my future, loving someone so much my heart would leap across great divides to find him.

Father Time kneels and opens his arms to younger me, and she jumps into them. My anger festers, raw and furious. The lass will lose her parents and home. She will forget what it is to run with abandon and spin circles by the sea.

Choked with despair, I look away. The wild mare still gallops up and down the beach. Her mane and tail fly into the sky, her coat glistening. I lean closer for a better view of her. The ivory mare leaves no prints behind her. She flies over the beach without her hooves kicking up sand or marking a trail.

It's said that where the sea meets the land, Eiocha comes to shore in a drift of foam and emerges from the water in her mortal form as an ivory mare, free and powerful. She stays until nightfall and then rides a wave back into the sea and disappears in a moonbeam.

The ivory mare halts and looks up at me. My lips part in wonder, and a warm buzzing cascades over my spirit. While our gazes are connected, my spirit begins to rise off the ground. I continue upward as swiftly as an updraft. The ivory mare shrinks beneath me until she blends in with the foam along the beach.

I lift my gaze as I ascend toward the heavens and into the soft cloth of the eternities. The drop is always less gentle. I plunge into my body and dizziness grips me.

Muriel catches me before I fold over. "Did you see Father Time? How did he look? Is he still as handsome as ever?"

I just flew to the past and that's her first question?

"I . . . I need to sit down." I stagger back into the main room ahead of her, trying not to trip over the cats. Radella has fallen asleep on the back of a sitting chair, clutching her full belly. Osric and Laverick rise in alarm. Jamison was waiting by the door, so he helps me to the sofa.

"What did you do to her?" Laverick accuses the sea hag.

"Nothing," replies Muriel. "Everley is faint from spirit jumping."

Jamison and Laverick gape at her and Osric's eyebrows raise.

"I'm fine," I say before she divulges anything I don't wish to share. "We were talking, and I got woozy."

Muriel lifts her chin, clearly still offended by Laverick's harsh accusation. "Osric, come join me in the kitchen."

He pats Laverick's shoulder in understanding and follows Muriel out. Several cats run after them, I suppose for food.

"That woman is mad," Laverick says, throwing up her hands.

Jamison sits at my side and stares at me, prodding me for further explanation. I stare right back at him. He wishes for me to explain what Muriel said about spirit jumping, but I can scarcely fathom it myself. What am I supposed to say? That I spent several minutes outside my childhood home, which has since burned to the ground, and I saw my mother, who is long dead? And that I may have seen the Creator out for a run on the beach? Muriel would not be the only one accused of madness.

Our standoff continues for so long that the feeling in the room shifts to a level of discomfort that Laverick can no longer tolerate.

"I'll help in the kitchen," she says.

Halfway to the door, she pauses out of Jamison's sight and motions at me to talk to him. She's making a big sacrifice by choosing to go into the same room as Muriel, so I nod a little to assure her that I will speak with Jamison. Laverick salutes me, pivots on her heels, and marches into the kitchen.

"Everley," Jamison says quietly, "you aren't well. I don't want to ask you again, because I know you'll tell me everything is fine, but I know it isn't."

I would tell him what's wrong with my heart, but I cannot even think about taking years from someone else without feeling ill. Father Time may have said that what Muriel does is worse, trading fortunes for time, but both methods are monstrous.

I select my words carefully and with sincerity. "I've shared more about myself with you than anyone else. Everything I've told you is true."

"What about our wedding vows? Did you mean them?"

"You didn't mean your vows either," I say on a strained laugh. His expression tightens into a pained look. "Jamison, you couldn't have meant them. We hardly knew each other."

"A promise is a promise." His hand tries to touch mine, but I pull back.

I have touched him too often of late and savored his touch more than I should have. Every time I allowed a physical connection to happen between us was out of selfishness. We have come a long way since we made our marital vows, but I've fooled myself into thinking this could last.

Jamison sits away from me, giving me the room between us that I silently asked for. "Everley, you're my wife. No matter what happens, I swore that I would be your husband forevermore."

I stop myself from rubbing at my building headache. I have to share something, confide in him in some way, to stop the rift widening between us.

"Muriel told me she's a seer. She can look into someone's past, present, or future and show her customers what they wish to see. In return, she takes time from them."

Jamison sits up straighter. "She takes time as payment, as in years off of someone's life?"

"I assume that's how she's lived this long."

His attention turns inward as he scratches the head of a calico. He must be speculating about what he would ask the sea hag to show him if they struck a deal. I would return to a quiet evening with my family. I presume Jamison would wish to see a moment from the past where he was with his mother and sister, but the possibilities are endless, so I cannot say for certain.

Osric carries in two steaming teacups. "This is seaweed tea. It sounds worse than it tastes. Actually, it's atrocious, but it will tide you over until dinner."

I accept a cup. Jamison declines the second cup, so the elf drinks it himself.

"Is it true?" Jamison asks. "Can the sea hag see through time?"

Osric sits on the corner of the sofa, pushing off a cat. "Reading someone's lifeline is Muriel's specialty. People come far and wide to see their fortunes."

"What did you ask to see?" I ask, sipping my tea. The drink tastes abominable, like hot stewed lagoon water.

The first mate stares down into his steaming cup. "My parents. I wanted to know how they were faring without Brea and me."

"And?" I press.

"And I suggest you be careful about what you ask to see." Osric rises, startling another cat from around his feet. "Muriel asked that you two join us in the kitchen. She's thought of a way to send us to Everblue."

Chapter Eighteen

Muriel lays the fish in the pan over the fire. For a sea hag, her kitchen is missing the expected identifiers of a sorceress's home. She doesn't have a boiling cauldron of frogs' legs and toad eyeballs, or a broom in the corner, or jars of miscellaneous body parts floating in amber liquid. Except for the cats roaming in and out, her kitchen could be a match for my uncle's. I'm beginning to wonder if human storybooks depict anything right.

Jamison and I join the others at the long table. Instead of chairs, Muriel has two settees stuffed with pillows pushed up to it. Before sitting, Jamison checks under the throw pillows and finds a loaded pocket pistol. He puts it on the table and then pours us both glasses of grog. He finishes his and speaks up first.

"Muriel, how much time does it cost for someone to see their future?"

She shoots him a sly grin over her shoulder as she sprinkles green flakes on the fish. I pray the seasoning isn't seaweed. "I deal in yearly increments. Two, four, ten . . . The contract depends on what it is that my customer wishes to know."

"Contract? Time?" Laverick asks, glancing from face to face. Jamison quickly summarizes Muriel's powers, with Osric chiming in. At the end, the Fox has her own question. "Do the years come off your customers right away or later in life?"

"Whichever they prefer. All the terms are written in the contract. Most request their life be shortened instead of abruptly aging."

"What if someone only has months to live?" Jamison asks.

Muriel smiles again as she flips the fish over in the pan. "I've never had anyone die, if that's your worry. I always leave my patrons with at least a year of life, but many of them are elves and giants. They typically have more time to give than humans."

"Which is why this is a bad idea for any of us," I state.

"A human's time is limited, so it's worth more to you, but a year is the same to me regardless of whom it comes from."

"Can we ask to see someone else's future?" Jamison says. At my widening eyes, he adds, "Of course, this is all hypothetical."

While the fish in the pan is cooking, Muriel stirs a small pot of boiling potatoes and then goes to a cutting board and chops apples with a cleaver. "You've a mind for strategy, Lord Callahan. But I'm afraid the answer is no. For my customers to give away time willingly, they must see their own fortune." She slams the cleaver into the cutting board, sending two cats at her feet scattering.

Laverick taps her foot against the ground impatiently. "Can we discuss how you plan to send us to Everblue now?"

The sea hag wipes her hands on her apron. "I had the idea while I was with Everley. You cannot swim to Everblue as yourselves, so you should travel as someone who can." We stare at her in confusion. "The solution is simple. I can transfer your spirit to someone else, and you go to Everblue disguised."

"Transfer our spirits," Jamison says slowly, trying to puzzle the words out. "You want us to steal someone's body?"

"I prefer to think of it as borrowing." Muriel tosses a bit of fish to the cats, and they all crowd around for their part. She smiles at them fondly. "Sometimes when I cannot sleep in my own body, I transfer spirits with my cats and sleep and sleep. It's very restful."

I glance at Osric as if to say, *You brought us to this lunatic?*

"Whose body do we 'borrow'?" asks Jamison.

We all lapse into contemplation while Muriel slides the fish out of the pan onto a platter and carries it to the table. The fish still has its head and tail, its dead eyes looking at me. I glug down another glass of grog.

Osric brings the bowl of boiled potatoes along with the plate of apples for himself. Neither Jamison nor Laverick appears hungry.

Laverick sits up suddenly. "We can catch merrows."

"You and Markham already tried netting them," I remind her.

"This time we'll use bait and a decoy." Laverick gestures at the fish on the platter. "You catch a fish with a worm or a fly. We can dangle something appetizing in front of the merrows to draw them in."

"Wonderful idea," Muriel says, clasping her hands together. She makes no comment about whether baiting them will work, but this is the same woman who professes to switch bodies with her cats, so her opinion doesn't hold much merit. "Each of you will need your own merrow to trade spirits with. Are you going as well, Osric?"

His winces, torn between his reluctance and my silent pleading. "They'll need a guide," he surrenders at last.

"How safe is the transference?" Jamison inquires, pouring us both our third glass of grog. "Are there any long-term effects?" He does not reference me, but I suspect he's concerned about my low stamina.

Muriel answers while studying her frown lines in her hand mirror. "None at all, but the longest I've been out of my own body was one day. I wouldn't wait any longer."

"What happens if we do?" Jamison asks.

"Your spirit will switch back on its own. The sudden switch can be very disorienting."

Spending any amount of time with my spirit in the body of a merrow seems like a terrible idea. "Can we swim to Everblue and back by then?"

Osric chews another bite of apple while he weighs the question. "If we take the underwater highway across Skull Reef, we should be back within the day."

Laverick twists toward him. "How do you know so much about it? Have you done this before?"

"I went to Everblue using the bubble tonic once to settle a dispute with a merrow trader. The journey was . . . unforgettable."

Muriel jabs her fork into the eyeball of the fish and lifts it out. "The depths of the seas are directionless and bottomless and lonely. A stranger to the currents could be easily disoriented. You won't even notice you're being swept away until you're lost. But with Osric as your guide, you have a real chance."

Her lukewarm encouragement scrapes at my throat. I cannot think of another plan, and apparently neither can Jamison because he doesn't argue. Or perhaps both of us have had too much grog to argue effectively. It does seem odd that Muriel should present this option now, yet it's plausible that it didn't occur to her until I spirit jumped.

Laverick swallows a forkful of fish. "It's settled. At nightfall, we go fishing."

We row out of the grotto between low tide and high tide, racing the sunset back to land. I'm grateful to leave the sea hag's lair. I was beginning to smell like a cat.

The sea hag's gnome ties off our skiff. Osric continues to row the other boat, traveling by water with our supplies while the rest of us trudge toward the spit on foot. Muriel suggested we go there, since merrows are often seen lounging on the rocks. Radella stayed behind to help Muriel prepare for the transference, plus her glowing light could have given us away.

Laverick and Jamison pull ahead, him with the short sword and her with fuses and the lantern. I carry the fishing pole and brush tufts of white cat hair from my cloak.

The lavender sky to the east darkens, and in the west, the heavens around the sinking sun are a wash of fiery oranges and yellows. We go straight to Hangman's Tree. The finperson we saw the other day still hangs there, strung up by a noose. Its rotting scent wafts toward us on the breeze, and I struggle not to gag. Our plan involves getting much closer, for me, really close. This is the only way we could think of not to scare the merrows away.

While the flashy colors in the sky deepen to dusk, Osric casts the weighted nets he brought. The nets fade into the water until I lose sight of them.

Jamison treads up to the dangling body of the finperson and rips the sack off its head. It would look like a man, considering it has legs, if not for its bulbous fish head. The finperson has begun to decompose, yet not to the point where any of us change our minds. The flesh on the finperson's bottom half is in worse condition than its scaly head, and even its eyes are still intact.

Laverick goes to meet Osric, who is rowing to shore. I step back from the tree. Jamison swings the short sword at the rope, severing it, and the body drops to the ground.

I wave away pesky corpse flies from my face and then start up the tree. Jamison undoes the noose and moves it to the finperson's feet, then throws me the rope. I grab the end and heave while he lifts the body off the ground. The dead finperson leans against him while I tie the rope to the tree.

"You can finish anytime," he grunts.

"I'm going as fast as I can."

Jamison wriggles a little, shifting the rope.

"Stay still!" I say.

"I had a fly on my nose."

"There," I say, finishing.

Jamison lets go of the body, which now hangs by its feet instead of its head. I climb back down to the ground. He has already started the skinning process, cutting a line from the finperson's knee, where its scales begin, straight up to its groin, and then back down to the other knee. The body swings too much, so I have to hold it steady.

I turn my face away. "This is the most disgusting thing I have ever done."

"That may be a premature sentiment," says Jamison.

Laverick and Osric work by the shore, tying the fuses to the black-powder bags they found in Muriel's storage. They're very careful as they put them together and then stack them up from the waterline in the rocks.

Jamison finishes his strategic cuts and then grabs the loose skin around the knees of the finperson and begins to peel down. I watch the fading sky to mitigate my revulsion as he disrobes the corpse, skinning it like he would peel off an undergarment.

The skin drops to the ground, and Jamison sets to work gorging the eyes out of the finperson's sockets. He pauses to wipe his brow and smudges his skin with something yellow and oily. I clean it off with my sleeve, unenthused about the next step of this process.

Osric finishes helping Laverick with the black powder. Before we left the grotto, he explained that Hangman's Tree is where patrons of Eventide are executed. Few rules exist in this mostly lawless world, but stealing someone else's slaves is punishable by death.

Jamison washes the finperson's skin in the sea and then lifts it up and frowns. "You don't have to do this, Everley. We can manage without you."

"No, we can't," Laverick calls out in reply. "The plan doesn't work without all of us."

We all have roles, but my clock heart limits mine, so I draw on my hatred for Markham and gather the courage to touch the skin. The outside isn't slimy, but what the exterior lacks the inside more than makes up for. I slip out of my trousers, down to my knickers, and then lift my arms over my head.

"Let's get this over with," I say.

Jamison tugs the skin down over me, putting it on as he would a frock. The thickness reminds me of wool, but the similarities stop there. The inside feels like oily fish skin. I may never get this rotten scent out of my hair.

I hold my breath as long as possible, and when I inhale again, fresh air pours in where Jamison cut a slit for my mouth. He works to fit the tight skin over my arms and hands. This finperson had a much larger head and thicker chest, so the skin sags in spots, but its arms and hands were smaller. Finfolk also have no fingers, so I squish mine together as though I am wearing mittens.

Jamison finally finishes and steps back.

I hold out my arms to show him how I look. "Well?"

"It's disturbing how well this may work," he replies.

Laverick finishes stacking the black-powder bags and then puts the lantern near them. Osric passes pieces of beeswax from the sea hag's storage room to Jamison. With the skin covering my whole head, Osric didn't think I would need any. Jamison plugs his ears and picks up the fishing pole.

"Can you hear me?" I ask.

"What?" Jamison replies.

"You're ready." I place my hand over his heart. It's pounding so fast I can hardly count each beat. If this plan goes awry, he will be the first person we lose. I didn't know such terror could exist. He lays his hand over mine. I let that little act of comfort be enough, and then leave him to crouch behind the rocks with Osric.

Laverick gets into the skiff and lies down at the bottom. She wanted to stay on shore, but Osric is too large to hide in the boat, so he will run the explosives according to her instructions.

Jamison sits at the water's edge, by all appearances a lone fisherman who rowed out here, anchored his boat, and came ashore to hook his next catch. My anticipation simmers as I watch the sea. So much life hides below its surface; the sea is like a big secret I want to be part of yet don't want to carry the burden of knowing.

The finperson's skin has begun to itch, and my ears are folded where it clings too closely. I gag down my nausea and force myself to think of something other than how close I am to vomiting.

"Why are the finfolk helping Markham?" I whisper to Osric.

"I suspect he promised them your seas."

"Our seas?"

"Killian will allow them to migrate to your world. The finfolk have been at odds with King Dorian for centuries. Without the merrows to compete with for territory, they would be unchallenged."

I want to dismiss his theory, but it would be typical of Markham to offer such a bargain. He thinks the worlds are his to control. "What gives Markham the right to trade away our seas?"

"Elves are appointed overseers of the Land of the Living. One could argue that your world falls under our dominion as an independent territory."

"I hope you're wrong."

Laverick shushes us from the boat, and we quiet.

The waves lap against the shore, mimicking the soft beat of my ticker. The ticktock isn't slowing or winding down, like one would think a clock on a countdown would do. I fear its beat will grow fainter until, eventually, without warning, it halts midtick.

Osric perks up beside me. "They're here."

A soulful voice begins to sing offshore. The merrow's head, a bump on the surface, rises directly in front of Jamison, a distance off the beach. She slides closer, moving like a water viper across the surface. Her hair floats around her pale-green shoulders, and a string of pearls sits atop her head, reflecting the starlight like miniature moons.

Jamison bobs his fishing pole, playing his role as her bait.

Another merrow swims into view, flanking the first. Jamison waits to respond, giving the second merrow time to come nearer to the skiff and net. The two merrows combine their voices, their harmonious duet a far-off noise to my covered ears.

Jamison drops his pole and rises. He wades into the water with all his clothes on, soaking his boots and trousers. His movements are slow and weighted, as though he's made of solid wood. My ticker beats faster, and although my pulse is harder to detect, my chest aches from the speed.

Osric creeps around the rock pile to crouch low near the black-powder bags and lantern. He holds up two fingers. Then three.

We have three merrows in total.

He holds up two more fingers. No, five.

The combined force of their singing presses through the scaly skin covering my ears. A slight buzzing from their enchantment starts to hum through me. I press down on my ears, sealing the skin tighter and lessening the noise.

Jamison wades up to his waist in the sea. The merrow with the pearls on her head grabs a hold of him and pulls him out into deeper water. All five merrows surround him and pet his shoulders and face. He floats with his head above the water along the surface, relaxed and motionless. His submissiveness is so convincing I cannot tell if the merrows have enchanted him or if he's brilliant at pretending to have fallen under their influence.

Laverick stays low in the skiff, hidden from view, and Osric waits for more merrows to surface. He must think this is all of them, because he signals that it's time for me to make my entrance.

I loosen the finfolk skin around my head so I can hear better and step around the rock pile into open view. The merrows' singing quiets to one voice, and they all direct their luminous eyes at me. Osric assured us that the merrows would never run from a lone finperson, yet the merrows scan the spit for my possible accomplices.

One merrow addresses the group. "It's a scout. The others must be coming."

"No," says the merrow with the pearl crown, "he's alone. He must be a messenger. What message do you bring?"

She speaks our language even though her song is in another dialect. Muriel told us before we left that the finfolk and merrows can communicate as humans do.

"Um"—I clear my throat so my voice is deeper—"have you ever heard black powder go off?"

"Go off of what?"

Osric lights a fuse and tosses the black-powder bag out into the water, away from the merrows. Laverick measured the powder perfectly, so it explodes in midair before it hits the sea.

The merrows cover their sensitive ears and gape at the raining ash. While they are overwhelmed, Laverick slides out of the boat and into the water. The merrows don't appear to notice, but their confusion won't last long. Laverick needs to close the net from a U-shape to a circle without detection. If the merrows catch sight of her, they will try to return to the safety of the deep sea.

"What sorcery is this?" one of the merrows asks.

The one with the pearls has already lost interest in me. She presses her lips to Jamison's and sinks low in the water, an anchor pulling him under.

Osric throws another lit black-powder bag, and it explodes closer, startling the merrows so much that they shriek. The one clutching Jamison resurfaces, bringing him up for air. He doesn't gasp or sputter.

Bloody bones. Their enchantment has him.

Laverick is a third of the way done closing the net, but the merrows are so startled by the explosion that they start to swim out to sea, taking Jamison with them. I grab a black-powder bag and draw all eyes to me. Osric hisses at me to be careful as I light the fuse and toss the bag high into the air. It explodes above the water, directly over the merrows' heads, and ash smears the sky.

"If you run, we will capture you!" I shout.

They all halt. I quickly pick up another black-powder bag, and the skin around my wrist tears straight up to my elbow, revealing my real arm.

The merrow wearing the pearl headpiece spots my skin through the rip and glares. "I can see you're human," she says. "Who are you?"

I tear the finperson's skin off me and stand before them as myself. "I'm that man's wife. Let him go."

The merrow peels her green lips back over her pointy teeth and shoves Jamison underwater. He doesn't struggle or flail, nor does he send up strings of bubbles. "Come and get your man, woman."

Laverick swims faster with the net, near to closing it. Osric holds on to the other end where it is staked into the rocks and waits for her to finish. Laverick pulls the net shut all the way, completing the circle, and hollers, "Now!"

Osric yanks on the other end, and at the same time, Jamison leaps from the water and wraps his arms around the merrow's neck and his legs around her middle.

The other merrows take off for the open sea. Laverick and Osric hold the line, tightening the net. Osric goes into the water for a better hold on his end. I light the black-powder bag and toss it over the net to the other side. The explosion scares the merrows back, and our friends begin to gather the netting, narrowing the circle and pushing them toward shore.

Jamison hangs on to his catch as she tries to buck him off. He will not let go, so she bites his arm and holds on like a mongrel. He elbows her in the head again and again until she goes slack. Laverick gathers in the netting, tightening it around Jamison and catching him too.

Before Laverick and Osric close the net entirely, two merrows thrash and wriggle over the top. The last I see of them are their fins as they dive for open water.

I run down the shore. Osric tows the bundle of netted merrows toward the boat. Laverick climbs in and begins to tie their netted catch to the side of the watercraft. The two conscious merrows screech and thrash, tossing water over Laverick and into the boat. Osric knocks each of them over the head with a mallet. Their sudden quiet is jarring.

Jamison untangles himself from the netting with Osric's help and wades to shore. The merrow's teeth tore into his arm, and the wound bleeds heavily, soaking his shirt. He drops on the sand and lays his head in my lap.

I remove my waistcoat to use as a bandage. "I believed you were under their enchantment."

"I tried to be convincing," he pants.

His flippancy exasperates me. I don't know whether to cuff him or kiss him. I settle for smoothing his wet hair from his eyes.

"I heard you shouting," he says, clutching his sore arm. "What did you say to them?"

"I told them I'm your wife and to let you go."

He blinks up at me. "You've never said that before, that you're my wife."

I sense that he wants me to say it again, so some part of me is annoyed that he's making this more significant than it should be. "I'm your wife, and you're my husband. What else was I supposed to say?"

"I like how rosy your cheeks get when you're annoyed." He grins and then wrinkles his nose. "You smell horrendous."

"Oh, get off my lap."

I gently push him away and help him stand. Osric heaves himself into the skiff beside Laverick. The bundle of netted merrows is tied shut and tethered to the back of the boat.

"Return to the grotto," Osric says, "before the others come back with reinforcements."

Jamison and I start off on foot, while he and Laverick row slowly down the coastline, dragging our catch behind them.

Chapter Nineteen

Radella hovers in the archway of the sea hag's cave. Osric and Laverick rowed straight to the grotto, while Jamison and I walked to the second skiff, dodged growls from the gnome, and traveled the last leg of the trip by water. The pixie darts back inside the cavern ahead of us.

Our friends are tying off their docked skiff, our netted catch still in the water. One of the merrows has woken up, and she is livid.

"My father will kill you for this, Muriel!" Her voice bounces off the stone ceiling, amplifying her rage.

"Osric, do you know who this is?" Muriel asks.

The elf studies the screeching merrow in the torchlight and blanches. "Princess Nerina?"

"We kidnapped the king's daughter?" asks Laverick.

"His eldest," replies the sea hag, "the crown princess and two of her closest friends."

For a moment, no one moves. We are collectively undecided about what this means for our next venture. Should we let her go or continue with the transference?

"Well," Muriel says, "let's get on with it."

Osric binds the merrows one by one, and then he and Jamison drag them out of the water. Princess Nerina lies on her side, her arms behind her and her long tail flopping. Her pearl crown has slipped and is now sitting crooked on her head. She is more human looking out of the water, despite her furious hissing. I will never again struggle to carve a merrow figurine.

In the grotto, the cats begin to yowl. Their forlorn sounds echo down the narrow tunnel and off the ceiling. Muriel ushers us into her grotto and shushes her felines.

"Won't the merrows die if we leave them out of the water?" Laverick asks.

"They'll be fine for a short while." Muriel whirls on Osric. "You were supposed to bring back four of them, one for each of you."

"We lured in five, but two escaped. Muriel, we can stop this now."

"We certainly cannot. The injury is done. King Dorian will never forgive me, and my frown lines will be permanent." By her tone, she believes the latter is the worse fate. "You caught three merrows, and there are four of you. Decide which of you is staying and we will begin the transference." She murmurs to her cats during her return to the cavern. "They can't hurt you, my pets. I won't let those nasty things eat you."

Osric wears a troubled frown. "Was Muriel acting strange to you?"

"Compared to what?" Jamison answers.

The four of us dodge each other's gazes while we form arguments for why we shouldn't be the one left behind. I won't leave whether I live or die up to someone else, and Osric has to go because he's our guide. Jamison is the only one injured, but his arm has stopped bleeding and he seems to be managing the pain.

Laverick meets my stare. "No, Everley. Claret is down there. I'm going."

"Let the rest of us find her and bring her back."

"Why don't *you* stay and let us bring back the sword?" she counters.

Objectively, I understand her frustration, but personally, my panic mounts at the thought of not having a hand in what becomes of the sword—or me. This is something I must do myself. "I have to go because Father Time asked me to."

"If Everley says that she must get the sword herself, then she must," Osric proclaims. "Let's all remember whose weapon it truly is."

Laverick's posture sinks. "Then what do we do?"

If I had a few years to spare, I would ask Muriel to show me the result of this expedition for each different pairing of our group so I could make an educated decision.

"I'll stay," says Jamison.

"No," I reply, even though I don't have a good reason besides wanting him with me. Laverick should be the one to stay, not him.

"You need Osric as a guide," he says. "I'll stay and guard the merrows."

"It's settled, then," Osric declares. He goes back to the cavern, and Laverick trudges out behind him.

"I want you to come with me," I tell Jamison.

"I do too." He skims his thumb across my cheek and smiles cheekily. "Be careful, my treasure."

I cannot come up with a playful nickname for him in return. This transference scares me, as does losing a whole day of my life. I should have that much time left in my ticker, but what if I'm wrong? My clock heart is beating so faintly I can scarcely feel it. What if it stops while I'm underwater? This could be the last thing I ever do.

"Jamison, I think you should know something."

His countenance becomes somber. "I have something to discuss with you as well."

"You do?" I ask, my ticker skipping a beat.

Osric appears in the passageway. "Hurry up, you two. We're ready to begin, and may I remind you that Prince Killian has a head start?"

"We'll speak on this later." Jamison presses his lips to my forehead. I lean into him and will my heart to keep beating long enough for our future conversation to happen.

My leaden legs carry me into the pool cavern. Muriel stands beside the section of the wall where I etched my name, arranging three chairs in a line. All the merrows have awoken, and they are blindfolded and gagged.

"Are the gags necessary?" I ask.

"They are if you don't want to hear what scathing things Princess Nerina had to say about you." Muriel fingers her pearl necklace with one hand and touches the princess's crown with her other. "Osric, you'll take the form of the princess."

Princess Nerina stiffens. She can hear what's happening, which could be detrimental to us once we let her go. Muriel must not be concerned, though, as she has made no effort to whisper or take our discussion elsewhere. The princess's companions, her friends, are still as well. One of them is tall and the other stocky. They both look terrified.

"The other merrows will think you are the princess," Muriel goes on, "so be mindful of what you say and do."

Osric's glower turns grave. Acting as the princess will be a substantial burden to bear. We would have blended in more easily as civilians. Still, with him as Princess Nerina, our group should have better access to the castle and sword.

"Please sit so we may begin," Muriel says, her tone too chipper, considering we're about to commandeer three bodies. We sit in the chairs facing the pool, our backs to the wall and the merrows lying on the path to our right. "To transfer your spirits with theirs, we must connect your creation powers. Much in the same way the Everwoods unite the worlds, creation power unites us all."

She extends a fingernail and punctures the merrow princess's fin. Nerina bucks in anger as Muriel squeezes several drops of green blood into a cup of water. The sea hag does the same to the other merrows, each of their blood going into a separate water cup. As she brings the cups to us, Princess Nerina swipes her tail out, nearly tripping her. I take the first two cups from Muriel while she balances herself and swap mine with Osric's before passing it to him.

"Do we have to drink it?" Laverick asks, taking her cup. The blood has diluted so it's no longer visible, but the concoction is still unappetizing.

"Oh, my, no. Now, we prick your skin and add your blood." Muriel passes us a needle to do the work ourselves.

I brace myself against the incoming discomfort and poke my finger. Blood beads up, and I squeeze three droplets into the water. Osric and Laverick do the same, and then we stare into our cups at the unappetizing mixture. I'm glad we don't have to drink this, because I doubt I could force it down.

"Next, set your cup on the floor in front of you," says Muriel. "Lord Callahan and I will bind you to your chair. We don't want the merrows running away with your bodies." The hag cackles as if that's the wittiest thing she's ever said.

Princess Nerina hasn't moved since her blood was taken. She's listening to our every word.

Jamison ties us up while Muriel prepares our gags and blindfolds for the merrows after we've switched forms. The reason for them disquiets me. I'm giving temporary rule over my body to a fish. Had I the choice, I would rather wear the finperson's skin again.

Muriel sprinkles granules of sand into each cup and backs away to our left. "To finish the ritual, you must each kick your cup into the sea."

"That's it?" Laverick asks. "We just knock the cup over?"

"Did you expect me to feed you a potion or cast a spell?"

"Noooooooo," Laverick replies, drawing out the word in indecision. Osric lifts his foot and waits for us, but Laverick has another concern. "What happens if we die while we're switched?"

"If you perish, they will too, and the opposite applies."

The princess protests, her voice muffled by the gag.

Muriel takes on the same tone she uses to pacify her cats. "Lord Callahan, Radella, and I will keep close watch over your bodies. Go find Claret."

Laverick closes her eyes, her muscles tense. I hold myself still so I can sense my ticker. Its faint murmur is so alarming I almost withdraw.

"Everyone on three." Muriel raises her hands like a conductor and counts us down with overexaggerated hand motions. "One. Two—"

We kick the cups over at the same time. As the water-and-blood mixture pours into the sea, my spirit drains out of me and I float above myself. The princess's spirit has left her form as well, her expression petrified.

I flow past her spirit and pour inside her body in one quick rush. When I open my eyes, I'm blindfolded, and my wrists and mouth are bound. Other than the absence of having knees and feet, I feel like myself.

A peculiar sensation greets me that I haven't felt in too long.

Thump . . . thump . . . thump.

The beat of my heart. I still to listen to its rhythmic pulse; it is the most beautiful song in all creation.

Someone removes my blindfold. I look up at Muriel as she pulls the gag from my mouth and unties me. Jamison does the same for the other two merrows.

"Osric?" Muriel asks.

"Here," replies a feminine voice. His spirit occupies the shorter merrow with bulging eyes and frayed hair.

Muriel frowns. "Then who . . . ?"

"Everley, you didn't," Jamison breathes.

"Ah." The sea hag steps back. "Clever lass."

I explain in my new, shriller voice, "I brought us to this world and got us into this, so I should take the biggest risk."

"You did this to gain an advantage," a voice snarls.

Laverick transferred spirits with the taller, thinner merrow. She thinks I'm hurting our chances of succeeding.

Across the way, my head rises and my blue eyes blink at me. Princess Nerina glances around in horror and then down at herself. "What did you do to me? I'm—I'm *hideous!*" Jamison starts to blindfold her, and she snaps, "Don't touch me, land vermin."

"I still owe you for the bite you gave me, so quit moving." He wraps the blindfold around her head.

Nerina stops writhing and gasps. "What's wrong with me?" She wheezes twice as hard as a moment ago. "I'm Princess Nerina of the merrows! You could have at least transferred me into a stronger body. Something is dreadfully wrong with this one."

"Would someone please calm her down before she stops my ticker?" I say.

"Is that what's wrong with you?" Nerina replies. "How do you swim with this mechanism in your chest?"

"I don't."

The princess's gape widens. "You live half a life, woman. This heart is weak. *You* are weak. I could never withstand your—"

Jamison shoves the gag in her mouth. Though I am no longer in my body, he brushes back her disheveled hair and adjusts her shirt. His tenderness with her—with me—stirs something far down inside me.

I care about Jamison. I care about him very much.

He crouches down in front of me in the merrow body and searches my face for some sort of connection. I sense his disappointment in me, but more so his anger. I see the moment he recognizes my spirit in the softening of his troubled eyes. "Evie, it's just a sword."

"I had to do this." The second I return, I will tell him everything. I want him to know all of it, even the things Father Time warned me against revealing. Secrets are a form of protection, but I've no reason to protect myself from Jamison.

Princess Nerina tugs furiously at her bindings, rubbing red marks into my skin. I trust Jamison will prevent her from doing too much damage to my body.

"Can someone help me into the water?" Laverick asks. "My tail is starting to feel stiff."

"Your tail," I remark, smirking.

She completely ignores my attempt at humor.

Osric rolls into the water and goes under. Jamison slides Laverick in and then me. As I'm submerged, small flaps cover my nostrils. Bubbles billow out of my mouth, and when I inhale salt water, the water flows out of gills along the base of my throat.

Laverick practices breathing underwater beside me. Once we let go of the concept of depending on air to breathe, the three of us swim about the lagoon. My eyesight is remarkably clear, although the farther I descend from the torchlight, the less colors are visible. Our surroundings deepen to purples and blues.

My powerful tail drives me into a wall on accident, and in correcting myself, I bump into Laverick. She scowls and swims across the pool. We do two more laps, and then Osric points his thumb up, motioning for us to surface. We've used up our practice time. Dawn is only a few hours away. We must go now to arrive at the castle before the merrows go to sleep for the day.

Muriel smiles widely at us, the corners of her mouth stiffer and the lines around her eyes deep. Something is amiss.

"Muriel, is there anything else we should know before we set out?" I ask.

"Only that this is precisely what you should be doing and where you should be." She takes off her pearl necklace and slides it over my head. "Tell the king my debt is settled."

"We'll add that to the list, after we rescue a human and steal an eternal relic," Osric says dryly. He points his thumb downward to indicate he's diving.

I connect gazes with Jamison, send him a reticent smile, and then sink down into the true Land Under the Wave.

Chapter Twenty

Heart pumping, tail swishing, hair floating, and chest stretching, I swim the labyrinth of passageways out of the grotto. Breathing in and out through the gills along the base of my throat, I fight the inclination to return to the surface. Instead, I normalize my inhales and exhales to a relaxed rate and keep swimming so I don't sink like a stone.

When we enter the cove alongside the spit, the current tugs at me, attempting to shove me off course. Relying on the strength of my tail, I remain on track and stay close to Osric and Laverick. My tail does most of the propulsion, my arms and hands perform tiny course corrections to stabilize my direction.

We exit the cove and set out into the open sea, angling downward into the abyss. The water grows colder, yet the merrow body regulates its temperature masterfully.

Without this acute eyesight, the darkness may have closed in around me and brought upon panic. Remarkably, the colors are saturated, the blues rich and soft, lovelier than a dream. The seafloor is covered with corals of all shapes and sizes. They grow tall like trees with branches and round like bushes, almost like an underwater forest.

The reef, which I assume is Skull Reef, is filled with fish of every size and color. Whereas my human nose would only smell brininess, my heightened sense of smell picks up many scents—a tangy fragrance, something floral and sweet, and something clean and bright. My father would have enjoyed exploring these watery depths, whereas my mother would have advised me to stay on land. My perspective lies somewhere in between. I am apprehensive about venturing deeper yet keen to descend farther into unseen trenches.

Several gray creatures shoot past us, startling me, and then circle back. They are seals, eyes big and yellow and skins pale silver. I cannot tell if they're selkies, but regardless, they dart in between us, their swift movements like underwater dancing.

Not too far offshore, the seals split away from us, and we swim toward the blue lights in the deep. The small, glowing shellfish form long roadways through the midnight waters. Osric selects a highway for us to follow. I have no sense of which direction we are swimming, only that we are plunging farther into the heart of the sea.

My tail works effortlessly to push me forward, and it isn't until a smaller fish speeds past without moving its fins that I realize the road coincides with a current. I relax my tail, surrendering to the sea's power, and soar. Laverick and Osric do the same, each of us taking turns spinning upside down in corkscrews.

My heartbeat speeds up from the thrill of propelling effortlessly through the water. I haven't had a real heart in so long that I delight in the strain of its quick beat, the sensation of living on the edge of its might. Part of me wishes I could keep this heart and stay here forever, careening through the Land Under the Wave with my pulse hammering boldly.

We race along the sparkling-blue highway, past jellyfish and squid, but no other merrows and no finfolk are visible. Our path widens as it veers sharply downward. I lost sight of the surface long ago. I have no concept of how deep we are as we plummet farther.

"Osric," I say, "when were you here before?" My voice carries out and comes back to me as though someone else spoke. Sound travels faster underwater, muddling the origin.

"I was smuggling goods at the time," he says, referencing the smuggling business he and Markham ran.

"You've grown up since then," I remark.

"We never quit growing and learning, no matter how old we are."

"Muriel has proved that," Laverick says, her opinion of the sea hag harsher than my own. "She still acts like a child."

"Muriel believes age is a mind-set," Osric explains. "Her efforts to remain eternally youthful and evade death include a childlike sense of optimism for what's to come. Despite her many years, she has not allowed herself to become jaded."

As someone else who is not yet done living, Muriel's approach to life speaks to me. But what is the cost of evading death? Muriel relies on other people's desperation to feed herself more years. Osric has done something similar, in that he must always keep a supply of charm apples for his consumption. Both of them refuse to give in to time and aging, while it has always been my fondest dream to live long enough to grow old.

A vast glow off in the distance radiates up from the seafloor. Osric doubles his speed, and I keep up, savoring the quickening of my pulse and rush of cold water over my gills. He verges away from the highway to a narrower path of lights and motions for us to slow. The road extends close to the rocky seafloor. He swims to a dip in the road, and Laverick and I join him, stopping for our first glimpse of Everblue.

Roads pour into and around the underwater city like rivers of azure. The kingdom itself is similar to those on land, enough so that it could have been sunk by an earthquake and flooded by the sea. All the roofs, balconies, arches, and bridges are uniquely curved. Even the walls have a roundness to them, as though the builders and architects took their inspiration from the curl of a wave. The result is a flowing gentleness from one structure to the next.

Much like musical notes progressing up ledger lines, the height of the castle builds until the apex at the middle. Spiraling stairways, lofty arches, and swirling spires bridge the domed central structure and its cylindrical towers.

At a distance, the shape of the curved exterior walls and turrets appears to form an octopus, the main tower representing the animal's head and the smaller towers situated around it in the fashion of long arms. Each gaping window and doorway, high or low, glows a haunting blue. Two large doorways have the ominous appearance of eyes.

"Where is everyone?" Laverick asks.

"Probably gone home," Osric says. "Dawn is coming soon. Merrows sleep during the day and come out at night. The king should be waiting up for his daughter."

I straighten my pearl crown. Maybe I *should* have let Osric play the princess.

A whistling noise sends us all jumping. Suddenly, we're surrounded. A dozen finfolk riding upon armored sea turtles encircle us and point tridents at our chests.

Although my experience with the hanged finperson was excruciatingly intimate and repulsive, the corpse was nowhere near as frightening as these robust soldiers. They are positively revolting. Their bony legs and feet are emaciated, the skin transitioning to scales around their thighs. Though they are shaped like humans, their webbed hands and underarms and the spiky fins standing atop their heads are aberrant. Open mouths bearing fangs and flat, dead-looking gazes lock their expressions in perpetual sneers.

The largest finperson, twice the width of my merrow body, lifts his staff for light; the ball at the top is filled with squirming glowworms. With his strapping chest, gnarled fish face, and razor teeth, he is the most intimidating of the bunch.

Markham rides with the armed group. A close-fitting bubble surrounds the prince like a second skin floating above his clothed body. The bubble's exterior is as slimy as a snail's trail, yet the opaqueness lets outsiders view him clearly. It is almost as though he's been swallowed by a jellyfish.

"Princess Nerina," says the large finperson, his coarse voice small compared to his hulking size, "we've come to escort you home. King Dorian will give much to have his beloved firstborn returned to him."

Webbed hands lock around me, and rope binds my wrists and tail. They use the line to drag me behind one of the turtles and tie me to its armor. I quell my shaking while Osric and Laverick are also bound and tethered.

"The princess is less ill-tempered than her reputation implied," the big finperson says.

Markham floats over the seafloor to me, sets his feet on the ground, and bends down, staring into my eyes. "She's just shocked to see us, aren't you, Princess?" He leans in and says more quietly, "You suit your scaly tail, Evie."

I flinch away. "How did you know it's me? Do the finfolk know?"

"Tell them who you are, and I will say you're trying to trick them." Markham smirks as he takes in my changed form. "Did you think I wouldn't recognize you? These tides could never rule your spirit, Everley Donovan."

"Don't waste your flattery on me."

"No? Then I must compliment your flaws. Your obstinance and strong will. Nay, your preoccupation with my sword. Truly, your obsession knows no bounds. Reminds me how very alike we are."

I growl low in my throat and snap my teeth at him, an instinctual response that comes from my merrow form. Markham chuckles loudly with the finfolk. He wanted me to lash out at him, to perpetuate the lie that I am the temperamental princess.

"Do you still wish to kill me?" he asks softly.

"You still deserve to die. I would settle for turning you over to Queen Aislinn so she can burn you on a pyre."

Markham grabs my chin and lifts it. I repress a growl, refusing to give him the satisfaction again. "How does it feel to have a heart of flesh and blood? You think of me as a great deceiver, but look at yourself. You stole a merrow's form."

"I borrowed it," I counter.

He grips my chin harder and speaks more loudly so his companions can hear. "You, Princess Nerina, are the key to unlocking the past and awaking our future." His grip on my face lessens as he bends closer to whisper. "I had intended to catch the princess myself, but why do the work when you could do it for me? You should be more careful who you trust."

He shoves a huge kelp ball in my mouth, gagging me, and then floats over to Osric. The prince speaks in the first mate's ear too, more obnoxious gloating, I am sure. Osric snarls at him, and then a finperson gags him and Laverick while Markham mounts his sea turtle.

Unable to stomach his smirk any longer, I shut my eyes. My heartbeat thunders in my chest, a roar rising to my head. The inner beat of dread grows as our captors take off and drag us by our tails into the merrows' stronghold.

Chapter Twenty-One

My hair flies in my face, disrupting my view of the city. The lampposts stuffed with glowworms brighten the night to day, yet I feel stuck in a never-ending nightmare.

Our captors parade us through the narrow streets, their ugly heads high and proud. Voices cry out, and the merrows swim in the opposite direction or disappear inside buildings, fleeing from us, or, more specifically, the finfolk. Our captors' sneers are ugly and wide; they relish the fright of their enemies.

Muriel deceived us. She's the only one who could have alerted Markham about our plan to transfer spirits with the merrows, and it was she who recommended that we fish for them off the spit. Did she know Princess Nerina would be there?

Markham knew where we would be. He never intended to race me to the sword. He needed a bargaining tool against the king, and we gave him the perfect treasure to hold for ransom.

Our captors halt before the castle gates, and I bounce against the ground again. Two merrow guards swim out to meet us, armed with tridents.

"We've come for King Dorian," the lead finperson says.

The high doorways of the castle radiate pale-bluish light, like the color of someone's lips when they're cold. Or dead.

The guards must have been notified that we were coming, because they open the gates without a word, and the finfolk enter the bare castle grounds. An oval of iridescent water swirls over the royal towers like a halo. That must be the undersea portal, the one Dorcha brought us through.

The finfolk untether Osric, Laverick, and me from the back of the sea turtles and haul us by rope through the main door. We enter directly into the throne room. The bumpy walls are made of coral, and light glows from plankton suspended near the arched ceiling. The finfolk haul us down a center aisle through crowds of onlookers. Word must have spread that we were coming.

The male merrows are huge, bulky in the chest, their noses lumpy, chins long, and eyebrows bushy. They are twice as intimidating as the merrow females, though both genders growl lowly at the finfolk as we pass. A few also whisper to each other about the prince. Even leagues under the sea, Markham's reputation precedes him.

All the patrons of the castle seem to have gathered, including servants kneeling off to the side. From the corner of my eye, I spot Claret among them. Laverick hiccups in surprise. Our friend has a transparent skin around her much like Markham's, only hers is thinner, like a bubble stretched too far. As we pass her, Claret stares straight ahead and pays us no notice.

The finfolk dump us on the unlevel ground at the end of the aisle. I gaze upward at the dais high above the floor. Unlike a human throne room, no steps lead up to the royal perch, which is set at least fifteen hands above my head. On the dais, two stone thrones face the rest of the room, and a huge pipe organ covers the wall behind them.

It is the largest organ I've ever seen. Its dozens of pipes are layered from one wall to the next and extend to the ceiling. Oddly, the instrument is covered with daisy designs. Is this a sign of the kingdom's allegiance to our deities or merely decoration?

A merrow, thin as a reed through his chest and lean tailed, occupies one of the thrones. His pale skin sags over the sharp angles of his ribs, shoulder blades, cheekbones, and chin. The merrow's sheer tail fin swishes side to side like a hunting cat's, and his onyx eyes are empty of feeling. Behind him, between the pipes of the organ, two sets of round yellow eyes glare out at us.

The finfolk still hold most of the audience's interest, but King Dorian commits the full force of his attention on Markham.

"Leave us," says the king.

The attendees abruptly swim out, disappearing behind the archways that fringe the room. Claret follows a set of female merrows—princesses, judging by their pearl-encrusted tiaras. A handful of guards armed with tridents linger and form a half circle behind us, blocking the way out.

Once it is quiet, the king speaks again. "Killian, I heard rumor that you had returned to my seas. Captain Redmond was eager to assure me that he had disposed of you. He seems to have overinflated his effectiveness." The king clutches his armrests, his black-nailed fingers tense. "I suppose you expect my thanks for bringing home my daughter."

"Muriel had her, my liege."

The king's voice takes on a purr. "How is the old hag?"

"You know Muriel. Insatiable as always."

"Hmm," replies King Dorian. "What do you want, Killian?"

"We've come to deliver your daughter . . . for a price."

The large finperson grabs me and places a stone dagger to my throat. The merrow guards shuffle in closer behind us. The blade is so close to my skin I dare not move.

The king taps a finger against his chair. "You require use of my portal?"

"Now, now, Dorian. Your daughter is worth more to you than that." Markham sighs theatrically, as though he would be traumatized to see my blood spilled when he would gladly slit every throat here to get what he wants. "I've given this considerable thought, and I think you would agree that your heir is worth a substantial amount to you."

King Dorian's eyes burn. "Again, I ask, what do you want, Killian?"

"Give me the name of Father Time's helmsman."

"I cannot. Father Time entrusted me with the name so I may know who is running the sands of time and, therefore, keeping the pace of our tides. The information was never to be used."

I listen intently, confused as to why Markham wants the name of the helmsman. The tale of the infinity sandglass must be true, then, like so many others that humans think are fantasy.

"Father Time doesn't care for your happiness or welfare," replies Markham. "Had he cared, he would have warned you that your wife was ailing and given you more time together. It would be a shame to lose your heir too, especially so close to the passing of your wife."

The king snaps his fingers, and two eels shoot out from the organ pipes. The pair bare their fangs and hiss as they circle above their master defensively. In response, the finperson restraining me presses the blade closer to my throat. My gills quiver. In my side vision, Laverick and Osric have gone still.

"You're bold to question my allegiances," King Dorian states coldly.

"I question your future," Markham corrects. "What legacy will you leave your daughters? Will you leave them these limited waters or let them rule the unclaimed seas of the Land of the Living? You can give your progeny an opportunity no one has—a future of their own making."

The finfolk do not protest this arrangement. Despite what Osric said about Markham promising them rulership over my world's seas, Markham wants the merrow king and his kind to evacuate, and, in doing so, surrender this world to the finfolk.

My blood chills as I imagine the chaos the merrows would create in Dorestand. The Skeleton Coast would be cheerful compared to the disruption they would cause in our seaside cities.

The king stays motionless, his expression inscrutable. He makes a beckoning motion with one hand, and a moment later, a servant swims in carrying the sword of Avelyn nestled in a pillow of seagrass. The sword's thin blade gleams starlight and its gold hilt shines.

It takes everything inside me not to leap for my weapon.

The king takes the sword and holds it out. "Accept the sword of Avelyn in return for my daughter."

"I've no interest in the blade." Markham puts on a lethal smile. "I will accept only the name and location of the helmsman."

I should feel more shocked, but Markham said the king had something else he wanted. He came all the way to the bottom of the sea and laid this trap so he could gain something more valuable. He wants another ancient relic, and it must be the one the helmsman is responsible for: the infinity sandglass.

The finperson pushes the blade deeper against my throat, scraping the skin. I tilt my head away to try to avoid it, and the bulbous gag slides into the back of my mouth. Any farther and I will choke.

King Dorian taps his fingers in time with his swishing tail. "You will give me reign of the waters in your domain?"

"You have my word, as prince of the Land of Promise, that you may possess the seas of our territory, the Land of the Living."

"Your sister will permit this bargain to give away a portion of her territory?"

Markham's voice toughens. "I am prince of the elves. My sister will honor my word."

"I can only give you the helmsman's name. I know not his location."

"His name will suffice."

King Dorian stares at the sword as he answers. "His name is Holden O'Shea."

Markham angles sharply toward me. I hear nothing over the quickening booms of my heart.

Uncle Holden—*my* uncle—is Father Time's helmsman?

The blade lowers from my throat. The finperson ungags me and cuts my bindings. I hover in the water as Osric and Laverick are released as well.

"My liege, you may claim your new territory after the new moon." Markham bows, and then, without acknowledging me, he and the finfolk swiftly depart.

The guards file out to ensure they leave the grounds, and the king sets down my sword, leaning it against his throne with the tip of the blade scraping the floor. His eels go back to hiding in the pipe organs.

"You have a new pearl necklace, Nerina."

It takes me a moment to realize King Dorian is speaking to me. "Yes, sir."

"Sir?"

I rush to correct myself. "Yes, Father. I took back the pearls the sea hag stole from us."

"You shouldn't have risked yourself." He presses a finger to his temple. "It's late, Nerina. Go to bed. We'll discuss your carelessness later."

I rip my gaze from my sword and hurry out. Osric and Laverick follow me from the throne room into an empty corridor. The castle has quieted, the other patrons having gone to sleep for the day.

"I could kill Muriel for what she's done," Osric seethes.

"Why did she betray us?" Laverick asks.

"Time. Markham must have promised her more time, a painless thing for an immortal to pass around. The transaction costs him nothing." Osric growls to himself and then quickly regains his decorum. "Everley, get the sword. We'll find Claret."

"Holden O'Shea is my uncle," I reply in a daze.

Osric grabs my arms. "Does Killian know where to find your uncle?" I nod, and he lifts his gaze upward. "Mother Madrona, this is worse than I thought."

"Father Time said Markham isn't after a 'what' but a 'who.' I never guessed . . ."

Osric shakes me a little to bring me out of my stupor. "We don't have time to discuss this now. Meet us outside the city, up on the ridge where we were before."

"But my uncle—"

Laverick grips my hand. "Get the sword, Everley."

I nod several times to let her words sink in, and the princess's pearl tiara slips down my forehead. Laverick readjusts it and pulls me in for a swift hug. "We're almost finished, and then we go home."

The promise of an ending, and that ending being home, rekindles my determination. Osric and Laverick go one way, and I return to the throne room for my sword.

Chapter Twenty-Two

The quiet throne room is empty. Hiding behind a pillar near the outer edge, I peer out at the lofty dais and pipe organ. The king has left and appears to have taken my sword with him.

I cautiously swim up to the dais. The stone thrones are built into the floor, so I search around and behind them. Finding nothing, I investigate the bench in front of the underwater organ. I have never seen a more curious instrument. The organ does not have keys like our pipe organs back home. Instead, it has tiny finger holes for pressing.

The eels dart out from two of the pipes, and King Dorian is suddenly behind me.

"You aren't Nerina," he states, his tone smooth. His eels snake around me, preventing me from fleeing. "You may look like my daughter, but you are not her. The body without a spirit is an oyster without a pearl. Yours doesn't fit right. It is too . . . loud."

I force calm into my voice. "But, Father, it's me, your eldest daughter."

King Dorian sits at the organ and begins to play darkly rich treble chords and bass clef downbeats. The song has a sinister tone, like a death march. "If you're my daughter, then sing."

"Sing what?"

"Sing," he says more forcefully. "Princess Nerina has a lovely voice, or didn't Muriel tell you?"

After the long night I've had, I have little patience for games. "My name is Everley Donovan. I'm a human from the Land of the Living."

The king pauses, his webbed fingers poised over the finger holes. "Where's my daughter?"

"Safe with Muriel. You'll have Nerina back if you cooperate." The threat slips out without a thought. He offered my sword to Markham in exchange for his daughter, so he may do the same for me.

He starts to laugh, his thin shoulders shaking. "You, a human, threaten *me*?"

"I'm presenting you with a bargain—the sword in exchange for your daughter. You offered the same to the prince just moments ago. Why did Markham ask for the name of the helmsman?"

King Dorian begins to play the pipe organ again. "What's stopping me from locking you in the dungeon until the transference wears off? I know the sea hag helped you switch spirits with Nerina. It's a common trick Muriel plays. Or didn't she tell you how she stole those pearls? She switched bodies with a selkie, swam into my wife's chamber, and swiped them right off her table. When I asked for them back, Muriel insisted she keep them. But there is no cause to worry. The transference will lapse soon, Nerina's spirit will come home to her body, and you will return to your weak human form."

The princess's flesh-and-blood heart bangs away, a barometer for my desperation. "Father Time sent me for the sword of Avelyn."

"Did he?" replies the king, still playing the dreary song. "Why?"

"I'm dying." My voice catches on the bluntness of my statement, said without pity, but I'm not above appealing to his compassion. "The sword can save me. Without it, my husband will become a widower like you."

King Dorian quits playing and narrows his eyes at me. His eels continue circling, so close their sleek bodies brush my hair. "Who are you?"

"I'm Everley Donovan, the girl with the clock heart."

"The Terrible Dorcha mentioned your name to me." He turns around on the bench, swinging his tail toward me. "Why have you come to our world, Time Bearer? We have no place for you here."

"Father Time wants his sword. Give it to me and I'll be gone."

King Dorian rises from the bench and swims to his late wife's throne. He reaches beneath it, into a narrow gap I did not see, and pulls out the sword of Avelyn. Raising it between us, he points the gleaming blade at my chest. "Tell me, Everley Donovan, what would you give to have more time with your husband?"

"Anything," I say, my voice breathy. "I would do anything for more time."

"There isn't anything I wouldn't do to have one more day with my wife, but my daughters are all I have now."

He swims closer and the eels back away. The king rests the sword over my pounding heart. Though I doubt he will harm his daughter's body, I dare not move.

"My family will soon build a new empire in your world. Mankind is too weak to have inherited the Land of the Living. Merrows may never possess your land, but we will surely dominate your seas." He lifts the sword higher between us, aiming it upward, and considers the blade. "Prince Killian is recrafting the worlds in his image." He offers me the sword. "Take the weapon, Time Bearer. You must have seen or been shown what's to come, so you know just how badly you'll need it."

I hesitate, not trusting that he won't lunge at me, and then swiftly take the sword.

"Upon your return to the grotto, tell Muriel to release my daughter or I will tear her home down stone by stone and throw a grand banquet for the whole castle to feast upon her precious gaggle of cats."

The king sits back down and resumes playing the pipe organ. His eels lie on the dais near his tail fin, like mongrels at his feet. His dismissal confuses me into stillness. King Dorian gave me what I wanted, yet I sense that, in taking the sword, I have lost something much more valuable.

My hand starts to loosen on my blade, almost to the point of dropping it. I hold up my other hand and see my spirit starting to peel away from the princess's body.

As I turn to go, the king says, "Leave my wife's necklace."

I remove the string of pearls, set them on her throne, and flee.

As I approach the exterior gate, the castle guards take off toward a small group swimming away from the highest tower. Osric and Laverick are holding Claret between them, her bare feet sailing out behind her.

I rush after them, my sword at the ready. "Leave them be!"

The guards withdraw and offer their apologies to their princess.

Claret hardly appears awake. Her pale skin is pruned like fruit rotting in the sun. When my friends reach me, we do not stop.

"Open the gates," I say.

The guards rush back to push open the gates. Lamps filled with glowworms highlight the quietness of the city. Osric guides us upward, over the city, instead of navigating the streets.

"We must hurry," he says. "I can feel my spirit slipping."

"Mine too," I reply.

The undersea portal swirls overhead. Markham has probably escaped through it by now and must be on his way to my uncle and the infinity sandglass.

Past the city, we swim into a swift current. The flowing water picks us up and propels us away from Everblue. Laverick, Osric, and I don't stop swimming despite the extra speed of the current. Claret's protective bubble is so thin I fear it will tear.

Osric soon guides us out of the current, and we start our ascent over Skull Reef. He and Laverick speed for the surface with Claret as I heft the heavy sword. Our dazed friend begins to rouse, the enchantment fading.

We break the surface with large splashes. As soon as Claret hits the air, her bubble bursts, and she gasps and coughs. She holds on to Laverick until she recovers and then starts thrashing.

"Let go of me, you monster!"

She lands a well-aimed hit to the side of Laverick's head. The Fox slips underwater to evade her strikes and rises behind her, locking Claret's back against her front.

"It's me. Lavey. You've been missing since you fell off the longboat. You were under the merrows' enchantment. We found you, and Everley's gotten back her sword."

I raise the sword of Avelyn as proof that what she says is true.

"Lavey?" Claret says, her acceptance dawning. "Why do you look like a merrow?"

Laverick lets go of her. "It's a long story."

Claret revolves to hug her friend. "I remember what happened now. I heard this sweet song, and then I was in a strange place far away from the light. The whole thing was dreadful."

The Fox holds the shaking lass at the surface. "Everything is all right now. You don't ever have to go back there."

The late-morning sun beats down on us, revealing our location off the southern coast of the continent, between the village and the spit. Traveling by sea is fastest, so Laverick carries Claret, and we follow Osric to the sea stacks. Seeing the familiar rock formations in the distance, I double my speed. I will miss having a heart of flesh and blood, but the thought of returning to myself doesn't trouble me.

It's time to go home.

At the entrance to the sea stack, I leave my friends at the surface and dive into the clear blue water. I arrive at the cavern pool first and search the landing for Jamison and Muriel, for my body, and for Radella. Everyone has gone.

I lay my sword on the side of the pool and rest while the others catch up. On the ground near me is Muriel's hand mirror, its glass shattered. My senses jump and stay on high alert.

Osric and the others swim into the pool. "Where did everyone go? Why did they move our bodies?" he asks.

I show him the broken mirror. "Something must have gone wrong."

"I suppose it's true what they say," says a surly voice. "Even a broken clock is right twice a day."

Captain Redmond steps out of the passage from the grotto. The giant wears his gaudy red jacket with black embroidery and gold toggles, the collar and sleeves of his white shirt a frilly lace.

In one hand, he has a sword. In the other, the severed head of the sea hag.

Chapter Twenty-Three

Captain Redmond has not a splash of blood on his fine white shirt. I don't know why that's my first thought at seeing Muriel decapitated, her head hanging from his big hand, but I must look away from her face or I may retch.

Her glamour spell has fallen. She is herself, every wrinkle and gray hair showing. I saw her true appearance, so this doesn't startle me, but she would hate to know she's lost all her beauty in death.

Several members of the pirate crew march out of the grotto and flank their captain. I snatch up my sword and swim away from the ledge, closer to my friends. Daylight filters down from the gaps in the cave ceiling, shimmering off the water and reflecting onto the walls. Claret gawks up at the well-dressed giant, her first view of him.

"Osric," Captain Redmond says, "you must know I wouldn't forget your betrayal." He tosses the head of the sea hag into the water. We all cringe away.

Osric restrains his tone with an admirable level of calm. "We don't want trouble, Mundy. Where are our bodies?"

"They would still be here if I had them."

Jamison and Radella must have taken us out of here. Regardless of where they are, the transference will fade, and our spirits will leave this space to find our bodies. Claret will be left behind, and I will return to my physical form without the sword. Our entire expedition to Everblue will have been for naught.

Something large moves behind me in the water. The captain's saltwater crocodile swims through the passageway into the pool, blocking our only exit. Tattler swallows the floating head of the sea hag, and again, I cringe.

"Mundy, listen to me," Osric pleads, shedding his composure. "Markham is pursuing the helmsman. All the worlds are in peril now. You must let us go."

The enormous croc swims closer, sliding silently through the water. Claret squeaks and grabs on to Laverick harder.

"It's high time we finish the war," replies the captain. "The Land of the Living doesn't belong to mankind. Prince Killian will recraft the worlds and repair this division. Then we can go home."

"The prince lies!" I say, my voice echoing off the high cavern ceiling. "He makes false promises so you'll serve him. He cares nothing for your kind."

"Prince Killian cares enough to release us from captivity while the rest of the worlds do nothing!" the giant hollers back. "He will return the worlds to their proper order, and you won't be here to see it." Mundy gestures at his crocodile. "Kill them and fetch the sword."

Tattler speeds at us, his jaws opening for Osric. The elf smashes his fist into the croc's nose and smacks him in the head with his merrow tail. The crocodile redirects from him to Claret, Laverick, and me. I dive to draw him away from them, and Tattler catches up in seconds. I twist around him and slash a shallow wound down his side with my blade.

Tattler comes back for a second pass. His teeth nip at my tail fin, and Laverick, who has dived down, grabs his neck and climbs on top of him. The croc rolls and rolls while she hangs on. I stab him in the tail, and the thrashing croc throws Laverick off. On the surface, I see Claret kicking away from the edge of the pool with Osric.

Diving under Tattler, I stab upward into his soft belly. Laverick races for the open passageway. Osric dives with Claret, who's obviously holding her breath, and speeds for the exit. I wrench my sword out of the crocodile's middle and race after them.

We surface in the passage outside of the cavern. Captain Redmond's howls boom behind us, echoing off the stone walls. Radella flies down through an opening in the ceiling.

"Radella," I say, "where's Jamison and our bodies?"

Zipping low, she motions for us to follow. We swim hard after her, out of the sea stack and into the cove. The *Undertow* isn't visible, but the captain's vessel must be close by.

Radella flies toward the mainland, staying over the water, and we track her path. Though we are exhausted, we are wary of the captain and his crew, so we keep swimming. She leads us down the coastline, following the same beaches we traveled by foot when we left the watchtower. We swim hard, but the sea is strong, and our strength is dwindling.

Osric and Laverick take turns carrying Claret on their back while the sword of Avelyn threatens to drag me down. For something I wanted so badly, I am awfully close to letting go and letting it sink back to the bottom of the sea.

Osric notices me struggling and leaves Laverick to help Claret. "Everley, let me."

I pass him the blade and swim alongside him as he works twice as hard to combat the waves with the heavy weapon. My tail twitches as my control over the merrow body wanes. The sun is too bright, the current too powerful.

Laverick flails at the surface behind me. "Everley! I'm going—"

Her spirit lifts from her borrowed form and sails off into the distance. Osric stops suddenly. We lock gazes. He throws me the sword, and as I catch it, his spirit also flies away. I immediately lose sight of the merrows in the waves.

Claret grabs on to me to keep afloat, her grip weak. "Don't leave me, Evie."

"I won't."

Radella hovers over us. I swim harder after her, towing Claret and the sword. My spirit starts to lift farther off my body, like a snake shedding its skin, but I charm it back in with my stubbornness.

Stay here. Stay for Claret. You must stay.

Radella veers toward land. I spot the watchtower and my strength is renewed. Using the tower as my beacon, I redirect for shore.

Several minutes later, land is still too far away. The extra weight I'm dragging grows heavier, and my spirit starts to slip again. I will not leave the merrow body until Claret and the sword are safe. Although I try, I cannot push my spirit fully back in, but I do stop it from leaving.

Radella stays just in front of us. My movements are slow and heavy, my slipping spirit making them less precise. I swim to her, and then she darts away and waits. I swim to her again, and she flies ahead. She is a more attainable marker than the watchtower, but she keeps moving.

And I am so tired.

"Everley!" Jamison stands on the beach, waving his arms.

I push harder to catch up to Radella, but Jamison is my new marker. The pixie darts ahead of us two more times until she's with him. Suddenly, I can see more land than sea in front of us.

Claret slides off my back and grabs my arm, and we both kick for shore. I swish my tail the last few lengths into the shallows. Her feet touch the bottom, and we let go of one another. Claret collapses and crawls for shore. Jamison runs into the surf. My arm shakes as I lift the sword to him. The second he takes it, I release my hold on the body.

My spirit shoots above the merrow princess and soars over my friends to the watchtower and through the open door. I slam into my body, where it is lying on the floor. The falling sensation dissipates— and then the emptiness comes. The absence of a solid pulse, a beating heart of flesh and blood, is stark. My limping ticker has never felt more fragile. The desolation carves me out and leaves me hollow, like carrion-picked-down bones. I lie on my side and try not to compare my heart to Princess Nerina's, but it's more evident than ever that my time is almost spent.

Sometime later, I don't know how long, someone touches my cheek. I open my eyes, and a blurry face peers down at me.

"Welcome back," says Jamison.

As he unties my bindings, I try to push to sitting, but everything hurts. My body is fractured, like a splintered bone that was reset wrong.

Osric lies beside me, still unconscious. Laverick and Claret are together on the stoop, Claret with her long, wet hair hanging down her back and Laverick with her arm around her. Claret glances over her shoulder at me and touches the center of her chest. The Fox must be telling the Cat about my ticker. Radella is with them as well, and they appear to offer the pixie condolences for Muriel's death.

The sword is propped against the wall. Seeing it sends the day's events back to me in a wave of dizziness. I shut my eyes and recount the worst of it to Jamison. "Captain Redmond killed Muriel."

"Radella told me. A lot happened while you were gone." His monotone voice restricts his sorrow, but it comes through in his slowness of speech. "When we spotted the *Undertow* off the coast, I loaded you three into a skiff with all the supplies I could carry. Muriel stayed behind to point the pirates away from us. Before I left, she told me . . . she told me many things. Foremost, she wanted me to ask you to forgive her. She said you would understand what she meant."

"She told Markham where we were, and he and the finfolk ambushed us." My head finally clears and I reopen my eyes. "Markham didn't want the sword from King Dorian. He wanted the name of Father Time's helmsman. My uncle Holden."

"Your uncle?" Jamison asks, rubbing his chin. "I suppose he *is* a clockmaker."

Now that I have time to think back, my uncle wasn't shocked to see Father Time the night they installed my ticker. He knew who Father Time was without an introduction. They weren't strangers.

"Where are my apples?" Osric asks, groaning. Jamison hands him a small bag that he must have brought from Muriel's. The elf gets up stiffly, moving like someone a few hundred years old should. He bites a huge chunk from his charm apple and swallows before he speaks. "Captain Redmond won't give up until he finds us. How soon will you be ready to go?"

"I'm ready now." I rise gradually to prevent myself from having another dizzy spell. "My uncle is in Dorestand, in the Land of the Living."

"Then that's where we'll go. If we hurry, we may beat Prince Killian. The bubble tonic he took wouldn't have been strong enough to protect him as he traveled through the undersea portal, so he'll be heading to the land dwellers' portal too." Osric polishes off his apple and cranks his neck right and left, setting off several loud pops. He fills his pockets with more charm apples, his movements faster. "I don't know what the prince wants with the infinity sandglass, but the helmsman has sworn to guard the timepiece with his life. Your uncle will protect it."

This is meant as a comfort, but it makes me more anxious to get to the portal.

Osric takes swords to Claret and Laverick outside while Jamison helps me into my cloak. The sea hag's spyglass is in his breast pocket. He shoves a pistol into the front of his belt and hands me another one.

"It's loaded," he says. "The extra black powder got wet, so we each have one shot."

I tuck my pistol at my waistline, pick up my sword, and start for the door. I almost make it outside when light-headedness grips me. I brace against the doorframe, my chest heaving and my fingertips tingling.

"Are you still recovering from the transference?" Jamison asks.

"No, I have something to tell everyone." I sit on the stoop, my face sticky from perspiration. Jamison sits beside me. He waves Laverick, Claret, and Osric over from where they are sheathing their weapons, and they encircle us. My inclination to bite my tongue flares, so I outwit it by opening my mouth until the words finally fall out. "I haven't told you all how my clock heart functions because I haven't known. But recently, I learned from Father Time that my uncle gave me ten years of his own life to animate my ticker. Much like Muriel would take years as payment from her customers, Uncle Holden gave me those years nearly a decade ago. My ticker has been growing fainter because that time is almost spent."

"How much is left?" Laverick asks quietly.

I stare at the ground to avoid seeing Jamison's reaction in my side vision. "I don't know exactly. The tenth anniversary isn't until next month, but it feels closer."

"Time moves at different intervals in every world," says Osric. "One day in the Land Under the Wave is equal to one month in the rest of the worlds. Your visit to the Land of Youth, then to your own world, then to this world in so short a period may have confused how your ticker counts time."

Of course time is working against me. I can never seem to get ahead of it, but my ticker will not stop me from going home to my uncle. I will make time for this.

Jamison drops his head in his hands, his fingers digging into his hair. "How long have you known?"

Osric clears his throat and rises. "We'll wait over here."

The lot of them step aside. Claret does well walking on her own, but her scarecrow body moves as though her joints are understuffed with straw. Laverick supports her until she's steady on her own, and Radella flits off to hover by them.

"I've known something was wrong since before we came to this world," I admit. Jamison cranks his jaw from side to side. "I didn't know

I was running out of time until I met with Muriel. I wanted to tell you in the grotto, but we were in a rush to do the transference."

He lowers his hands and stares at a tuft of grass between his feet. "Did Muriel tell you how to fix this?"

"I need to go home. My uncle will know what to do."

"After your uncle saves you, then what happens?" he questions in a low voice. "Will you return to your old life? Is that what you want?"

What I want is very different than what waits for us. I have evaded the obvious truth for too long. Jamison deserves my honesty, even if it is unsatisfactory. "I can't change who I am or who you are."

His gaze jumps to mine, and the amount of hurt I see there steals my breath away. "Do you know what I wanted to tell you in the grotto? I wanted to assure you that I'll make your life as Lady Callahan a happy one. I don't care to participate in high society. Though I still have my title, I gave up that lifestyle when I lost my inheritance. For me, going home means having a life with my wife. Everything I've done in this world was so we could go home together."

He's trying to compensate for complications that aren't his to solve. My clock heart and criminal sentence are my burdens to bear. "I would never ask you to live as a shut-in."

"You don't have to ask. Being with you is the only homecoming I've imagined." Jamison pushes to his feet to leave and then hesitates. "I wish you had told me. It's difficult to trust someone with your cares and dreams when they refuse to trust you with theirs."

Laverick bites her lip and looks away. All our friends are watching or listening, and upon reading their expressions, I realize they agree with Jamison.

"I'm sorry," I say, extending my apology from one friend to another. "I should have told you all, but I was afraid of what was happening and didn't want to admit it was true."

"I'm afraid too—afraid of losing you," says Jamison. "Above all, I'm afraid *for you.*" He reads the sun, discerning the midday hour. "Markham's lead on us is growing. We need to get Everley home."

He picks up my sword, lightening my load, and marches past our friends. Osric and Claret follow him down the path toward the village, Claret moving steadier each step she takes. Radella flies to the front of the group to ride on Jamison's shoulder, a clear indicator that I've lost her favor.

Laverick walks by my side, our gaits falling into sync. "Do you know what I do when I'm afraid?" she asks. "I light a fuse and blow something up."

Though that may not have been my intent, I fear that's precisely what I've done.

Chapter Twenty-Four

We hurry down the steep footpath, traveling around the lagoon to the village. Osric finishes eating another charm apple and signals for us to stop. Upon the elf's request, Jamison passes him the spyglass.

"What is it?" he asks Osric.

The first mate peers through the spyglass at the structure atop the mountain, the stairway that seemingly leads to nowhere. "Someone is climbing to the portal . . . It's Prince Killian."

I grab the spyglass to see for myself. Markham is indeed scaling the stairway. If we hurry, we won't be far behind.

Jamison doesn't need to set the pace now, because I race down the pathway ahead of everyone. But as we round the bend into the village, Claret slows down and points behind us out to the sea.

"Lavey, isn't that the pirate ship you told me about?"

I pause to look through the spyglass at the *Undertow* entering the harbor. I lower my sight to the upper deck where Captain Redmond stares back at me through his own spyglass. I snap mine closed. "We need to hurry."

I was pushing my limits before, yet I still dig further for strength and dash for the village. Radella flies alongside Jamison, her little wings easily pacing us. I grip my aching ribs and start to slow. Laverick slides her arm around my waist, and Claret does the same on my other side, helping me along.

As we near the houses, the residents go inside and shut their doors and windows. Osric slows, as though something is wrong, and then Neely steps out from behind a building, a mace in one fist.

"Osric," says the giant, "the captain said if you came this way, I was to bring you all to the ship." Neely spots me supported between my friends and sends me an apologetic smile. "Hello, poppet. How's your ticker?"

"It's not so good, Neely. I need to go home."

"I can't let you do that. The captain found a way for me to go home to the Hollow. I'm sorry, poppet. I would like to see my world again before I die."

"I understand," I say.

Osric draws his sword at the giant. "Everyone keep going. I'll handle him."

We hasten past him while he paces the giant. Jamison resumes the lead, urging us onward, my sword in his right hand.

The switchback roadway is endless, the crushed shells beneath our feet difficult to run on. I hear Neely smashing apart buildings below with his mace, trying to strike Osric. His mace finally connects, and the impact tosses Osric over our heads. He lands in the hills above us.

Neely stomps after us, gaining ground with his long strides. Jamison hands my sword to me and draws his pistol.

"Get to the portal," he says.

"But, Jamison—"

"Go, Everley!"

I pull away from my friends and push myself to run. Claret and Laverick stay close, their swords drawn. We round the end of the switchback and jump all at once at the boom of gunfire. Down the slope, Neely has dropped his mace and is clutching his shoulder from where Jamison shot him.

Jamison sprints after us, waving for us to keep running. We set off again, but so does Neely.

Radella, who has been switching between flying beside Jamison and me, now darts behind us and flutters her wings, releasing pixie dust. The dust opens a hole in the ground. The giant's foot lands in the ditch, and he flings forward, landing hard.

Up ahead, Osric gets up from where he was thrown. We run toward him, and he signals for us to keep going, then walks to the center of the road with his sword to confront the giant for another round. Radella stays back this time with him.

We leave the seashell-strewn streets and set out on a dirt trail. Jamison is limping, but I dare not mention it. Our footing pulls out loose rocks and sends little stones bouncing downward. The Fox and the Cat are tiring, so I do my best to hike without their help on my wobbly knees and ankles.

Neely's heavy footfalls close behind us cause us to pause. I don't see Osric or Radella, so the giant must have fought his way past them. Laverick glances at Claret, and they seem to agree upon something.

"Everley," Laverick says, "go ahead of us."

"No, we stay together," I reply. "I'll run faster."

Laverick groans at my stubbornness. "Stop trying to do everything alone. Let us do this as your friends."

The top of the giant's head appears down the slope.

"Be careful," I say to the Fox and the Cat, and then Jamison and I continue up the trail.

We run until we are high above them, then I look back and see Laverick standing face-to-face with the giant. Claret leaps out from behind a boulder, and Laverick gives her a boost, lifting her onto the giant's back. The Cat wraps her arms around the giant's neck, clinging to him while Laverick hacks at his knee with her sword. Neely lets loose a howl. Jamison and I start up a steeper incline and lose sight of them.

The tingling in my fingertips worsens to include my toes. Numbness in my extremities is a warning sign that time is leaving me. Pressing a hand over my tight chest, I sense little movement in the gearwork of my ticker. I plod around the next bend and stop to read the clockface. The minute hand is at the seven and steadily moving toward the six, soundlessly rotating counterclockwise. Once it counts downs to a zero hour, I sense my time will be up.

"Evie, we have to go," Jamison says.

"Take my sword to my uncle," I pant. "It's my ticker the captain wants."

"Don't be a nidget." Jamison hoists me over his shoulder, my arms draping down his back, and starts uphill. "We may disagree from time to time, and you often pretend you don't like me very much, but we were just starting to fancy each other."

"You've always fancied me."

"What's not to fancy? Your frosty temperament or your mannish attire?"

He sets into a jog, his knee barely holding. My view of behind us shows me longboats full of pirates rowing from their ship across the lagoon to the dock. Reinforcements are coming to aid Neely, but we should be long gone before they catch up.

Jamison starts up the final section of rocky path, the stairway to the portal well in sight.

A boulder soars over our heads, hurled by the giant, and decimates the trail in front of us. Dirt and pieces of stone spray down, the pathway crumbling. We slide downhill, Jamison and I falling and skidding to a stop in a cloud of dust. I cough and wave away the dust plume.

"Jamison?"

"Here." His trousers are torn and his legs cut and scraped. I rise to help him, and the air clears to reveal Neely rounding the lower bend of our trail.

"Damn bastard won't give up." Jamison pushes to his feet and passes me the sword of Avelyn. "Get on up there."

"I want to go home together."

"I'll be right behind you." He draws his sword and confronts the giant. "Go, Evie!"

My pistol still has one shot, but unless my aim is perfect, firing it will only serve to further anger Neely.

I scramble up the path, over unstable rocks, and crest the mountain. The wooden stairway is bigger from this vantage point and endlessly tall. The many stilts that hold up the structure appear rickety and old. As my uncle would say, the craftsmanship has no soul. The stairway is strictly functional and not well maintained.

Markham is nowhere to be seen, so I heft the sword and climb.

The stairs go on and on. After the thirty-fifth step, I reach a platform and a boggart rises through a trapdoor in the floor. The creature can assume the shape of anyone or anything. His current form is of a skeletal cloaked figure, his hood drawn to cover his skull. His jawbone juts out from under the shadow of his hood, the rest of his face hidden.

"Name," he says in a crackly whisper.

"Everley Donovan."

"You may pass, Time Bearer. But first, the sea hag requested that we deliver this to you."

The boggart's skeletal fingers slide out from under his sleeve. In his bony hand is a folded piece of paper. I take it and quickly read the message.

> *Dearest Everley,*
> *Some sacrifices are so immense they change the course of*
> *the future.*
> > *This was always my end and your beginning.*
> > *All my love,*
> > *Muriel*

The stairway starts to shake. Neely has topped the mountain. Neither Jamison nor any of my friends are anywhere in sight behind him. The structure creaks and groans as the giant begins to scale the steps after me.

I shove the letter in my pocket and dash upward. The taxing climb grays my vision around the edges like singed paper. When I glance over my shoulder to gauge Neely's progress, I spot Jamison bounding up the steps after us.

Neely lunges upward two and three steps at a time. I run faster and summit the final dozen stairs. An iridescent cloud hovers and swirls at the end of the platform at the top, floating above the ground in midair. One could step off the platform into the portal, akin to stepping on a cloud. As I have never stepped through a portal without a guide, the security of its structure is uncertain.

The giant barrels after me, his heavy weight and fast movements making the stairway quake. I wait for a moment for Jamison to catch up so he can come with me, but he's still too far behind.

I shuffle to the end of the platform, my toes hanging over the edge. The ground is a very long way down. Up close, the color of the portal varies from red to green to blue, and every color in between, a rainbow through the mist.

Neely ascends the final stairs and towers over me, bleeding from his leg and his shoulder. His weight unbalances the structure, swinging it from side to side.

"Jump, Everley!" Jamison yells.

Jump into what? I would feel more confident if the portal were a doorway or a tunnel, something more substantial than colorful brume.

The giant lowers his big hands to catch me. I duck down, avoiding his swipe. Though I don't want to leave Jamison or our friends behind, I have nowhere else to go. I ready myself for a big drop and leap from my crouch into the portal.

Chapter Twenty-Five

I am standing atop a lofty pinnacle. Stars race around me, chasing each other like flitting butterflies. Far below, I see the worlds, all of Avelyn lies at my feet.

My clock heart spins, then the gears inside it yank and the floor opens beneath me.

I plunge through the darkness, plummeting through the bottom of a star. A soft, soulful melody played on a violin fills my head, and a warm, velveteen blanket engulfs me.

The sudden silence jolts me awake. I blink fast to clear the starlight from my eyes and find myself standing in a forest of colossal elderwood trees. Their trunks are as wide as wagons, and their treetops so high I cannot find the sun beyond their leafy crowns.

I didn't know portals could transport me to the Everwoods. Perhaps they only do this for Time Bearers.

My ticker has paused its countdown and instead spins and spins like a compass struggling to find magnetic north. The sword of Avelyn glows as brightly as a new star and vibrates a little in my hand, as though it's happy to return to this wondrous forest.

No one else is here—not a pixie or sprite or gnome in sight. The trees are all the company I need. I tread to the nearest elderwood and press my palm against its velvety bark. A word comes to my mind with firmness.

Hurry.

A patch of daisies sprouts beneath my feet, extending out in a path. I follow the trail of flowers through the trees, the rich scent of damp greenery fresh upon my skin. Warm sunshine filters through the leaves and dapples the forest floor.

Through a gap in the leafy branches, the daisy path leads me to a clearing. On the opposite side stand several doors, seven in total. The doors are not built into a wall but stand independent of each other, as though a house has fallen down around them and only they were left erect.

Each door is constructed from the same wood yet carved with individual designs. The first door is the most ornate, decorated with etchings of apples with crowns of leaves encircling them. The second door has markings of mountain peaks, and the third has wild lilies, but the markings have faded and the brass doorknob is rusty.

The fourth door is carved with acorn trees, its craftsmanship finely detailed. I linger by this door the longest and then move on to the fifth door, which is set apart by its etchings of shooting stars. The sixth door is also distinct, with images of various seashells. But the seventh door is the most unique, and not for good reasons.

Dead vines choke the door itself, and faded leaves are strewn in front, the only fallen flora I have seen in the Everwoods.

I tug away a patch of the scraggy vines and reveal the door's cloud designs. Someone has placed a large hanging lock around the handle, and, more oddly, the lock has no keyhole. While the other doors appear to be in service, this one is obviously in a state of disrepair.

Down the row, the acorn door slowly opens and muted light spills out. I cautiously tread back to it, and a daisy sprouts near the opening. The flower shoots up and up, tall as my outstretched hand. I touch the pure-white petals, and something shifts in the forest behind me.

I raise my sword and whirl around. "Father Time, is that you?"

Nothing else moves in the forest; however, the acorn door swings inward wider. No wind pushes it, and as far as I can tell, I am alone.

A familiar sound carries out of the door—a chorus of ticktocking clocks. Curious, I touch the door, and it swings fully open into a room filled with timepieces. My uncle's creations.

I step inside the store, and when I look back, the door from the Everwoods has disappeared.

The shop smells of sawdust and fresh lacquer mixed with a mustiness that accumulates after endless spring rainstorms. I sheathe my sword and lay my palm on a mantelpiece clock. Its beats ring through me with purpose. My own ticker has resumed its counterclockwise beats, its voice too weak to hear. The minute hand has crept farther backward and is now between the three and two.

My uncle's shop is just as I recall, except the shelves haven't been dusted, the floor hasn't been swept, and the "Closed" sign has been hanging in the window so long an outline has been smudged on the glass. I run a fingertip across a dusty shelf and leave a trail.

This is not a dream or a visit to the past. I'm home.

Voices come through the cracked door to the workshop.

"Hand it over and I'll leave you be," says Markham.

"I can't do that," replies my uncle.

I draw my pistol and throw open the door.

Markham stands across from my uncle, armed with a pistol as well, the workbench between them. The prince switches his aim from my uncle to me. "Everley, your timing is impeccable."

"Get out of here, Evie," barks Uncle Holden. "Let me handle this."

He has no weapon and no defense against the prince's gun.

I pace sideways into the room, my back to the wall. "Get out, Markham, or I'll alert the constable corps. One gunshot and they'll come running."

He jerks his head at my uncle. "Tell him to give me the infinity sandglass, and I'll happily take my leave."

"Not on your life," says my uncle.

"What about her life?" Markham counters, his finger tightening on the trigger. "I made a hole in her once. I'll do it again."

I take aim at the prince's smirking face. "Not if I shoot first."

Shakiness carries up my arm. I don't drop the gun, but my strength is buckling. I'm like a windup toy on its last turn, and both my uncle and the prince see it.

Uncle Holden starts to walk around the workbench to me.

Markham switches his aim back to him. "Sandglass first, and then you may go to her."

My uncle's gaze darts between us, weighing his offer.

"Don't listen to him," I reply. "He betrays everyone, even those he claims to love." The prince does not balk at my accusation, infuriating me all the more. "What happened to Harlow?"

"She fell behind and the elven guard took her," he says, finger tight on the trigger of his pistol. "Harlow is safe in the Land of Promise. My sister takes good care of her captives." He issues this statement not as a compliment but a fact, with little respect for his sister's authority.

Uncle Holden speaks, his voice grave. "Everley, it's nearly midnight. Any moment now, I must turn the sandglass. It's my duty."

"And, of course, you must fulfill your duty to Father Time." Markham's words hold explicit venom. He arrived at the end of my uncle's watch. With the timekeeper on the ship, I waited beside the naval sandglass and promptly turned it over when the sand ran out. Had I not, the only repercussion would have been our time skewing from the mainland's. But the infinity sandglass sets the time for all the worlds, so the consequences will be far reaching.

Tears wet my uncle's eyes. I leave my pistol aimed at the prince as Uncle Holden crosses the room. He lifts a tall wooden box off a shelf, sets it on the workbench by Markham, and pulls off the three-sided cover. Underneath is a sandglass filled with pearly moondust. The bottom of the vessel is nearly full and the top almost empty.

Uncle Holden's hand hovers over the sandglass. The vessel is attached to a wooden base, and when the last granule falls, the bolts locking it to the base snap away to reveal hinges. My uncle pushes the top of the vessel, spinning the sandglass upside down so the sand within waterfalls without pause.

"Thank you for fulfilling your duty, Holden," Markham says, and then cracks him over the skull with his pistol.

My uncle's eyes roll into the back of his head, and he crumples to the floor.

Markham goes for the infinity sandglass, and I pull the trigger. My shot goes high, hitting him in the side of the neck and throwing him back against the wall.

He bends forward and clutches his throat. I run around the table. My uncle is unconscious and his head is bleeding. Conversely, Markham sheds no blood, but, damn him, I hope he suffered the pain of my gunshot.

He raises his pistol at me. I hit his wrist, and his shot goes through the ceiling. We lunge for the sandglass at the same time and both get a hold of one side.

"You really are the most infuriating girl," he says through gritted teeth.

I kick him in the kneecap and wrench the sandglass from his hold. He springs at me, his weight throwing me to the ground, my sword still undrawn at my side. The sandglass falls out of my grasp and lands in front of us.

Markham reaches over me to grab it and elbows me in the face. I roll away, clutching my nose, and he rises with the sandglass, his eyes gleaming like a boy who has uncovered the worlds' greatest treasure.

"Don't do it," I say. "Don't stop time."

"Is that what you think I want to do? Oh, my dearest Evie. I don't intend to stop time—I mean to rule it."

He starts to unscrew the top of the sandglass, where the vessel meets the stand. With each rotation of the lid, his spirit begins to pull away from his skin.

I leap at him and try to wrench the sandglass from his grasp. The second I touch the vessel, my own spirit begins to slip away from my body. I pull harder, but he finishes unscrewing the top, and a rainbow bursts out of the glass.

Our spirits jerk out of our bodies, and the geyser of light shoots us up to the heavens. We whirl past the worlds and stars, across seas of velveteen skies. Markham tries to shake free of me, but I hang on to him.

We land in a heap and roll apart. As I push up, I find that my sword is still sheathed at my waist. The ancient weapon has clung to my spirit, its vitality immortal.

I grip its hilt and rise. We crashed in a desert filled with piles of discarded belongings. Mountain after mountain of furniture, tools, old toys, broken parts, faded clothes, and scraps of lumber surround us for as far as I can see.

"You stupid, stupid girl," Markham spits out, rising from the dust. His ears, nose, and chin are pointy, his dangerous good looks sharper than usual. The glamour charm only altered his outward appearance to resemble a human. His spirit looks like the real him.

We are both opaque versions of our physical forms, faded and ashen, as though we have been washed and hung to dry in the sun too many times. This desolate world is stained yellow and gray. The daylight is insipid, casting a ghostly pallor over the dusty landscape. There is no sign of any living thing. Our spirits are untouched by the terrain, yet considering the glare of the sun and lack of foliage, this desert would be a harsh environment to survive in.

"Where are we?"

"The moon." Markham begins rooting through the nearest pile of junk. "Opening the infinity sandglass opens time. Time is not bound to the portals or gates; it moves freely, with some exceptions, of course."

I survey our surroundings again. "*This* is the moon?"

"Some know it better as the pixies' treasure trove, a dumping ground for the worlds. This is where everything goes that the pixies vanish. In the Land of Youth, pixies were rubbish collectors. Haven't you ever wondered what happens to the things they disappear?"

I did for a moment after Radella vanished my comb.

More rubbish rains from the sky and lands in the piles. How many times did I stare at the dark spots on the moon and never once wonder what they were?

Markham continues to root around. Strewn about his feet are countless hats and mismatched socks. "One of them should be here somewhere . . ."

"How are you doing that? You're a spirit. You shouldn't be able to touch things."

"Spirits have power in the present. To some extent, we can interact with the worlds."

Before when I was a spirit, I was in the past as a witness that could not act or be acted upon. In the present, as spirits, we must have some power over our surroundings. How much influence I have must depend on where I am in time. I kick at a piece of rubbish and it goes flying. The reasoning for how all this is possible still confuses me. I refocus and draw my sword. "Why did you bring us here, Markham?"

He digs into the pile up to his elbows. "Nearly a millennium ago, when the giants were cut off from the rest of Avelyn, Eiocha ordered the pixies to vanish all signs of their kind as punishment for starting the triad war. There are things here from the Silver-Clouded Plain that cannot be found elsewhere."

I march up to him and point my sword at his head. "You hurt my uncle so you could come here and pick through rubbish?"

"Holden will recover. If he doesn't, Father Time will find another helmsman. The bastard always does. 'Time must go on' and all that overdramatic drivel."

I jab the sword at his nose, restraining myself just short of slashing him. "My uncle's death is not for jest!"

Markham frowns up at me. "Why do you protect your uncle when it's he who taught you to fear others? You shouldn't have been hiding as a clerk in a shop. With the sword of Avelyn, you are mightier than them all."

"You have no idea who I am."

"You're Everley Donovan, and we are the same," he explains plainly. "From the moment you were born, until the moment you die, our fates are entwined."

I lower the point of my blade. This may be the most honest thing he's said to me. He tied our fates together when he stabbed me through the chest as a child. I cannot be anything other than what I am, and I will always be what he made me.

"Ah, there's one." Markham slides a burlap pouch out from under a woman's hat and shakes it upside down over his palm. Out fall four sky-blue seeds the size and shape of beans.

"That's it?" I say. "That's why you did all this?"

"Not all treasures glitter." Markham drops the seeds back into the pouch and, to my utter surprise, offers me his hand. "Come with me, Everley. Step out of your uncle's shadow and let me show you what all this is for."

Repulsion swamps me, second only to curiosity. What's so valuable about the seeds, and what could possibly be next?

"You feel the wonder," he says, smiling to himself. "You inherited your lust for adventure from your father."

"Go sit on a pike."

"Always with your threats," he says and sighs. "You of all creatures should understand how difficult it is to break free from the past and why I must return home a victor or I will never be at peace."

"Plowing over people is a cold victory. What about Brea and Amadara and Harlow? What about the unborn children you let die? Muriel told me Amadara was with child."

His clamps his teeth together. "Muriel lied."

"Not everyone lies as much as you do. Osric is right, you don't love anyone. Everywhere you go, you inflict pain, and pain and peace can't coexist." I raise my sword again, this time to strike. "You will always be a monster."

He pushes to his feet. "You've used up my patience, Evie. Find your own way home."

The prince looks up and starts to rise off the ground. I swing at him, slicing his arm, but he floats higher and faster. I grab his leg, and he pulls me up, the two of us launching off the moon. He kicks his leg to shake me loose. My grip slips down to his ankle, but I hold tight until we tumble back down to our bodies in my uncle's workshop.

The impact knocks all the air from my lungs. I slowly turn over and push onto my knees. My uncle is still unconscious on the floor, and I am back in my brittle body. Markham sits up and winces. He touches his forearm, and his fingers come away wet with blood.

"You're bleeding," I breathe.

Neither of us moves. My sword cut him, and the wound isn't healing.

As more blood wells from his cut, my mind sharpens. Everything I have been waiting for, training for, praying for, lifts me from the floor. I stand over him on rickety legs, my sword in hand. "You're not laughing now, are you?"

His face goes ghostly pale. "Everley—"

I raise my sword and swing with all my might. The blade connects with his chest, and he buckles over in pain. I double-fist my weapon for a final blow, and he straightens again.

"Now may I laugh?" he asks, smirking.

His shirt is cut, but no blood seeps from his chest. The strength of my arms gives out, lowering my blade. How is this possible? How is he bleeding from one blow and not the other?

Someone bangs at the shop door. "Constable corps! Let us in!"

They must have heard the gunshots.

Markham picks up the infinity sandglass. I lean against my sword, the blade pressing into the floor. All my muscles have tremors now, trembling harder by the second.

He cocks his head to the side. "The sword of Avelyn is nothing but a broken star. It's fitting that you found each other. But you're naive if you believe that the sword or its master will protect you."

The constables bang harder on the front door. Markham flashes his white teeth in a rigid smile and ducks into the kitchen. I limp to the doorway and prop myself against it, too tired to run after him. He flees into the alley and leaves the back door ajar.

The door to the storefront bangs open, and two constables rush in. The men in scarlet jackets file into the workshop, pistols raised.

"We've been robbed," I whisper, pointing at the back door.

They view my uncle's injured state and run after Markham.

I sink to the floor and rest my hand over my ticker. The minute hand is before the one, almost to the end of my time.

Another hand presses down on mine. Uncle Holden has awoken and crawled over to me. "Everley, where is the infinity sandglass?"

"Markham took it. I'm sorry. I couldn't stop him."

"You did your best. Let me take a look at you."

I lower my hand from over my ticker.

"No, let me look at *you*." He grasps my face in his palms. "Did you have an adventure?"

I choke on a breathy laugh. "More than I ever imagined I would."

"Did you find love?"

Thoughts of Jamison purge my mind of previous assumptions and notions about clocks and hearts and metal and flesh. This clock heart— this machine—was not supposed to be capable of falling in love, but by some miracle it has.

Because love doesn't care what's impossible. Love does what it wants.

"His name is Jamison Callahan. You met him once, remember?"

"The earl?" My uncle smiles, and in that smile, I see my mother. "Oh, Evie, you grew up so fast. You were just a lass, and now look at you, a woman. The passage of time is swifter than you know."

"I've missed you," I whisper.

"And I've missed you. I should have told you that I'm the helmsman, but you had so many other burdens to bear. You didn't need to take my duties upon yourself as well." Uncle Holden sets his forehead against mine. "I'm grateful I got to see you grow up. Your mother and father would be so proud of you. Brogan and Ellowyn wanted the very best for your future. I hope you think of what you meant to them and of me often."

His countenance clouds with pain, and then he pulls back to reveal his sliced palm. His blood wets the blade of the sword of Avelyn.

He presses his bloody hand over my ticker.

"No!" I try to pull away, but light bursts between us and flares out.

The stream of brightness expands, sending a current of warmth over me, straight down to the marrow in my bones. I feel something far down inside me flip upside down, like an inner hourglass turning over and restarting with the top of the vessel full of sand. The light slowly fades, and my uncle sinks to the floor beside me.

I push onto my elbows and bend over him, clutching at his work apron. "What did you do?"

"The years I had left would have meant nothing without you." His bloody hand over my clock heart weakens. "Take the last of my years and create something beautiful."

His grip falls and his head lolls to the side.

"Uncle Holden?"

I shake him, but he gives no response.

"No." I lay my head against his chest, hot tears spilling from my eyes. "You cannot leave me. You cannot leave me here alone."

My clock heart beats with renewed vigor, the heartwood reanimated with time. The ticktock booms throughout me. Time has a voice again: my sorrow.

The pair of constables run back into the workshop. I hardly hear them over my sobs. I scarcely feel them pull me off my uncle and help me to my feet.

They release me suddenly.

"A clock heart," gasps a constable. "This is sorcery."

"See the blood?" replies the other, drawing his pistol. "She murdered him."

I make no attempt to cover myself or to run or to explain. They manacle me and lead me at gunpoint out of the shop. Onlookers and neighbors line the street to watch them load me into a detainment wagon. They see the blood on my unbuttoned shirt, see my clock heart ticking away boldly. I have given life to their fears that the heretic Children of Madrona are hiding among them and threatening the queen's Progressive Ministry, and I cannot muster the strength of spirit to give a damn.

A constable remarks that the robber I encouraged them to pursue was not found. The other constable expresses doubt that there ever was a robber, and his partner agrees that I sent them away as a ruse.

They shut the wagon door, casting the cell into darkness. Compared to the light, I prefer the shadows, for the light took the last of my kin from the world.

Chapter Twenty-Six

The underground labyrinth of Dorestand Prison is just as I remember, a gloomy pit filled with dank and putrid cells. I am alone, my arms and legs chained to a stone wall. The guards tried to jam me into a cell full of women, but several of the prisoners started to wail when they saw my clock heart. More than one spat at me and called me names, so the guards transferred me to the lowest floor of the prison into a windowless private cell that's as frigid as the sea is deep.

In the hours that I've been alone, I've tried to make sense of why fate led me here. Muriel's part in this is still unclear. The prison guards confiscated her letter before I could reread it, but its overall sentiment was that her death would change the course of the future. Because of her, Markham got the name of the helmsman from King Dorian. I would blame her for my uncle's death too, but the blame falls on Father Time for not interceding.

More time passes. The cold in the cell becomes almost as torturous as my loneliness. I didn't think I could miss anyone more than my parents and siblings. But there are two people I miss even more fiercely. One of them is gone forever, and I'm worlds apart from the other.

I should have known I was falling in love with Jamison. Anyone who can bring me this much yearning and worry must be someone I care for deeply.

A guard unlocks the door and lets in the queen's secretary. How did Secretary Winters return to Dorestand so quickly? The last time I saw him, his ship was intercepting the *Cadeyrn of the Seas*. Oh, but Osric said time moves faster here, one month for every day we spent in the Land Under the Wave.

"Everley Donovan," says the secretary, "Her Omnipotence will see you now."

Queen Aislinn fills the doorway. She has come in her regal finery, her gray hair pinned up and an ivory broach of a mare set at her bosom. We have not seen each other since the day in the courtroom when she sentenced me to seven years at the penal colony. I'm amazed by how much has happened since then, how much has changed. How much I have changed. I'm not the naive girl she interrogated, yet she has the same large, suffocating presence.

The queen is not a woman of substantial stature or enviable beauty. Her power comes from the graceful control of her movements, her elegant mask of aloofness, and the iron influence of her carefully constructed words. Her calculating eyes do not seek truth. She crafts lies as adornments and conceals them behind her grandeur. Her thin gold crown entitles her to interpret principles and enforce them with cruelty and bloodshed. I fear her, but I fear her propensity for distorting the truth more.

Her expression reveals no opinion of me. Her detachment comes with a callousness that is impenetrable, a condemnation that was decided before she entered the room.

The queen removes my sword from behind her back and drops it on the floor with a clang. Her disrespect for the sword of Avelyn appalls me, but of course she doesn't know its value.

"Where is Killian Markham?" she asks, her voice deceivingly soft.

"I don't know."

She lifts her chin. "I've no patience for lies. You colluded with Killian to destroy my penal colony. You aided him in the ruin of a naval warship and then commandeered my first-rate vessel and fled across the seas. You must know where he is."

"Shouldn't you know?"

"My gift of sight is not for you to mock."

After meeting Muriel, I'm astounded that Queen Aislinn ever convinced me or her people that she's a seer. She's nothing more than a charlatan in a crown. Palm readers have more ability than she does.

"Markham isn't who you think he is," I say. "He isn't even human."

She stomps up to me, her heels clicking on the stones, and tugs down the front of my shirt. "Do you expect me to believe that outlandish lie while you're marked with a talisman of sorcery?"

"You and I both wear our loyalties," I say, referring to her broach of the ivory mare, her favorite symbol of the Creator. "Markham deceived us both. He doesn't belong to this world. But you don't want to ally with the truth, do you? Because then you'll be held accountable for what he does next."

"You lecture me on truth? The girl who has lied about her identity and pretended her death while others mourned her family's passing. Your father was the bravest explorer in all of Wyeth. You shame him and his great name."

Her condemnation would have pulverized the girl in the courtroom, but I understand that every word she says is deliberately chosen to fortify the decision she made before she walked into my cell.

The queen leans in, the scent of her amber perfume smothering me. "The Creator has shown me your true nature, and you are indeed heartless. Any girl who kills her uncle, her own blood, deserves a million deaths."

I glare back at her. "You can call me what you'd like, but you will never be a seer, and I will never be what you think I am."

"You're an abomination." She swings around in a whirl of silk. "Burn her."

A blow I expected, but a blow nonetheless. The queen knows very well that Markham is dangerous, but he humiliated her and got away, so she will punish me instead.

"What about my trial?" At least in a courtroom I could explain my story to a magistrate, warn him and everyone in attendance that they're in peril. More people should hear the threat that Markham presents to the worlds.

"You're undeserving of a trial," replies the queen. "That thing in your chest condemns you." She beckons Secretary Winters. "Announce her execution far and wide. She will burn at sunset. Invite every able-bodied citizen to attend."

"Everyone answers for their deceptions in time," I say, my heart beating so loudly I know she can hear it ticktocking. "Even you."

Queen Aislinn marches out. The secretary picks up the sword of Avelyn and takes it with him.

The guards do not wait long to unchain me. They release my confines and stay nearby while two servants bathe me with damp cloths and dress me in a thin white shift with a low neckline that reveals my scar and ticker.

I have never worn anything this revealing in public. The queen hopes to portray me as a trollop, a brazen, unscrupulous sorceress. She wants me to appear more formidable before she terminates me, a ploy to demonstrate her power. I am her retribution, a pawn in a big game of chess that I was never allowed to play.

Sitting cross-legged on the floor, I wrap my arms around my knees and battle off shivers. The servants who dressed me let me keep my red gloves until we leave for the execution. They are faded and worn, and one of the seams is torn, but this little piece of my family, of me, makes me feel less alone.

The only sound to listen to is my ticker. I try to cover my ears to silence it, but the beat is even stronger inside me, drumming in my head. The noise reminds me of Uncle Holden, and when I can stop myself from thinking of him, instead I think of Father Time. He didn't stop Markham from killing my parents or siblings, yet this is worse, because he chose my uncle as his helmsman. Then he let him die. And he will probably let me die too.

A guard delivers my last meal, a bowl of gruel, and lets in an unexpected visitor. Dr. Huxley comes in with his medical box, and the guard waits outside the open door.

"Alick?" I say, rising from the floor. "How did you get here?"

"The queen requested a surgeon, Miss Donovan. She wants reassurance that your clock heart isn't unsafe for the crowd. The surgeon who works for the prison was daunted by your ticker. He and I were mates in school, so I volunteered. I would have been here sooner, but I had to wait for approval from the warden." Alick comes closer, his gaze flickering back and forth from my face to my ticker. "Does it hurt?"

"Not anymore."

He touches the old scar from Markham's sword and then finds the scar on my back where the blade exited. "You should have died."

"I almost did. The ticker saved me."

Alick accepts my explanation without a blink. "Are you hurt anywhere?"

His concern for me is too much to bear. I throw my arms around him and hang on tight. He goes still and then embraces me back.

"We were so worried," he whispers.

"Where's Quinn? How did you return to Dorestand so quickly?"

He releases me, his expression puzzled. "Everley, Quinn and I have been home for months. You left for the Land Under the Wave half a year ago."

"That's right," I remind myself. "Time moves slower there."

Alick checks that the guard is still outside and goes on. "Quinn, Vevina, and I were captured by the navy ship. We told them we were taken hostage during the mutiny against Lieutenant Callahan. Because of my good standing with the queen, they believed us and determined that Quinn's time overseas fulfilled her sentence. We received the terrible news that Quinn's mother passed away while we were at the penal colony. Quinn would have gone to an orphanage, so I adopted her." He smiles a little. "And her cat."

"Is Quinn all right? What about Vevina?"

"Quinn is settling in. You should see her. She's so grown up, and she can read and write on her own now. Vevina was turned in to the constable corps when we returned from our voyage. They were bringing her here to the prison when she escaped the detainment wagon. She came to my home a few weeks later to hide. She, Quinn, and I spend a lot of time together. You would be proud of Vevina. She isn't gambling or running bets. She's been teaching Quinn needlepoint."

I am so aghast at the thought of Captain Vevina sewing, let alone teaching Quinn, that I give no response to that. "What of Jamison? And the Fox and the Cat? Have you seen them or heard of their return?"

His face goes still except for his eyes, which dart to the left. "I have not."

My hopes crash and crumble. They mustn't have made it past Neely to get through the portal. All of them worked so hard to help me get home, and I left them behind.

Alick's mouth falls in a frown. "My most heartfelt condolences about your uncle."

"I miss him constantly." My eyes sting with withheld tears.

"Hurry up in there," says the guard.

Alick opens his medical box and removes a silver tool. He turns his attention to my ticker and whispers, "You could have told me."

"I couldn't, not because of anything you've done. I couldn't tell you or anyone because I was afraid of this happening."

His touch is as soft as his voice. "The queen's council wanted you to stand trial. They did *not* appreciate her sentencing you without their approval. She's lost favor with them since the ruin of the colony. Things in the realm have been tense. The queen called the entire naval fleet back to port and interrogated every man and woman who knew Markham and every sailor who worked for him. Anyone who gave an unsatisfactory answer was jailed or released from duty. Every day, we see more burnings and hangings. Those named a worshipper of Madrona go straight to prison. Most of them see the noose. I live in fear every day that Vevina might be found and that someone might falsely accuse Quinn or me. Everyone is continually on guard, concerned about their family's safety."

I bite my lower lip. "Will you tell Quinn not to come tonight? Neither of you should attend. I don't want you . . . I don't want you to see that."

The guard hits his baton against the cell-door bars. "Time's up, Doctor."

Alick puts away his instrument and closes his medical box. His troubled gaze briefly meets mine, and then he says under his breath, "I would like to respect your wishes, but as your friends, we will not let you be alone."

A hot thickness cramps my throat. I pull my gloves off and hold them out. "Please, take these to Jamison. He and the others were still in the Land Under the Wave. When he gets home, tell him . . . tell him I'm sorry."

Alick takes the gloves and nods. I wait until he and the guard are gone, then I press my lips against my shoulder to muffle my sobs.

Chapter Twenty-Seven

The walk from the prison to the pyre is jammed with people. The courtyard is packed with more attendees than I have ever seen here before. Little children sit on their parents' shoulders. Boys climb onto barrels, and girls huddle in the windows that overlook the quad. Merchants have left their shops, and residents have walked from their homes. People have traveled from all over Dorestand, their wagons and carriages cramming the streets and halting daily responsibilities. The whole city has come to a stop for my execution.

Four guards march me around the perimeter of the quad. The sky is overcast, the faint scent of char from an earlier execution hanging in the air. My rope bindings scratch my skin. It's a minimal discomfort compared to the gasps and murmurs from the onlookers. Parents cover their children's eyes, and others watch closely to see if my clock really runs, then they turn to those behind them to report that my ticker is indeed sorcery. I drop my chin and let my hair fall in front of my face as my heart hammers away.

Her Omnipotence is stationed on the wooden platform with her councilmen, several magistrates, and the high priest from the Progressive Ministry. The secretary of state has my sword at his side. He must have taken ownership of the blade. I hope it brings him nothing but misfortune.

As we climb the wooden stairs to the top of the platform alongside the stone pyre, we pass by the line of officials.

"Eiocha protect us from this sorcery," says the priest.

"It's hideous," adds the queen's lead councilman.

A magistrate replies, "A tragic end to the Donovan family name."

I would rather burn at the stake over and over again than let them see how much that hurts, so I lift my chin and stare out at the crowd.

Alick and Quinn are near the front. She's older than I remember, her face thinner and her physique more mature. She has become a poised young lady, an immense change from the dirty-faced girl I met on our voyage to the penal colony. Alick's hands rest on Quinn's shoulders for support. He must not see her expression, because the lass isn't crying. She wears a mask of defiance.

Before I am led up the pyre, the priest steps forward holding a bowl of water with lilies floating in it. His pure robes symbolize the color of Eiocha when she came to shore as an ivory mare. He dips his fingers in the water and draws them across my forehead.

"Great Creator, deliver us from this evil." He finishes washing my brow and says, "May Eiocha forgive you."

He pulls away, and the queen glances at my clock heart without even a sneer. She feels nothing for me, not even revulsion. Her apathy is the final denunciation I need to accept that this is truly happening.

I am going to die.

Guards prod me up three stone steps flecked in ash. Before I arrive on the stand, they stop me to remove the boots that were given to me for the march across the courtyard. I step onto the circular stand, and my bare feet sift through cindered logs and piles of ash. The stone is still hot from the last execution, enough so that it hurts my soles.

When I reach the stake in the middle, an inescapable calm comes over me. Is this how Father and Mother felt when they realized they had lived their last day? I imagined their final moments were of terror and pain.

That must still be coming.

The guards won't waste a good section of rope, so they untie my bindings and retie my arms and legs to the stake with burlap cut from an old feed sack. At the same time, more guards heft loads of kindling up the stairs from a pile at the bottom of the pyre and stack the bundles around me until the mounds are as high as my knees.

Down on the platform, the executioner lights a torch and holds it up. The audience quiets, and Queen Aislinn steps forward to address them.

"Everley Donovan," she starts, speaking to me while she faces her people, "you have been found in possession of a clock heart and accused of sorcery and murder. What say you to these charges?"

I didn't anticipate an opportunity to speak, nor did I prepare something to say. I raise my voice to the wind. "Holden O'Shea was a great man. He raised me and took me in when my parents were murdered. He was a father in every way. I loved him. He taught me that people fear what they don't understand. So understand this, Dorestand—your queen is a fraud!"

Shock and outrage ripple across the audience.

"Light the pyre!" Queen Aislinn hisses.

The executioner scales the steps. I shout louder.

"Queen Aislinn is no seer. She cares not for our people, only her own greatness! A war is coming, and with her as your leader, you will lose!"

The executioner lowers the torch to the kindling, and the fire begins to engulf the stand. The flames start low but speedily spread. Smoke pours up, stinging my eyes and throat, and the flames prowl closer, snapping and hissing at my thin shift.

I wriggle against my bindings. The burlap holds. I cough hard to clear the smoke out of my lungs, but with every inhale, I draw in more.

As I lift my chin to find clearer air, I don't believe my eyes when a pixie lands on top of the stake. Radella flies down through the smoke behind me.

"Radella?" I ask. "How did you get here?"

The burlap around my wrists vanishes. My arms come free. As I untie my legs, an explosion goes off across the quad. Now not only is the pyre on fire but so is the roof of the courthouse.

People scream and dart about as bricks fall into the courtyard, landing on carts and crushing a wagon. I wriggle free and back into the only corner of the stand untouched by flame.

"Everley!" Alick calls from below the pyre, by the woodpile. "Jump!"

The wind changes, pushing the flames and smoke at me. I shield my face and leap over the edge. Radella flies ahead of me, sailing downward as she flutters her wings and sprinkles dust over the woodpile. I hit the mound hard, but it's less bruising than I anticipated. Sliding down the side to the ground, I notice straw bales were hidden under the layer of wood that Radella vanished.

People around us scatter in every direction. Secretary Winters pounds down the stairs of the platform with guards. Alick tosses me a loaded pistol, and I cock it. A second explosion goes off in a building diagonal to us.

The blast throws Alick and me to the ground. I cover my ticker as I land, my shoulder taking the worst of the impact. Radella disappears some debris before it falls on us, and then she pulls on my hair so I'll get up.

Screaming and yelling come from the direction of the platform. Three out of four of the pilings underneath it have been weakened by flying debris. The queen cries out as she goes down with the toppling platform. The structure crumbles, along with the top half of the pyre. The tower falls toward the middle of the courtyard, throwing flames and raining ash.

Ears ringing, I rise and help Alick to his feet. The queen's secretary lies on the cobblestones near us, dazed and disoriented. I yank my sword out of his hand and aim my pistol at him as I back away.

"I worked too hard for this sword. No one is taking it from me ever again."

Queen Aislinn staggers out of the rubble, her dress stained and torn. The fallen pyre crackles between us, flecks of embers sparking off it and feathery ash floating down. The queen and I stare at each other across the blaze. I shift my pistol toward her. One shot. Just one pull of the trigger and the realm will be free of her.

I lower my firearm and call across the flames, "You aren't worth it."

Her mask of coldness melts away to fury.

A horse-drawn wagon sprints into the emptying courtyard, dodging piles of bricks and abandoned carts. Vevina occupies the driver's bench, and Quinn calls out from where she's crouched in the back.

"Come on!"

Pistols raised, Alick and I back up toward the wagon and then jump inside with Quinn.

"Hold on!" Vevina snaps the reins and the horses take off.

Our wheels shoot over the cobblestones, bumping down the street. Gunfire sounds behind us. As we all drop low, Radella dives into my hair to hide. Once the gunfire ceases, I lift my head to see where we're going. The streets are mostly clear behind us, but ahead, the constable corps are setting up a blockade.

Vevina snaps the reins harder, driving right for the barricade. A second later, a third explosion goes off in a building in front of us. The structure crumbles into the road between us and the corps. Vevina takes a sharp turn down an alleyway, and everyone in the back slides into each other. She makes a few more turns, and the tall buildings begin to disappear from our view as the bumpy cobblestone street turns into a dirt road.

Quinn arranges a wool blanket, covering all of us entirely. "We need to stay hidden and quiet," she explains. "The constable corps will be looking for us."

I hold myself still and wait to speak until the wagon slows to a less aggressive pace. "Where are we going?"

"North," Alick replies. "We'll arrive by morning. Everyone try to rest."

Quinn slips her hand into mine and tips her head against my shoulder. I want to hear everything I missed, particularly how Radella made it back from the Land Under the Wave. Still woozy from the smoke, I set aside my urgent questions for now and just breathe.

After a while, I press two fingertips to my lips, and my mind drifts far away to a man in another world, my heart crossing great divides with longing to bring him home.

Chapter Twenty-Eight

The wagon rolls to a stop. Alick throws the blanket off us and sits up. I stretch out my sore back and stare at the cloudy sky. I have no idea where we are, and I don't particularly care because I've lived to see another day.

Radella curled up in the hood of Quinn's cloak, and the two of them are still asleep. Alick slides out of the wagon carefully so as not to disturb them and helps me with my sword.

An early morning mist hangs over the rolling hills, which are dotted every so often by a lone tree. A large countryside manor is set before us, three stories tall, with a rectangular shape, a simple roofline, and dozens of windows. Daisy bushes grow alongside the wide stone stairway that leads to the main entry.

Vevina meets us at the rear of the wagon with her arms full of clothes. "We're far north in the highlands, well out of the city. We should be all right here for a while." She passes me a cloak, a pair of boots, and my mother's red gloves. "Alick saved these for you."

"Thank you," I say, slipping into the clothing.

Vevina tucks her hair behind her ears nervously. "I owe you an apology, darling. When we attacked the Terrible Dorcha—"

"I understand why you did it, and your reasons weren't wrong. The Land Under the Wave was worse than any of us thought."

"Alick said you would understand." Vevina stands back to look me over. "I see you got your sword."

"Yes, and I'm keeping it." Father Time initially asked me to bring the treasure to him, but I would be hard pressed to give it away. I need the blade for the ritual that adds more time to my ticker, so the sword is staying with me.

Radella wakes up and flies to me, perching on my shoulder. I tense and wait for Vevina's negative reaction to the pixie, but she smiles at her.

"You look very pretty today, Radella," she says.

I forgot they must know each other from planning my escape together. I'm glad Vevina has adjusted her opinion that all magic is foul. She and Radella will get on well. The pixie trills and flutters her wings. Though her language is still a mystery, I'm almost certain she thanked Vevina for the compliment.

A horse with two riders trots up the long carriageway. Laverick and Claret come into view and cross to us. Laverick dismounts and grabs me in a hug. Her hair and clothes reek of black powder.

"You set off the explosives in the city," I say in awe.

"I told you I blow things up when I'm afraid." Laverick leans away and beams. "They tried to execute my friend. I think that qualifies as a fair reason."

I gape at Alick next. "You said they hadn't returned."

"I couldn't risk the guard overhearing," he answers, grinning shamelessly.

Claret dismounts beside us. She moves like a broken piece of pottery that was pasted back together. She may be frail and delicate still, yet she's holding strong. She brushes black powder from Laverick's nose. "Lavey organized your prison escape."

"I had help," says the Fox.

"Don't be humble," replies the Cat. "You were brilliant."

I raise my brows, expecting a report later from Laverick on the status of her and Claret. Everything appears to be going well between them.

"Everley," calls another voice. Radella jumps into the air, and I reel around as Jamison comes down the front steps of the manor.

I start off toward him slowly and then quicken my pace. He sweeps me up and squeezes me against him. "I'm sorry I couldn't come to the city. I—"

I press my lips against his. He goes stock-still and then crushes me closer, his soft mouth a stark contrast to his embrace. I tip my forehead against his own. "How? When?"

"We went through the portal soon after you. Neely had an unfortunate accident and fell off the stairway." Poor old soul. All he wanted was to go home. "The portal dropped us along the coast, not far from here. I rode hard for Dorestand, but you were already in prison. Your uncle did a brave thing."

I shut my eyes and reopen them, not wanting the reminder that he's gone. "I have so much to tell you."

Jamison's voice goes oddly quiet. "And I you. Was there trouble leaving the city?"

"Plenty." Vevina smiles mischievously. "But we make a good team."

Osric calls from the open doorway. "Lord and Lady Callahan, the tea is ready." His expression warms at the sight of me, and he tips his head in greeting.

I start up the steps of the manor with Jamison. "Whose home is this?"

"My family's summer estate. Per my mother's deathbed wish, it's mine."

"It's large."

"Embarrassingly so." He adjusts the cuffs of his silk jacket. He's wearing the finest clothes I've ever seen on him, and he's freshly shaven.

We step into the entrance hall. Radella catches up, sitting on my shoulder. Every piece of furniture and each wall hanging is immaculate and old. Plaster molding, high ceilings, polished floors, gleaming furniture—this manor is much grander than my childhood home.

A butler waits inside, along with two servants. They are unmoved by the presence of the elf and pixie, yet one of them side-eyes my sword. Alick comes past us carrying Quinn, and a servant escorts him upstairs to put her down.

"We'll take our tea in the study," says Jamison.

He leads us to a room off the entrance hall. Laverick, Claret, and I go straight to the fire to warm ourselves. A chessboard is set out on a low table, and a grandfather clock keeps time in the corner. Jamison's violin rests on a stand by sheet music in another corner by a pianoforte. The last time I saw the violin, it was floating in water on the *Cadeyrn of the Seas*. Muriel's promise that Jamison would have it again appears to have come to fruition.

Vevina cases the room, admiring the fine furnishings. "Lord Callahan, I do think I've underestimated your importance."

"Oh, I doubt that." He gestures at a sofa. "Have a seat."

She selects a striped sofa, and Claret joins her, sipping a cup of tea. Alick must have turned in after putting Quinn to bed, and Radella curls up on a footstool by the hearth to sleep.

"How has Claret been?" I whisper to Laverick.

"Her time in Everblue shook her." The Fox speaks even softer. "She keeps up appearances, but she isn't sleeping. She'll do better here in the countryside where it's quieter. The city is too much for her nerves right now."

I glance at the Cat. Her hands are wedged between her thighs, her gaze skittish. "Did you tell her . . . ?"

"She mentioned her feelings for me first." Astonishment colors Laverick's voice, her expression alight with joy. "While under the enchantment, she said she could see and feel everything that was happening around her but couldn't participate, as though she were trapped inside a glass case. During those lonely hours, she realized she loves me."

Even though we have a bit of an audience, I cannot help but embrace her. "I'm thrilled for you. After all you've been through, you both deserve a happy ending."

"You'll find your happiness with Jamison too."

I pull back, my smile unsteady. "Maybe so."

Osric clears his throat, signaling the commencement of our meeting. "The queen launched a manhunt for Prince Killian, but as of now, he hasn't been found."

"She won't find him," I say, my voice dragged down by my festering dissatisfaction. "He stole the infinity sandglass. By now, he could be anywhere. The sandglass acts as its own portal through time. He used it to spirit jump to the pixies' treasure trove to retrieve some sort of blue seeds."

Jamison scratches the back of his head. "Markham did all this to get *seeds*?"

"They're called sky seeds." Osric has gone still, his expression pensive. "Sky seeds have a high concentration of creation power. The infinity sandglass gives Markham the ability to travel through time to anywhere in the worlds without a portal, except for the one place the Creator has restricted."

"The Silver-Clouded Plain," I say, remembering the eerie door in the Everwoods with the dead vines blocking it.

"Why was that world restricted?" Vevina asks.

"The giants were cut off from the rest of the worlds after they very nearly decimated mankind," Osric explains. "They must have something Markham wants."

"Markham wants an ancient relic, though Father Time didn't say what." My frustration for Father Time seeps into my voice, shortening my tone. "He hid the artifact where Markham could never find it."

Osric nods solemnly. "We'll discuss this with the elves when they reply to the letter I just sent the council. My queen may know which relic Prince Killian is after. Whatever it is, he intends to win back his power as prince of the Land of Promise, even if it means starting a war."

A curtain of silence drops over us. I listen to my ticker moving in time with the grandfather clock across the room and cannot help but feel that Father Time is watching us. I wonder if he's sorry about my uncle, if he even cares that I'm the last of my bloodline.

The first rays of dawn glow through the window, moving us from night into day and reminding us of our exhaustion.

"Everyone should rest," Jamison says, rising. "You're free to walk about the property as much as you'd like. The manor and grounds are yours to explore. My servants will show you to your bedchambers." He opens the door and reveals his people-in-waiting.

Vevina exits the study, her gaze glittering as she examines a gold-framed painting on the wall. "Thank you, Lord Callahan. I think I will."

They all file out, done in by the long night, except for Radella, who is still fast asleep on the footstool. I stay behind with Jamison, not quite ready to part ways with him, even for a few hours. He tosses another log on the fire, and we settle on a sofa together. I still reek of smoke and soot. I almost feel bad for letting him sit next to me in his finery. He keeps his distance anyway, rubbing his hands together between his knees.

"Everley, I'm sorry. I wanted to be there last night, but I must keep away from the unrest in Dorestand for a while. My superiors have put me on temporary probation for disappearing at sea. I told them I fell in the water and was rescued by fishermen, and had been trying to make my way home since." He stares thoughtfully at a portrait over the fireplace of a man and a woman with two children, a boy and girl. His resemblance to them makes it clear they're his parents, the girl is his sister, and he's the boy. "My father passed away while we were gone."

I release a protracted exhale. He had told me the Marquess of Arundel was ailing, but this loss is still a shock. "I'm so sorry."

Jamison gives a heavy nod. "On his deathbed, my father reinstated me as his heir. I hoped we would make amends, and I suppose he did too."

I shift closer to his side and loop my arm through his. Jamison doesn't say anything more, but his grief bows his head and drags down the corners of his mouth. He's listless, still recovering from the blow of finding himself without a family. I recognize that heartache too well. He will speak about the loss of his father in his own way, and in his own time. Right now, he doesn't need empty platitudes. He needs someone to keep him company so he feels less alone.

Opening his palm, I trace his heart line. "What if I told you something I thought was true at the time but now I realize wasn't?" I ask.

"You mean a lie?"

"A misunderstanding," I amend. "You and I work well together."

He pops a brow. "Is that the misunderstanding?"

"No, I'm getting to that part." I tuck my quivering fingers under me and flatten my feet to the floor, grounding myself before I go on. "I thought I was incapable of falling in love. I thought my clock heart thwarted my chance of growing close to someone. How could a machine made of wood and gearwork feel anything? How could I be a friend? A wife? A mother? All the love I had for others felt behind me, carried over from before I had my ticker. I didn't understand that love is endless. My uncle may not be here anymore, but his love will always stay with me, and your father's love will always be with you. My heart may be different than yours, it looks odd and sounds strange, but I love you, Jamison Callahan. You're my family, and I'm your family for as long as you'll have me."

He smooths back my hair, his gaze roaming my face, and then he touches his lips to mine. A rush of tingles fires across my skin. He kisses me deeper, the two of us sinking into the sofa and each other. After I don't know how long, my skin radiates warmth, and all I want to do is touch every part of him that I can reach. I will find no end to this connection. Having him only makes me want him more.

He kisses me again, long and slow, the ache inside me stretching like warm taffy. Then he pulls back. "I left the city so no one would suspect you're here."

"Good."

"No, Evie, I mean that they won't come looking for you."

I frown, more confused. "That's ideal, isn't it?"

"Yes and no." He pulls away and walks to the hearth, propping one arm against the mantelpiece. "You recall that we were wed aboard the *Lady Regina*?"

"I'm unlikely to forget."

"Soon after the colony was destroyed in battle, the ship was found unsalvageable, and the captain who wed us was killed in the line of fire."

"I was there. Jamison, what are you saying?" My anxiousness broadens, and some part of me is a little hurt that I told him I love him and he didn't return my sentiments. Though, at this point, I would be happy just to receive another kiss.

Jamison becomes restless by the hearth and sits beside me again. "Evie, the logbooks from the penal colony were never returned to Dorestand. Our government has no record of the proceedings that took place on our voyage. I'm absolved of all suspicion, just like Alick and Quinn, but this freedom has come at a cost."

A leaden sensation sinks in my gut. "Just tell me what you're upset about."

"All right." He pauses briefly, then barrels on. "We've no record of our wedding ceremony. In the eyes of the law, you and I were never married."

I swear time stops. I need a long pause to push myself back into this moment. "I'm not your wife?"

"No."

"And you're not my husband?"

"Not according to the realm, but this doesn't change anything." Jamison kisses the palm of my hand. "I love you, Everley Donovan. I will be here tomorrow and the day after and the day after for as long as you'll have me."

I have the most irrational need to kick something, an odd response to hearing that the man I love does indeed love me back.

But I was ready to be a wife, *his* wife. I feel robbed of the whole romantic notion of having a husband. Of declaring to the world through a marital contract that this is the man I love.

"Everley, are you upset?"

"Aren't you?"

"I was devastated when I first heard, but now I think back to an hour ago when I was pacing right there in front of the fireplace while Osric trumped me at chess, uncertain if I would ever see you again, and I'm damn grateful you're here, alive and whole." Jamison pulls me closer, his blue eyes engulfing my sight. "I don't care what a piece of paper doesn't say. You're family, Evie. Nothing anyone says or does will change that."

I lean into him, chest to chest, and brush my lips over his. His soft mouth pushes back, a light pressure that flows down the length of me and warms my toes.

Golden morning light pours in through the windows. I cozy into his side and gaze ahead at the fire. The pendulum of the grandfather clock swings away in my side vision. I focus on Jamison, but the persistent ticktock of the timepiece disrupts the quiet and reopens my worries about what's to come.

"What do we do now?" I whisper.

Jamison tips his head against mine. "For as long as possible, we sit still."

I'm so exhausted that's about all I can manage.

"This may turn out for the best," he muses. "The constable corps will never guess that you or the others are here."

Our security, even if temporary, means so much that I let the conversation lie and leave our worries for later. For now, I will take advantage of this moment. I will sit beside the fire with Jamison for as long as possible and let the future take care of itself.

ACKNOWLEDGMENTS

Big thanks to these tremendous individuals:

The joys of my life—John, Joseph, Julian, Danielle, and Ryan. What an adventure! Many, many more are coming. Expect more road trips where I plot out loud while you're stuck listening. And my mom and dad, Keith and Debby, my biggest cheerleaders.

My agent, Marlene Stringer, for reminding me that writing is supposed to be hard. Sometimes I need a verbal smack to the head. You also know when I need kind words of encouragement. Thanks for knowing which ones I need and when.

My editor, Jason Kirk. Dude, *six books together?* I hope (crosses fingers) we're just getting started. I can't say enough how much I appreciate you.

My developmental editor, Clarence Haynes. You steer my stories in the right direction. They are always stronger for it, and so am I.

Brittany Russell and Colleen Lindsay—you are magic! I don't know how you get everything done. A million thanks for working so hard on my behalf.

My indomitable friends, Kate Coursey, Veeda Bybee, Kathryn Purdie, Jessie Farr, Annette Lyon, Natalie Barnum, and Kim Swallow, you ladies are my go-to accomplices. Let's make more mischief together, shall we?

And last but not least, a shout-out to the amazing authors who were there for me during a trying few months: Shannon Hale, Robison Wells, Jessica Day George, Ally Condie, Wendy Jessen, and Sarah M. Eden. You know what you did, and you know why I appreciate you.

ABOUT THE AUTHOR

Photo © 2015 Erin Summerill

Emily R. King is a writer of fantasy and the author of The Hundredth Queen Series and *Before the Broken Star*, the first book in The Evermore Chronicles. Born in Canada and raised in the United States, she is a shark advocate, a consumer of gummy bears, and an islander at heart, but her greatest interests are her four children. Emily lives in northern Utah with her family and their cantankerous cat. Visit her at www.emilyrking.com.